The 4th Reich

-Book One-

Patrick Laughy

DEDICATION
This book is dedicated to all Second World War buffs out
there who wonder, from time to time...what if?

ACKNOWLEDGEMENTS
Thanks to Suzy for her hours of research and editing, David for another great cover and Linette for her continued support.

The 4th Reich is a work of fiction. Though parts of the book make reference to historical persons, places and events, the fictional characters portrayed in the story are all the products of the author's imagination.

PROLOGUE

On August twenty-third, nineteen thirty-nine, a ten year Non-Aggression Pact was signed between the Governments of the Nazi Third Reich and Russia.

This agreement provided Adolf Hitler, Germany's Fuhrer, with a guarantee that once he took on the rest of Europe in the west, militarily, he would not find himself having to face a two-front war, as his country had in the Great War of nineteen fourteen – nineteen eighteen.

He was, as were his generals, convinced that a future two-front war for Germany was doomed to failure.

There was also a secret protocol that went with that pact. That protocol included an agreement on the part of Russia not to join in the possible future war in return for Germany's promise to provide the Russians with the Baltic states of Estonia, Latvia and Lithuania. In addition Poland, once overrun, was to be divided between the two powers. Under the provisions of this protocol the new border between Germany and Russia was to be run along the Narew, Vistula and San rivers.

This would provide Stalin with a land buffer to protect his country from attack from the west, something that was a major concern for him at the time.

It would provide Hitler the security of not having to fight a two front war.

The Reich leader was confident that it would also be the straw that broke the back of the English. He was convinced that this diplomatic plum, in addition to the military pressure he was already able to put upon them, would cause England to disregard her treaties and guarantees with other European nations and convince the British to seek a workable peace, on Hitler's terms, with Germany.

Under the circumstances the deal between Hitler and Stalin was not just a non-aggression pact. It was the intrinsic tool needed by the

Fuhrer to facilitate his blueprint for the creation of the New Germanic Nation.

In so doing, it all but guaranteed a Second World War.

As they begin, the Fourth Reich series of novels are filled with the historical facts of the day so that these may serve to set the stage for the everyday lives of the members of one fictional aristocratic German family depicted within its pages. Throughout the series fact and fiction appear, mix, meld and fade in turn.

The story of the von Stauffer family begins in the period of the Nazi rise to power in Germany and follows them on their, at times perilous, journey through World War II and beyond, toward the creation of The Fourth Reich.

CHAPTER ONE

- A New Germany -

In nineteen thirty-three, when Hitler's Nazi Party came to power in Germany, Wehrmacht Generalleutnant (Lieutenant General), Count Karl von Stauffer had just turned fifty. The Count's family had an ancient military tradition going back many generations.

The Count was a well-educated man, holding a doctorate in business administration, who had joined the German army directly after leaving university in nineteen hundred and six. By the time the World War ended in nineteen eighteen, the Count, who had specialized as an expert in weapons procurement and production for the duration of that conflict, had risen through the ranks to the position of Oberst (Colonel).

After the war, von Stauffer chose to remain in the small peacetime German army, and in the early nineteen twenties when his father died he had stepped in to take up the reins of control for the family's considerable investment portfolio. To refer to the family as independently wealthy would be a gross understatement.

By the time the Nazis came to power, the Count had four children, had reached the rank of General, and managed to bring the considerable family fortune through the worst of the worldwide economic collapse relatively unscathed.

He had, after all, held a reasonably high position in the German Armament Procurement Department since the war and with an insider's knowledge of what equipment orders were forthcoming, been well positioned to make shrewd investments within the armaments industry throughout that period.

While never openly expressing them, the Count had had doubts about the new Nazi regime from the time of the Party's inception in the early twenties in relation to both what it could mean to the members of the Wehrmacht like himself in the short term and what it would mean for his family and his beloved Germany in the long term.

The Count had not joined the Nazi Party prior to Hitler's rise to a position of absolute power in thirty-three, giving his reasons at the time for not doing so as being based upon a personal and strongly held belief that those holding high positions within the military should not have political affiliations.

However, being an intelligent man and always concerned as to the future of his military career, he saw the writing on the wall and the Count did, if not enthusiastically, become a Party member the day Adolf Hitler assumed the title of Fuhrer of the German Nation.

The Count's wife, the Countess Erika, had a different outlook when it came to the Nazi party and specifically in regard to the new leader of the New Reich. She saw Adolf Hitler as a messiah sent to save a crumbling Germany and had joined the Nazi party in the nineteen twenties when it was in its infancy.

While he did not share his wife's early, unqualified, and to him seemingly blind and all-encompassing acceptance of the direction in which the Nazi party had chosen to begin the restructuring of the Fatherland, he could not disregard the fact he was part of a very slim minority and that her viewpoint was shared by the vast majority of German citizens; nor could he fail to realize that the solidly
nationalistic stance taken by the socialist party had a strong appeal to the vanquished, downtrodden and seriously oppressed German people as a whole.

The Count was an experienced soldier and an intellectual man who had no difficulty in understanding his wife's positive position with regard to the new path the Fuhrer had chosen for the restructuring of Germany.

He readily recognized that the status quo resulting from the loss of the Great War and the resulting war reparations determined by the Treaty of Versailles had made day to day life an impossible struggle for the German middle and lower classes.

Before the Nazi party's rise to power, inflation and unemployment had crippled the country.

Adolf Hitler made it plain to all that if he were to achieve power, he would remove the artificial chains that bound Germany and swiftly return the Fatherland to world prominence where it historically belonged.

The seeds of his promises found fertile ground in the minds of all Germans and from the Count's perspective this response was only reasonable for a once proud people who were being systematically stomped into the ground by the unfair penalties imposed upon Germany by the victors of the colossally disastrous Great War.

Count Karl von Stauffer did not disagree that the situation, in nineteen thirty-three when Hitler came to power, was unconscionable, that it was unfair or that it could serve any other purpose than to lead to the eventual destruction of his beloved Germany.

In addition he concurred with many of the aims of the Nazi party, and yet he could not help but wonder if the cure as envisioned by the Nazis might not be worse than the artificially invalided condition it strove to solve.

Hitler's dream of a socialist state designed for the common man, led by one omnipotent leader and structured and policed by a strong national government, looked to the Count very much like a proposed dictatorship in sheep's clothing.

As the new Nazi laws began to roll out, the Count seriously searched for any signs of moderation in the plans and programmes being released by the new government but could find no clear indication of any such consideration of temperance.

Between nineteen thirty-three and nineteen thirty-eight he'd been able to access the results of the many abrupt and radical changes resulting from and the implementation of these new laws. Many he agreed with and supported.

However he still had concerns about their overall long-term effect and internally questioned how far they would eventually go. The strengthening and expanding of many reforms seemed more like an ongoing attack being dribbled out in small bites that would be acceptable to the masses, an indoctrination over time, than a fait accompli.

Power was being centralized and while he did not fault that per se he did question the absolute control being legislated to enforce this government's policies. When time was taken to view them with an open mind, they appeared to him as both severe and uncompromising to a degree that smacked of enslavement.

For the Count, the questions remained.

Was the pendulum swinging too far and too fast? Was there to be any room left for free thinking among the masses or was the German race being led into the darkness, like an obedient lamb to the slaughter?

CHAPTER TWO

- Early Years -

Adolf Hitler was appointed Reich Chancellor of Germany by President Hindenburg on January thirtieth, nineteen thirty-three.

Until August of nineteen thirty-four, Hindenburg held the power to dismiss Hitler from that post, but upon the President's death in that month Hitler found himself in a position of strength that allowed him to join the offices of Chancellor and President into one and on the day he did this, he adopted the new title of 'Fuhrer' (Leader). From that moment on Hitler was in absolute control of Germany.

For all intents and purposes the Third Reich began on that day.

Very few German citizens had any real idea of what that fact would mean to them as individuals; Nazi internal propaganda provided up to that time had sold a political platform to the masses which was primarily based on appealing to a nationalistic dream of a resurgent Fatherland under a committed central government controlled by a strong leader.

At a time of deep world-wide depression further compounded within Germany itself by the unfair consequences of the 'Versailles Treaty' which had been imposed by the allies after the Great War, the country was falling into ruin. Germany was suffering from both rampant inflation and massive unemployment.

Nazi promises of an economic reversal had been received with open arms by a citizenry who had reached the point of expressing absolutely no hope of a better future.

Suffering from the naivety of the sense of helplessness inherent in the downtrodden, the masses blindly voted the Nazi party into power with the hope that Adolf Hitler would, as promised, prove to be their saviour in an otherwise bleak and uncaring world.

In general, the German people spent little, if any, time considering what this commitment would mean to them as individuals or to the future of their children; after all they lived in a democracy and had simply chosen to cast their vote for a specific political party. If they found in the future that the resulting government was not to their liking all they would have to do to change it would be to vote for a different party in the next general election.

What did they have to lose in giving the Nazis a try? The Nazi Party, under Hitler's leadership had espoused the fervent belief that the individual German had one duty and one duty only and that duty was to the State, and on the flip side of that coin, the State had the responsibility and duty to allow each individual to play his or her part in the rapid development of a strong and powerful Germany and be fairly compensated for their efforts.

Reduced to its simplest form this belief was to be extrapolated from an initial, gender-based division of responsibility on the part of a eugenically pure race of Nordic/Aryan males and females.

A strong central totalitarian government would ensure that men were trained and educated to become workers and soldiers to build and defend a strong Fatherland, while the women would be educated and trained to become housewives and mothers who would then have as many children as was physically possible.

The aim was a perpetuation of that cycle. All children would be trained in Nazi ideology and educated by the State with the sole purpose of repeating the scenario which had been begun by their parents.

This State-imposed system had as its goal the rapid cleansing of the New Germany of all its racial impurities. This removal of inferior citizens would naturally bring about an improvement in the genetic stock of the German populace which would in turn lead the Fatherland to the forefront of world power and into a position of leadership where, the Nazis fervently believed, Germany historically and naturally belonged.

* * * * *

- Unemployment -

In nineteen thirty-three, when Hitler reached power, he decreed that every citizen in Nazi Germany must play his or her part in the resurrection of the Fatherland. Unemployment was to be eradicated. All must work and be productive for the good of the state.

He immediately began working toward the achievement of this goal, doing so by way of two main thrusts.

The first of these was a very public and well- propagandized program of attacking the causes of unemployment itself. The second was broadly propagandized as well in a general sense but the specific steps to be taken to deal with that aspect of the problem were kept hidden from the public at large. It dealt with the physically and mentally handicapped who were, because of their disabilities, incapable of becoming productive working members of the New Germany, a group of people considered by the Nazis to be an unnecessary and unacceptable drain on society.

When Hitler took office six million Germans were listed as unemployed. By January of nineteen thirty-four, that number was down to three point three million. By that date in thirty-five it was two point nine.

The figure in thirty-six was two point five million; thirty-seven, one point eight and by thirty-eight it was down to one million. In January of nineteen thirty-nine Germany's unemployment number was three hundred and two thousand persons.

These startling numbers were broadcast by way of Nazi propaganda far and wide, not only for the eyes and ears of the

German domestic population but also as a message to the world.

That message was simple. Sit up and take notice everyone. Germany, under the leadership of Adolf Hitler and the Nazi Party was clearly demonstrating its capability of doing what no other government on the planet could do - wipe out unemployment.

It was an amazing accomplishment.

Hitler brought this wondrous feat to fruition by introducing a number of strict Nazi policies.

In the New Germany the responsibilities of the two genders in relation to the State were clearly drawn. Men would work and fight. Women would marry, look after their husbands and produce as many children as possible. Women were not expected to work and should therefore no longer be included in the statistics of the unemployed. Hitler instructed that they should be immediately removed from the unemployment rolls.

Nazi Germany was to be a crime-free Police State. The numbers of men needed to create the forces that would keep Germany's citizens safe under the Nazis would therefore have to increase in all three of the main police forces, the 'Ordnungspolizei' (regular police), 'Kriminalpolizei' (criminal police) and the 'Sicherheitspolizei' (security police). These organizations all absorbed manpower as they grew rapidly. In so doing, they lowered the unemployment statistics.

The vast majority of Jewish Germans lost their chances of employment after the Nazis formed government.

By law, in nineteen thirty-five, all Jews lost their Germany citizenship. When this happened the unemployed Jews became non-citizens. As such they were no longer considered to be unemployed Germans and therefore were no longer included in the unemployment statistics from that date forward.

At the end of the Great War, the Treaty of Versailles had restricted the German army to a strength of one hundred thousand men. Germany had also been forbidden U-boats, and an air force. Her Navy could not have more than six capital ships, and all German troops had to be removed from the industrialized Rhineland.

The Nazi party leadership reflected the German people's hatred of the Treaty terms and they began to ignore some of the requirements of that document piecemeal as rapidly as they could safely manage it. Conscription became law in nineteen thirty-five and by nineteen thirty-nine the miniscule force specified by the treaty in regard to the German Army had been expanded to a force of one point four million men. Unemployment statistics went down accordingly.

The expanded army required new equipment. Forty-six billion deutschmarks were earmarked by the Nazis for new weapons and military infrastructure which immediately resulted in the industrial barons of Germany expanding their factories and hiring tens of thousands of workers.

Hitler was determined that the New Reich would be self-sufficient in both food and materials and no longer dependant on imports from foreign states. He ordered German scientists to find artificial substitutes for all imports. The required funds necessary for research were immediately made available and results were rapid. Makeup was created using flour. Wool and cotton were produced from pulped wood, coffee created from acorns.

The list was endless and as a result many previously unemployed workers found employment in the new industries that were created as each new discovery made its appearance.

Hitler had promised to improve the working conditions of the average German worker. He had also promised the industrialists of the country a guaranteed and reliable workforce in exchange for their backing and financial support for the Party, which he had received in its early stages of development.

Within a few months of reaching absolute power, The Fuhrer moved to deliver on both promises.

CHAPTER THREE

- The Economy -

On May second, nineteen thirty-three Hitler ordered the SA or 'Sturm Abteilung' (Storm Troopers), the party's private army to arrest all of Germany's trade union leaders. He then created the DAF or 'Deutsche Arbeitsfront' (German Labour Front) the National Socialist Trade Union Organization whose stated aim was the creation of a true social and productive community throughout Germany. The DAF instantly replaced all the various labour unions that currently existed in Germany. This organization was set up to mutually represent both the worker's and the employer's points of view.

The DAF provided workers with relatively high wages, job security, social security programmes, canteens, set breaks and regular working times. The average working man was generally satisfied with the result and in exchange provided the system with solid support.

Employee membership in the DAF was theoretically voluntary but in reality any worker found it very difficult to gain employment without being a member in good standing.

Members were required to pay dues which in turn were used to provide them with free or inexpensive holidays, subsidized sporting and leisure activities as well as factory renovations, canteens, smoke-free rooms, and overall cleaner and more enticing workspaces.

Employers also got what they had been seeking. They received the guarantee of a stable and secure work force at a reasonable cost. All employment contracts in existence at the time were terminated and then renewed under the auspices of the DAF. The right to strike was abolished.

Workers were banned from quitting a job without the specific permission of the DAF and any new jobs had to be filled through them. All restrictions on the number of hours that an employee could be asked to work were scrapped.

In short order labour strife in Germany had become a thing of the past. The economy was beginning to boom, creating more jobs. The employers were raking in profits. By nineteen thirty-six the average factory worker was earning thirty-five marks a week. That was ten times more than the unemployment benefits paid to the six million unemployed people in nineteen thirty-two.

Working conditions in Germany had begun to improve and the citizens were beginning to taste hope and a sense of burgeoning pride in their accomplishments, the Nazi Party and its Fuhrer, Adolf Hitler.

* * * * *

-The Children of the New Reich –

A short two months after the torchlight parades of celebration over Hitler's appointment as Chancellor, the majority Nazi government of the Reichstag passed the Enabling Act.

As a result of that act Hitler instantly won dictatorial powers, which meant that all Nazi organizations suddenly had the official power of the State behind them.

This included the Hitler Youth groups. It signalled the commencement of the 'Gleichschaltung' (forced co-ordination); the beginning of the Nazification of all German institutions and organizations which the Nazis considered worthwhile had begun, immediately sentencing any of those that didn't meet the new standards of the party to an instant demise.

Hitler's plan for the youth of Germany had been formed for some time and the leader of the Hitler Youth, Balder Von Schirach, had been appointed personally to his office by the new Fuhrer.

Hitler, like most dictators, determined from the beginning of his power that he had to maintain personal control of the future development of all aspects of the New Reich, for only he knew what was best for the German people. Von Schirach therefore, like all administrators of the Nazi party's doctrine and policies was, upon his appointment, ordered to report solely and directly to The Fuhrer.

At that time there were nearly six million German children involved in a vast array of youth groups, and Von Schirach was immediately instructed to either absorb these into the Hitler Youth or eliminate the over four hundred youth groups who had been in competition with the party's own youth movement.

This was accomplished in short order.

Many leaders among the conservative and/or nationalistic organizations welcomed this change with open arms. Others, deemed by the Nazi party to be unsuitable to the needs of the New Germany, i.e. those of a Jewish or Communist nature were simply disbanded on the spot.

There was some hesitancy on the part of the Nazis when it came to dealing with those groups run by religious or worker's organizations. The Nazis, after all, were a worker's party and Germany was a Christian State.

Rather than autocratically terminate these youth groups the Nazis chose to aggressively apply pressure against them, using propaganda and bullying to bring them on board.

They did this by using the Police and 'SA' (Sturm Abteilung) brown-shirts, the party's personal paramilitary organization, in what they referred to as the enforcement of laws regarding "public nuisance".

They soon had these groups completely intimidated and prepared to become part of the new Hitler Youth programmes. The Catholic Youth Organizations were
however, a different kettle of fish.

The Catholic Church had eagerly and with open arms welcomed the newly formed Nazi government, and the 'Reich-konkordat' agreement had been signed between Hitler's government and the Vatican shortly after the Nazis had come to power.

This agreement provided all Catholic institutions within Germany with the promise of Government protection.

It was of course a two -way agreement, in that the Nazi Party had correspondingly been promised the generous, overt and public support of the leaders of the Catholic Church.

In the months after Hitler's rise to power, high rankingmembers of the party and military continued to attend Sunday Mass of the German Catholic Church.

Hitler Youth members of both sexes could be seen attending services in uniform. It became common practice to find male members of that organization serving as Alter boys with their robes of office openly worn over their Nazi uniforms.

If, due to the agreement signed with the Holy See, the Nazis couldn't immediately absorb the Catholic Church youth groups by way of the use of overt force, they could and did infiltrate them, therein taking control of those organizations from within. They accomplished this with little challenge and in many cases, with thinly veiled support from the Holy Church.

The Fuhrer promoted Baldur von Schirach to 'Jugendfuhrer des Deutschen Reiches' (Youth Leader of Germany) on the seventeenth of June, nineteen thirty-three.

New manuals for the Hitler Youth organizations which were now under one leadership umbrella but divided by gender soon followed that appointment.

CHAPTER FOUR

- Hitler Youth -

Male children of six to ten years were encouraged to join and observe older boys of the 'Jungvolk' (Young People), made up of ten to fourteen year olds at their meetings and invited these youngsters to take part informally in Jungvolk activates.

At the age of fourteen boys became full-fledged members of the 'Hitler Jugend' (Hitler Youth). From this point until they were eighteen years old, each boy was provided with a booklet of performance which served to record his progress of development in all facets of his training which included athletics, basic military training and strict Nazi doctrine.

Count Karl von Stauffer personally considered the starting age of these new Nazi youth programmes to be somewhat early in a boy's life; however, as a Wehrmacht Officer, he did manage to assuage his concern with an admittedly somewhat self-righteous personal opinion that "a dose of discipline never hurt any boy".

It was a New Germany and both his sons had quite understandably responded to the early propaganda blitz put on by the Nazis and as a result they had eagerly entered into the Hitler Youth programme in nineteen thirty-three freely and with fervent expectations.

The Count's wife, Erika, had decided at that time that it was also a good idea to start their daughters in the corresponding 'Bund Deutscher Madel Inder Hitler Jugend' (League of German Girls in the Hitler Youth) and he had supported her in the reaching of that conclusion.

The decision reached, both of Count von Stauffer's daughters had joined the 'League of German Girls in the Hitler Youth' organization in nineteen thirty-three shortly after Hitler came to power.

The Count had some concern as to whether or not they had done the right thing at the time, or had his children been forced to grow up too quickly as a result? Had it hardened them in some ways more than he would have liked? Would he have preferred a somewhat softer approach to their education? Perhaps, but in general he was both proud and pleased with the end results: polite, disciplined, respectful, and fiercely nationalistic young sons was after all a German father's dream. And surely it could not be harmful to his daughters to be introduced to instruction in motherhood and homemaking or assisting with the harvesting of crops and a gaining of a general appreciation and understanding of what a farmer, who is the salt of the earth, did to provide for his fellow countrymen.

By nineteen thirty-six Hitler had passed a law making membership in the Hitler Youth mandatory for all children who qualified under the stringent Aryan requirements and who fell within the required age groups.

When this law came into force and with its prorogation, both the Count and his wife had some reason to feel affirmed in their earlier decision with regard to their own children.

It made it easier for them to push aside any lingering doubts as to the validation of that earlier choice to enrol their children into the programs offered by the State.

At that time, Ursula, the eldest and twin to her bother Wilhelm, was sixteen years of age. Her sister Gabriella, the family's baby, was fourteen.

As had been the case with the boys, the two girls, due to their ages, had been too old when the Nazis came into power to be part of the initial indoctrination period mandated for all Germany's youth by the Nazis: this early training period had been designed for children aged ten to fourteen.

At the time of their acceptance into the programme, Gabriella had only been a month away from her fifteenth birthday and as a result she had been accepted into the older group along with her sister, thereby missing the 'Jungmadel'(Young girls League) portion of the girl's movement, and going directly into the full League itself.

The two parallel youth organizations based on sex and set up by the party mirrored the Nazi authoritarian structure for the school system in that males and females, were kept strictly separate and each received a unique educational curriculum although both sexes were to receive a similar type of political indoctrination within the educational system.

The Nazi party believed that a structured education system was the best tool to ensure the creation of a future adult citizenry loyal and committed to both Adolf Hitler and the State. The separate male and female Hitler Youth groups were set up to augment the educational system and were designed to cement the State's control over children by absorbing as much as possible of the free time that was left to students, once their studies had been completed for the day and week.

Because the instant adoption and implementation of the new Nazi school curriculum depended upon the teachers and professors working in the education system, all teachers who wished to maintain their employment or who were planning to enter the profession had to be vetted by local Party officials before they could be licensed to teach. Propaganda and indoctrination was common practice within the education system. Any teacher who did not meet the standards of these officials was summarily fired without recourse. Not surprisingly, all Jewish teachers were fired and ninety-seven percent of the remaining teachers chose to join the new Nazi Teachers Association.

Any teacher who valued his job had to be mindful of what he said to his students.

Children were encouraged to inform the authorities if a teacher said or did something that did not fit in with the strictly supervised Party curriculum.

The subjects taught in the schools underwent a major revision under the Nazi regime. Changes followed the party line, reflecting a nationalistic approach. For example, the German defeat of nineteen-eighteen was to be taught as resulting from the malevolent artifice of Jewish and Marxist fifth-columnist spies who had worked feverishly to weaken the wonderful German system from within.

The world-wide financial hyperinflation and the stock market crash of the nineteen-twenties was the result of Jewish money lenders and saboteurs.

The German national resurgence of the thirties had only begun when Adolf Hitler became leader of the Reich.

The teaching of the sciences had a military bent. Subjects taught included the principles involved in firearms, the impact of poison gases, military, aviation, and bridge building.

Biology courses centered on the study of various races, designed to give credence to the Nazi claim that racial superiority was something to be actively sought and that the suggestion of a superior Nordic/Aryan race was based on a solid foundation. Inter-racial marriage was demonized as an obvious step to a wanton sentencing of Germany to the depths of an obviously racially inferior abyss. Older pupils were instructed in the proper methods of selecting the correct mate prior to the production of any offspring. In the case of the von Stauffer boys, these changes didn't affect them until their late teens.

Eric, nineteen years old when the Nazis came to power in nineteen thirty-three had been out of school and attending university. Due to his marks and physical prowess he had been recruited for officer training with the result that he had volunteered for the Kriegsmarine.

Wilhelm, sixteen at the time and still in secondary school had been one of the boys the Nazi regime had considered as being special. Due to his family's historically significant Aryan background, being in outstanding physical condition and having good grades, he was immediately transferred to an 'Adolf Hitler' school, which had been specifically set up to educate the future leaders of the Reich. He would spend the next two years in the school and when he graduated he was immediately accepted into the SS officer training programme.

Education for the Count's daughters, Ursula and Gabriella, was to be guided by the new direction the Nazi Party had determined as mandatory to ensure the achievement of their aim to create the perfect German woman, although, as had occurred with the boys, the family's long Aryan roots coupled with the Count and Countess's social positions was destined to guarantee a certain degree of adjustment and embellishment to the workings of the standard process.

CHAPTER FIVE

- Retirement -

On March twelfth, nineteen thirty-eight, the fifty-six year old Count Karl von Stauffer went under the knife due to a disabling heart condition.

His Doctor, Baron Heinrich von Kliest, was the son of a good friend who had died only a year previously, and was arguably one the best in the world at his job. This operation took place at a time when Germany was leading the world in scientific discoveries. Advances in the area of heart surgery by German medical researchers were the talk of the members of the medical profession worldwide.

As a result of his condition and at the urging of his wife, the Count had decided to retire from active military service before his scheduled hospitalization.

The operation went well and he found after a few months recuperation that he'd completely recovered and was feeling better than he had in years.

His decision to retire early had not been an easy one for him and although his wife had played a part in the reaching of that decision, he had been primarily influenced to retire by Adolf Hitler's rise to power and the resulting government policies and laws produced over the five years that had followed.

Due to Erika's strong support for the new regime, the Count rarely discussed the current political situation with his wife, or with his children for that matter. Over those same years his progeny had all been subjected to ideological manipulation under socialist programs originated by the Nazi party, and thereby had also become strongly pro-Hitler.

For the sake of his family the General had obeyed his orders and kept his thoughts to himself. In so doing, he had to acknowledge that he'd demonstrated a personal complacency in regard to the activities of the new regime and therefore had to accept a degree of responsibility for the tolerance of the changes taking place around him as reflected by the masses of German society.

Perhaps the most personally demeaning examples of this complacency on his part was the fact that by biting his tongue, he now found it impossible to absolve himself from at least some of the responsibility for the indoctrination of his own children which had taken place since Hitler's rise to power.

As was historically the case, the responsibility for the guidance of the children within the Count's immediate family was based upon gender.

Count Karl von Stauffer was of the old school and as the current patriarch of a family which had produced a long line of military men going back over hundreds of years, he took direct control of his sons' education and military placement, while his wife Erika took responsibility for his daughters' early upbringing and eventual entry into proper positions within the German nobility and its elevated sense of society.

Karl had been present in Berlin, where the family kept a large residence, when on the evening of January thirtieth, nineteen thirty-three; the Nazi party had celebrated the appointment of Adolf Hitler as Chancellor of Germany by way of a massive torchlight parade.

At the invitation of the Nazi Party the Count had attended the gala affair. While viewing the celebration, he hadn't given a great deal of thought to the fact that Hitler Youth units had attended as a part of the columned uniformed formations marching past below the watchful eyes of the elderly President Paul von Hindenburg of Germany and those of the new Chancellor, Adolf Hitler.

He would however, have good cause to remember their involvement when in the years that followed, the State stepped in to take responsibility for the education and training of all the children in the New Germany.

* * * * *

- Children of the New Germany -

The Nazi philosophy of placing only males into positions of authority within the New Germany was initially reflected in the structure of the female arm of the Hitler Youth program.

When the party came to power in nineteen thirty-three and thrust its tendrils of authoritarian control into the various youth organizations then functioning within Germany, their initial aim was to ensure the drawing in of all of these divergent groups under a single umbrella association that could be directly controlled by the Party.

When in nineteen thirty-three Hitler appointed Baldur von Schirach as Reichsjugendfuhrer of the HJ (Hitler Youth), this amalgamation of all youth into the Nazi fold under a single administration, revealed a basic problem for the party in respect to the fact that, unlike most other Nazi organizations, both genders would be involved.

Not surprisingly, as was the case worldwide, the Nazis soon realized that the leadership of the majority of the female youth groups being gathered into the organized Hitler Youth by way of mandatory membership in the 'Bund Deutscher Madel' (League of German Maidens) or BDM, had adult female leaders.

When informed of the situation, Hitler decided to deal with this conflict between Nazi dogma regarding leadership as an exclusively male domain and the inherited female leadership of the feminine youth organizations in two ways.

Firstly, he would appoint a woman to act in the position of BDM-Reichsreferentin (National Speaker of the BDM). He did this in nineteen thirty-four, selecting a postal worker named Trude Mohr, who was to be a figurehead only and was required to fulfill her duties under the direct supervision and guidance of von Schirach.

The Fuhrer specified that this position would have to be restricted, as were those of all other females gainfully employed within the Reich, to the conditions that they could only be held by a woman who was unmarried and without children.

When Mohr married in nineteen thirty-seven she was immediately replaced by Dr. Jutta Rudiger who turned out to be somewhat more assertive than her predecessor, but was still kept firmly pinned beneath von Schirach's thumb.

Secondly, Hitler determined that in both arms of the Hitler Youth, male and female, the leaders of the youth of each gender were to lead their peers. Youth was to lead youth.

In nineteen thirty-eight a third age group was added to the BDM to include girls between the ages of seventeen and twenty-one. Nazi ideology dictated that all Aryan females were expected to marry and have children once they were of age, but since they were also now expected to work for the benefit of the State until that important time came, consideration was also to be given to some specific job training and education.

With this in mind, the purpose of bringing this older segment of females under the wing of the Hitler Youth was aimed at preparing these budding German Frauleins, for their looming marriages and domestic life. As well it would address their future career goals with a view to helping them prepare to take up employment in certain specialized fields until they were properly performing their duties to the State.

These were defined as becoming good Aryan wives for their husbands and the producers of as many children as possible. This to propagate the future generations of German
children that would be needed in order to bring the Nazi plan for a world-dominating Third Reich to fruition.

* * * * *

- A meeting with the Fuhrer -

Although he did his best to hide the fact, Count Karl von Stauffer soon found early retirement both boring and unrewarding.

In May of nineteen thirty-eight the Fuhrer chose to make a personal appeal to the Count for his return to uniform.

While certainly both surprised and pleased at having the leader of the New Germany request his involvement in the future development of his beloved Fatherland in these exciting times, von Stauffer was not a man who made snap decisions without a thorough examination of the pros and cons and the Count had not done so in this case.

Instead he had requested that the Fuhrer allow him a week to consider his response and that request had been granted.

During that week he had first discussed the offer in depth with his wife, who was absolutely thrilled at this turn of events. When told of the Fuhrer's request she had, admittedly only for a few moments, actually lost her much admired aristocratic cool and aloof manner, to the extent that she embraced her husband and danced him around in unhindered glee.

It was immediately apparent to the Count that Erika welcomed such an opportunity and she went on to inform him that she was of the opinion that the family had been, since his retirement, excluded from the social world revolving around the Nazi leadership.

This was something which disappointed her to no end, not just for herself but for the sake of the future prospects of marriage for their two beautiful and blossoming daughters.

For the remainder of the week the Count had been repeatedly reminded by his wife that the girls had now reached and were quickly moving past the optimum age for marriage.

They required the immediate availability of a selection of proper suitors. Young virile men of sufficient wealth and social position, and that his return to the Nazi fold would pave the way for a return of the family into the upper echelons of German society, thereby serving to meet the family's needs in relation to this serious matter.

Karl had of course spent a good deal of private time thinking about the consequences of the offer and had spoken to others he trusted implicitly, primarily high ranking officers of the military and the industrial leaders at the helm of the firms in which his ancestors had historically invested with the successful aim of achieving long term profits for the family and in which he still held large blocks of stock.

He did not rush his decision, using the full week to study both sides of the question carefully.

In the end, and despite some lingering doubts as to the correctness of some parts of the roadmap Hitler had so far plotted for the future of his beloved Fatherland, these urgings of his wife coupled with his own boredom were enough to convince Count Karl von Stauffer to accept the Fuhrer's offer to reactivate his commission, and he did so on May twenty-fourth, nineteen thirty-eight.

CHAPTER SIX

- Baltic port of Kiel, Germany -

- September 16th, 1938 - 06:45 hours -

Having taken the late evening train from Hamburg, clutching his sea-bag and still having some difficulty in believing his request for re-assignment to U-boats had been accepted, twenty-four year old Kriegsmarine (Naval) Oberfahnrich zur See (Sub-Lieutenant), Eric Stauffer, the eldest son of fifty-six year old Count Karl von Stauffer and his forty-two year old wife, the Countess Erika, stepped off the first class coach car and onto the crowded platform at the main train station in Kiel.

He watched as a final plume of black smoke cleared the stack from the big engine and heard the sharp hiss of steam as it was shut down.

At this early hour and this far north there was still a chill in the air, briefly causing him to regret not wearing his greatcoat for the trip. Excitement over his transfer to U-boats quickly had over-ridden any concern about the temperature, however, and he moved rapidly through the busy station, out the entrance and into the open, under an overcast early morning sky.

After moving through the milling crowd to reach the edge of the sidewalk he paused briefly to glance about until he found what he was looking for. He then crossed the street and slipped into the small shop.

His practiced eyes immediately took in the woman behind the counter.

Although she was no longer young, she was still attractive and had obviously dressed with an eye to taking the best advantage of her not yet plump, but definitely well-rounded body.

She looked up as the bell above the door announced his presence and her eyes ran over him in a blatant and unhurried inspection as he removed his cap and set his sea bag down near the door.

Eric, at twenty-two still had a somewhat boyish appeal about him. Blonde hair in a close military cut with highlights that immediately picked up any change in lighting, clear skin covering chiselled features with well-defined cheekbones, and a strong square chin with a deep cleft at its centre made his features almost too handsome to be seriously considered as boyish, but the dimples appearing on each side of his mouth whenever he parted his lips to reveal two white and perfectly even rows of teeth, had somehow and for some time, served to disguise that fact for most members of the opposite sex.

Naturally broad-shouldered but not heavily built, he had begun to work out regularly over the past few months and although he felt he still had some filling out to do, his six foot four and now well-muscled frame suited the cut of his uniform very pleasingly and he had become very conscious of how strongly women were physically attracted to him when they first set eyes on him.

Although, quite honestly, still unsure of what it was specifically about him that they found appealing, he had learned with much delight while in his very early teens that most young females were physically drawn to him.

That experience had blossomed during early sexual experimentation, initiated by and involving the younger female serving staff at his ancestral home when he was just fourteen and had, from his perspective, bloomed into a natural and eagerly accepted reality over the past ten years.

He was by now confident enough of this delightful phenomenon to be absolutely certain as he approached the counter to request a box of his brand of cigarillos, that with very little effort he could bed this woman before the day was out if he so desired. Unfortunately he had no time for such a dalliance at present, but the very possibility of its success if he so wished it, caused a familiar sensation of warmth to sweep through him.

This was inevitably followed by a stirring in his loins and he smiled broadly as he took pains to avoid the clerk's soft doe eyes and to ignore the lingering touch of her fingers while he offered payment and accepted the box from her hand.

As he closed the shop door behind him and began to walk back toward the train station his thoughts were still on the shop girl and while dwelling on the experience, he found his mind drifting back to the only negative he had seen so far as a result of his transfer from his last posting at the Naval Training Academy to his true passion, U-boats.

Just over six weeks ago he had met the most beautiful identical twins while he was attending a party at their parents' country home. Eighteen years old, blonde and each built like the proverbial brick outhouse, they had latched on to him late in the evening at the point where all three of them were enjoying the blissful glow of several hours of liberal alcoholic intake.

One thing had led to another and in the early hours of the next morning they had enthusiastically joined him in his rooms near the base.

In short order, after leaving a trail of cast-off clothing from the doorway leading into his apartment across the room to his bedroom, the twins had eagerly dragged him into bed. There he'd happily serviced them repeatedly, both singly and jointly to moans of appreciative delight and shrieks of pleasure.

As a result of his initial encounter with the twins Eric had very quickly found himself a willing member of a virtually inseparable threesome.

Their mother, who was quite obviously oblivious to the specific activities being enjoyed by her daughters and their handsome new friend and who was currently positioned about mid-point in the social society of the city and striving to climb higher if she could, openly welcomed this wealthy and well-connected new addition to the her daughters' circle of friends.

The woman had been openly impressed by both his old family name and the social positions held by the other members of his family. The girls' father, a Wehrmacht Colonel, was currently on course in Berlin and therefore at least temporarily out of the picture. As such he was not likely to pose any real threat in regard to Eric's plan to continue to enjoy what the eager twins had on offer.

Under the circumstances, Eric saw no reason to pass up the possibility of an extended liaison. That easily-reached decision had led to a month and a half of fantasy-fulfilling sexual encounters between the three of them. These had been conducted on an almost daily basis and with undisguised and totally uninhibited mutual enjoyment.

For a twenty-two year old male, no matter how sexually experienced he might be for that age, it was readily recognizable to Eric as a sensually-charged opportunity that was unlikely to ever present itself again in his lifetime. As such it had not been something he would have easily put aside, but his transfer had forced the issue.

Suddenly aware of increased pedestrian traffic around him he pulled himself out of his reverie and let out a deep sigh as he put the memories aside and turned his attention to finding a cab.

Fifteen minutes later he stepped out of a taxi in front of the naval dockyard's main gate.

He then crossed to the gatehouse to present his transfer and travel documents to the officer of the day. He was quickly sent on his way with a seaman now carrying his sea bag and leading the way to his newly assigned quarters.

As they passed the flag pole, the breeze coming in from the narrow six mile channel off the Baltic that served the port caused the cloth above to snap sharply and Eric looked up and took note of the pennant flying just below the Kriegsmarine Battle flag.

It was the pennant of the 'Fuhrer der U-Boote' (Leader of the U-boats), and it signified that the officer in charge of the U-boat fleet was currently present within the dockyards.

CHAPTER SEVEN

- Kiel Germany -

Kiel was home to the historic sea port which had been opened by the Prussians in March of eighteen sixty-five, and subsequently inherited by the Germans.

It was here that the first German U-boat, SM U-1was commissioned in nineteen hundred and six. The first U-boat flotilla had been formed in Kiel in nineteen hundred and ten. A short year later a fledgling Ubootsschule (U-boat school) had come into being.

The reason for Eric's current trip to Kiel was the recent formation of the 'Unterseebootsflottille Weddigen' (1st U-boat flotilla) and the resurrection of the U-boat school which he would now be attending in preparation for his new assignment.

The school was supported by the 'Schulverband der Unterseebootsschule' (the practical training unit of the U-boat school) which consisted of six U-boats selected for on the job training purposes. This training fleet was supported by its own supply ship, 'Saar'.

With the outbreak of the war on September first nineteen thirty-nine, the training boats attached to the U-boat school were re-assigned to active service on war patrol duties in both the Baltic and North Seas.

This change in assignment forced a restructuring of the training curriculum and the powers that be had decided that all new officer transfers to U-boats would be dealt with by having these new crew memberstake basic land-based instruction at Kiel. When that training phase had been accomplished theinstruction was to be completed by way of a direct transfer from Kiel to the training boats which were out on war patrols. Trainee U-boat officers would in this manner be distributed between the boats and complete the remainder of their training on a war footing.

This system was to continue until after the Norwegian campaign in nineteen-forty, at which time Germany was in a position to return the sub flotilla to the training school at Kiel.

These unique conditions for U-boat officer training led to Eric being assigned to a brand new submarine, U-62 on February tenth, 1940.

U-62 was a Type IIC U-boat built by Deutsche Werke AG, in Kiel-Gaarden. She had been ordered on July twenty-first, nineteen thirty-seven; had her keel laid on January second, nineteen thirty-nine and launched on November the sixteenth of that year. She completed her sea trials and was commissioned on December twenty-first, nineteen thirty-nine.

Her first Captain was Oberleutnant zur See (Lieutenant-Senior) Hans-Bernhard Michalowski, who remained in that position until May of nineteen forty-one.

Three days after Eric joined the U-62; she went to sea on her first active patrol, leaving the Port of Helgoland on February thirteenth nineteen-forty. After three weeks at sea, during which time Eric received little sleep as he worked through the crash course on the practical requirements of a sub Captain, the sub arrived in Wilhelmshaven on March sixth, nineteen-forty.

U-62 made its next patrol leaving Wilhelmshaven on April fourth, nineteen-forty for a second three week sailing to return to the port of Kiel on April twenty-fifth. Once again, Eric spent the majority of the cruise learning his new trade, commanding the boat under the direction of her Captain.

No one, least of all Eric, would have predicted what this combination of circumstances, plus some impending coincidences, would determine for the future of this young Oberfahnrich zur See.

On her third sailing of a war patrol, U-62 left from Kiel for Wilhelmshaven on the eighteenth of May nineteen-forty.

Although there were three trainee officers on board at this time, each taking turns throughout the patrol at commanding the sub under the auspices of her Captain, it happened that in the early morning hours of May twenty-ninth, it was Eric's turn at the con of the U-boat.

HMS Grafton (H 80) was a Royal Navy Destroyer, built by Thornycroft of Southampton. She had been ordered in March of nineteen thirty-four, had her keel laid down on August thirtieth of the same year and was launched on September eighteenth of nineteen thirty-five. She was commissioned after her sea trials on March twentieth, nineteen thirty- six.

The destroyer, while taking part in the emergency evacuation of members of the BEF (British Expeditionary Force) from the beaches of Dunkerque in France under the code name 'Operation Dynamo' was returning to Dover with a load of rescued men from that dismal military debacle when she was unfortunate enough to appear in the periscope of U-62.

Surprised, excited and unsure, Eric, who was peering with disbelief into that periscope and verbally sharing what he was seeing, moved back from the scope to make room for his Captain to step forward to access and handle the attack.

The Captain did step forward. He had a brief look and then stepped back and turned to face Eric.

"You found her Oberfahnrich zur See. Now, let's see if you can sink her!"

U-62 fired a single torpedo, striking the stern of the ship, blowing it off.

Her fourth active patrol sailing from Wilhelmshaven to Bergen on June thirteenth, nineteen-forty was uneventful, but her fifth patrol from Bergen to Kiel, which began on the tenth of July nineteen-forty, was of note.

After two weeks at sea, positioned at 55.23 North and 09.18 West at approximately 18:28 hours on July nineteenth, nineteen-forty U-62 came upon the British registered S.S. Pearlmoor, a four thousand five hundred and eighty-one ton cargo ship.

By way of rotation Eric happened to be the training officer at the helm at the time of contact. Again the ship in the periscope went down.

CHAPTER EIGHT

- Berchtesgaden, Bavarian Alps -

- July 30th 1940, 13:30 hours -

Precisely on time and under the delightful warmth of sunny cloudless skies, SS-Obersturmfuhrer (Lieutenant) Wilhelm von Stauffer stepped off the train and onto the platform of Bahnhof Berchtesgaden.

This recently completed construction, currently festooned with Nazi banners, followed the new Nazi architectural style for government buildings: imposing, solid, substantial, built to last. The design did not fail to impress the impeccably black-uniformed twenty-four year old.

He felt his heat rate increase slightly and paused momentarily as he proudly filled his chest with the fresh mountain air.

This was what the new Germany was about! A new Reich being built to last a thousand years!

He shifted his gaze from the station proper and swivelled to view the series of tracks within the marshalling yard, noting two other trains at rest, both of whose massive engines faced him and were marked with the swastika emblems denoting them as special trains of the Reich hierarchy.

The furthest away of these was nestled against a separate, special reception area which had been constructed for the exclusive use of The Fuhrer and his guests. It was immediately recognizable to Wilhelm, by the fact that it had two engines in tandem, as being the 'Fuhrersonderzug', Hitler's personal train, and he felt increased excitement welling up in him.

He was here! The Fuhrer was in Berchtesgaden!

Lost in his thoughts, he failed to notice the figure approaching from the rear.

As he closed the distance between them Hauptsturmfuhrer Joachim Peiper, Chief Adjutant to Reichsfuhrer Heinrich Himmler, approaching Wilhelm from behind, took note with some amusement of the arrogant and deliberate stance taken by the young Obersturmfuhrer.

He found himself wondering.

Was I ever that green, that susceptible? That proud?

It seemed like so long ago, but yes, he had to admit to himself, there had been a time.

The sound of Peiper's highly polished boots striking the wooden platform interrupted Wilhelm Von Stauffer's reverie and caused him to turn around in time to catch Peiper's controlled but unmistakeable smile.

The Obersturmfuhrer's right arm shot out and his heels met resoundingly as he barked.

"Heil Hitler!"

Peiper came to a halt and returned the salute then extended his right hand.

"Obersturmfuhrer Wilhelm von Staffer I presume? I'm Joachim Peiper – Welcome to Berchtesgaden."

Wilhelm had not anticipated the proffered hand, but he recovered quickly and shook it briefly but firmly.

"An honour Hauptsturmfuhrer; your reputation precedes you."

The smile returned briefly to Peiper's thin lips.

"Hopefully you've heard nothing but good things."

The question was rhetorical and he didn't wait for the Obersturmfuhrer to respond, instead he held out his right hand, palm up.

"Your orders."

Still stiff at attention, Wilhelm flipped open the top button of his left tunic flap and drew out his transfer and travel documents as well as his identification and then placed them in the

Hauptsturmfuhrer's hand.

Peiper took them but did not examine them immediately. Instead, for a few seconds he openly studied the young officer who towered in front of him.

"My God what a specimen: strong chiselled features, blond-haired, blue -eyed, at least six foot six inches tall and extremely powerfully built - no matter what else the Reichsfuhrer had in mind for this perfect example of Aryan manhood, he was an obvious choice for inclusion in the Lebensborn Program.

Wilhelm, still in awe of his secondment transfer orders and more than a little curious as to what his new assignment would entail, wanted very much to probe for some specific information about his new job, but knew better than to be so bold as to ask. Instead he remained at attention and waited for Peiper to speak.

The Hauptsturmfuhrer sensed the young officer was becoming uncomfortable under his extended examination and turned his attention to the documents in his hand. He perused them quickly and then handed them back as he, once again allowed the smile to return briefly to his face.

"All in order, now if you will just follow me, I will take you to the Reichsfuhrer."

* * * * *

Reichsfuhrer Heinrich Himmler's features hardened when the sunlight filtering in through the window briefly glinted off his glasses. He turned his attention from his guest and met the gaze of the white uniformed SS orderly who stood by the doorway leading into the Reichsfuhrer's now stationary office on wheels.

That single look was enough to spur the man into immediate action and within seconds the blind on the offending window had been lowered enough to keep the sun out of the diminutive figure's eyes.

Himmler made no comment as the man accomplished the task and returned to his position beside the doorway.

Once the uniformed orderly was back in place, Himmler

returned his attention to the fifty-eight year old, recently re-activated Wehrmacht Generalleutnant who sat in one of the comfortably upholstered chairs that faced him on the other side of his desk.

"As I was saying Generalleutnant, in consideration of the Fuhrer's decision in this matter and while it may not seem that your newly appointed position as Reich, 'Aufseher, Buro der Wissenschaftliche Forschung' (Overseer, Office of Scientific Research) at the Kaiser Wilhelm Institute would require it. I believe in the broader view that it would be of mutual benefit if you and I were to come to an understanding regarding your future responsibilities."

The Generalleutnant, who stood six-foot-four and was unbowed in stature despite his years, shifted his erect posture slightly in the chair as his eyes carefully studied the SS-Reichsfuhrer.

Take away the uniform, put this little man into civilian clothes and you would pass him on the street and take no notice. A jumped-up chicken farmer no less…and yet perhaps, if not yet, certainly well on his way to becoming one of the most powerful men in the New Germany.

Only a fool would knowingly make an enemy of this man. Not only his own future but that of his entire family rested on how he dealt with this physically unimpressive officer.

He chose his words carefully while he removed the envelope from his pocket and placed it on the desk between them.

"Herr Reichsfuhrer, while I'm sure you are correct in your assessment of the need for us both to be attuned to the concerns of the other with regard to the manner in which I carry out my duties, I feel obligated by my orders to point out the fact that, as this letter clearly states, it is The Fuhrer's wish that I be responsible to him and only to him."

A thin smile formed on Himmler's lips as he picked up the envelope and slipped out the single folded sheet of eggshell coloured paper it held. Two beady eyes took in the black embossed large 'State Eagle' and the simple 'DER FUHRER' at the top and the familiar signature at the bottom, and then narrowed as he read the text.

When he had finished he silently refolded the sheet, returned it to the envelope and set it back down onto the desk. He then leaned back into his chair and smiled.

"Yes, just so! However, I had an opportunity to discuss this matter with The Fuhrer only yesterday and as a result of that conversation it was the Fuhrer's wish that I offer you my full personal support toward the advancement of your important endeavours..."

He paused, drawing out his last words for emphasis before continuing.

"...The Fuhrer felt, as do I, that I should be personally in-volved due to the importance of your work which directly relates to the preservation of the new Regime and the assurance of the Reich's internal security in the period yet to come. As I am sure you are aware, these two concerns are the basis for the creation of the SS 'Corps d'Elite' which I lead as Reichsfuhrer-SS."

Pausing, Himmler opened the top drawer of his desk and slipped out a letter very similar in appearance to the one that now rested in its envelope on the desk between them. He then placed it with a flourish on top of and covering, the envelope, before he resumed speaking.

"This is a copy. You may take it with you. As you can see Generalleutnant, my letter from The Fuhrer is more recently dated than yours, and while it doesn't affect the general tone of your letter precisely - you will still report directly to The Fuhrer. It does provide you with a well-deserved promotion more fitting to the scope of your responsibilities and a change in uniform."

The thin lips took on a much broader smile and those small eyes sparkled brightly.

"Let me be the first to congratulate you on that promotion to SS-Oberstgruppenfuhrer. Welcome to our little family. You will be pleased to know that your promotion is now official and you will find new uniforms awaiting you in your compartment. I suggest you change immediately so that you can be properly attired to welcome my new junior adjutant who should be arriving shortly to take up his duties as my personal liaison officer with your organization."

CHAPTER NINE

- Bahnhof, Berchtesgaden -

- Reichsfuhrer Heinrich Himmler's Personal Train –

- July 30th 1940, 13:45 hours -

They walked side by side, Peiper slightly ahead, dropping down onto a lower walkway that led across the end of the various tracks and over toward the two stationary trains on the far side of the railway yard.

As they stepped down into the gravel, the Hauptsturmfuhrer nodded toward the closest unit.

"The Reichsfuhrer is in his mobile command headquarters, the fourth carriage there, the one with the blackout curtains drawn to keep out the direct sun."

Wilhelm nodded and as they changed course slightly to move directly toward the car in question, Peiper spoke again.

"So where did we drag you from? I don't think we've ever crossed paths before."

"'SS-Junkerschule Bad Tolz' (Officer's Training School for the Waffen-SS), I was sports instructor, boxing."

Peiper paused mid-step and rested a hand on Wilhelm's shoulder.

"Right, now I remember. You were National Boxing Champion in thirty-seven; I knew I recognized you from somewhere. When did you receive your appointment to Training School staff?"

"Thirty-eight."

Peiper nodded and climbed up onto the steps leading into the car.

He knocked once and when the orderly opened the door he stepped through and Wilhelm followed him inside.

The two of them moved across to the desk and gave the salute and 'Heil Hitler' in unison. Peiper spoke.

"Obersturmfuhrer Wilhelm Von Stauffer reporting for duty as ordered, my Reichsfuhrer."

Himmler returned their salute and then took off his pince-nez and laid it carefully on the desk in front of him before reaching up to rub the bridge of his nose where the spectacles had been resting. When he was finished he briefly looked up at the two men before turning his attention to the orderly who had admitted them.

"Leave us now. When I ring for you, bring in tea for four and show the Oberstgruppenfuhrer in when he returns."

When the man had left the car Himmler turned his attention back to the two officers who were still standing stiffly at attention on the other side of his desk.

"Sit Gentlemen, but Joachim, please move in another chair for our other guest before you do."

While Peiper went about the task, Himmler let his gaze rest on Wilhelm. Pleased at what he saw before him his thin lips parted in a smile.

"Gott in Himmel Joachim! He should be our poster boy!"

Peiper dropped a third chair in front of the desk, sat down in it and smiled.

"Yes Reichsfuhrer. Just so! I was going to suggest we have some preliminary photographs taken and forwarded for consideration. It also occurred to me that we should consider this young man for the 'Lebensborn' programme."

Himmler addressed Wilhelm for the first time.

"Stand up Obersturmfuhrer, let me look at you; that's it, now turn in a circle please."

An obviously embarrassed Wilhelm, who knew little of the 'Lebensborn' (Fountain of Life) programme initiated on December twelfth, nineteen thirty-five as one of Himmler's pet projects, did as he was bid and after a few seconds Himmler waved him back to his chair and turned to face Peiper.

The Hauptsturmfuhrer, who had been Himmler's Chief Adjutant since thirty-eight was well aware of the depth of the Reichsfuhrer's commitment and very strong interest in the programme which he had personally designed and was aimed at the reversal of the then currently declining birthrate. The aim of the plan was to increase the Germanic/Nordic population of a vastly expanded Germany to one hundred and twenty million. Under the direction of the Reichsfuhrer, this and several additional eugenic related programmes, had received massive allotments of funds and were entirely staffed by highly motivated and dedicated SS personal.

Peiper was therefore not surprised at his boss's obvious interest in the specimen of Aryan perfection now seated before him.

"Do it. Make the initial arrangements today and I think we might also make use of this young officer in an administrative sense with a view to the overall goal of reaching the targets of our future needs in that regard. That would of course be in addition to the responsibilities of the posting he is about to receive.

Place such a discussion on my calendar. I wish to address the matter personally, once the Fuhrer's Military Conference has been completed."

Peiper drew a small notebook and pen from of his tunic pocket and made a note while, baffled as to the meaning of the verbal exchange between the two other men, Wilhelm made no response but remained sitting erect and alert.

There was a soft knock, a short pause and then the door opened and, wearing one of his new black uniforms, the very recently promoted SS-Oberstgruppenfuhrer Count Karl von Stauffer entered.

Wilhelm was taken by complete surprise.

"Father!"

The Count, as surprised as his offspring at finding his eldest son as part of the grouping within the coach, but well-practiced at keeping his emotions under control at all times, demonstrated not the slightest change in his facial expression as his eyes moved from Wilhelm to those of the Reichsfuhrer.

"Am I correct in assuming that Obersturmfuhrer von Stauffer is to be your representative on my staff Herr Reichsfuhrer?"

Himmler beamed back at him and nodded.

"Yes Oberstgruppenfuhrer, among other duties, he will fulfill that responsibility. Now that that is out of the way, let us drop the formality and permit you and your son to have some private time together. I understand you have not seen each other in some time."

He turned his gaze toward Wilhelm.

"The Count has been allocated quarters on my train for the duration of this Military Conference. As you know gentleman, we have a war to fight and I have other responsibilities to The Fuhrer which I have been neglecting in order to facilitate the welcoming of the two of you into the central structure of our SS family and the team who will guide the very important scientific challenges facing the New Reich as we move into the future. I know the Count is a very busy man and will not be able to spend much time here, but I would suggest that you both take this opportunity to avail yourself of a few hours of private time together."

He glanced toward Peiper.

"Joachim, you will not need the Obersturmfuhrer until the morning will you…say about eight?

Peiper nodded.

"That would be fine; our first meeting with The Fuhrer is scheduled for nine. An hour will be enough for me to brief Wilhelm on his new duties."

Himmler raised his hand in salute.

"Heil Hitler gentlemen"

Peiper and Wilhelm got to their feet; all three men returned the salute and then the Hauptsturmfuhrer led the way to the door and opened it for them, nodding at each as they left the coach.

Closing the door behind them, Peiper returned to the Reichsfuhrer's desk.

Himmler replaced his pince-nez onto the bridge of his nose and closed the file on his desk.

"Well done Joachim, I believe we have gone a long way in ensuring that The Fuhrer's choice of Leader for the Fatherland's Science and Technology Advancement Ministry will fall under our direct control. We should now be guaranteed of our ability to keep up to speed with and to guide this particularly important department toward the goals we have identified as absolutely paramount for the success of the New Reich. We will of course need to keep our eager young Von Stauffer on a tight leash, but in consideration of his background, education and performance to date, there is every reason to believe that he will eagerly share our vision and in so doing serve to further fortify his father's loyalty to our cause."

* * * * *

Count von Stauffer was silent until he and his son were inside the spacious compartment situated in the coach two cars away from the Reichsfuhrer's office which Himmler had provided for his use while he remained in Berchtesgaden.

As he closed the door behind him his eyes met Wilhelm's and he pointedly raised his finger to his lips in a silent communication to prevent his son from speaking.

"Well this is quite a surprise. We have some catching up to do. Have you had lunch?"

His youngest son nodded in acknowledgement of the obvious warning with regard to loose conversation and responded.

"A late breakfast, but I'm ready for lunch."

His father nodded, and for the first time since they had found themselves together, allowed himself a smile as he wrapped Wilhelm in a firm bear hug.

When they parted his father spoke again.

"Good, I know a likely spot where we can get a drink and enjoy a first-rate meal."

They left the train and when they had made their way out through the front of the station and onto the street, Father turned to his son and spoke for his ears only.

"You have moved up into the big leagues now. You must be constantly mindful of what you say, whom you say it to and how loud you say it. The train is wired. The good Reichsfuhrer-SS makes an excellent patron, but do not forget for a moment that he is Germany's top policeman and he takes his responsibilities to The Fuhrer and the New Reich very seriously. Like most effective policemen, he has a very suspicious mind and likes to know not only what everyone around him is doing but also what they are thinking at all times. We'll be able to find some privacy in the beer hall while we eat and when we do, we will talk."

CHAPTER TEN

- The Berghof –

- Obersalzberg - Germany -

'The Berghof' was the name of Adolf Hitler's home, situated in the Obersalzberg of the Bavarian Alps above the town of Berchtesgaden.

The original small chalet built on the site had first been rented by Hitler and then subsequently bought by The Fuhrer in nineteen thirty-three by using some of the considerable proceeds from his political manifesto 'Mein Kampf' (My Struggle) which he had begun writing while serving the jail sentence resulting from the part he played in the Nazi party's attempted 'putsch' of nineteen twenty-three. Hitler had finished the book shortly after his release from prison.

With the use of party funds, the simple structure he'd originally purchased was renovated and greatly expanded between nineteen thirty-five and nineteen thirty-six and when completed the name of the property was officially changed from 'Haus Wachenfeld' to 'The Berghof'.

It was no secret that The Fuhrer preferred living in the Obersalzberg to any other place in the Greater German Reich and spent as much time as possible at his home at 'The Berghof', going so far as to have an airstrip built and ordering the extension of the Munich/Salzburg Autobahn onward to Obersalzberg to simplify the travel of his motorcades plus authorizing the construction of the rail station 'Bahnhof Berchtesgaden' to handle the increased traffic flow of tourists who wished to view The Fuhrer's home.

He was, after all 'the people's leader', with the support of ninety-eight percent of his citizens and arguably the most popular politician in the world.

Interest in the Berghof was not only local in nature as it had reached an international audience when in November nineteen thirty-eight an English fashion magazine published a three-page spread on the 'The Fuhrer's' home.

This popularity, combined with the excellent summer weather and the Military Conference currently underway at the Berghof, meant that the population of the town of Berchtesgaden had more than doubled. Finding a quiet spot for a bite to eat and a beer was not going to be an easy task.

However, the Count's SS-Oberstgruppenfuhrer uniform had a very definite effect on the staff of the first beer hall they entered and they quickly found themselves ensconced in a private room with their own dedicated waiter hovering anxiously in his eagerness to grant their every wish.

The man was advised as to what they would have for lunch, what they wished to drink, and instructed to take up a position outside the only door to ensure that they were not disturbed until, and after their order was delivered.

When the door closed behind the waiter the Count sat at the small table and waved his son into the chair across from him.

"Sit, we need to talk and we won't have many opportunities to do that before I have to leave in the morning."

Wilhelm had been biting his tongue.

"What is it with the change in uniform? The last letter I received from mother said you were brought out of retirement at the specific request of The Fuhrer and had taken up your old rank of Wehrmacht Generalleutnant at his request after being given a special assignment, something to do with heading a new agency or department with regard to scientific and weapons development?"

His father sighed deeply and nodded.

"Yes that is what I originally agreed to do; however the Reichsfuhrer-SS has since spoken with the Fuhrer and what you see…"

He lowered his eyes as he waved his hand down across his

chest.

"...is the result."

Wilhelm was impressed, not exactly the reaction his father had expected.

"You've been promoted to full General, and an SS position to boot. I'm really pleased for you Dad. You must be very proud to have the Fuhrer offer such a powerful position within the New Germany; and now it would seem that one of my duties will serve to ensure that, for at least part of the time, we will be working together! Mother will be ecstatic!"

The Count studied his son for a second and then took in a deep breath.

"I am pleased to answer my Fatherland's call to active duty in a time of war. However this is not the uniform in which I would have chosen to serve, had I been given a choice. I am not your mother who will, as you suggest, be ecstatic and immediately preparing for a new and full social calendar involving those within the New Reich's Hierarchy. I am a soldier, and no longer a particularly young one."

Wilhelm was a perfect example of the young males who had been carefully indoctrinated into the Nazi's totalitarian sphere of beliefs. At the age of fifteen, he had eagerly joined the Hitler Youth which catered to boys aged from ten to eighteen. At the time he had been old enough to retain some earlier teachings but still young enough to be malleable and easily manipulated under the Organization's meticulously structured nurturing.

He had gone from there directly into the SS Officer training program and was, as his father knew only to well, a passionate supporter of the SS, the Nazi party and The Fuhrer, to whom he had sworn a personal oath of allegiance and therein, to every aspect of the New Germany Hitler had brought into being.

The Count had no desire to relive the several political disagreements he'd had with his young son over the past few years, a son he deeply loved.

He searched carefully to find the words to express himself

without the inherent danger of re-entering that area of earlier discord.

Am I wrong to dislike and distrust this New Germany? Is what I see as indoctrination and propaganda simply the realization of true nationalism? Am I simply fighting change because I am from an old military family who has always thought and fought to maintain the status quo? Is it because I am old-fashioned that I believe it is dangerous to be too so easily swept up in what I see as a radical change in the basic historical values of the German people? Could it be instead that if not for me, then for my family's sake, I should see it as so many others do, as the simple and undeniable organization and recognition of a special people's right to their proper place in the world?

"In all fairness, perhaps I am simply too old to accept and understand the many changes which have happened so very quickly. Am I so representative of the old guard that I wear blinders against social change?"

Tension had been building in Wilhelm, who sensed that they had been about to argue again and he felt it dissipate as his father spoke. He relaxed his stiff shoulders as he smiled across at his father.

"We have entered a modern age, Father. Germany has been reborn under the leadership of The Fuhrer. For the first time in recent history the Fatherland has thrown off all its shackles and begun to assume its natural place as a leader among the states of the world."

The Count's eyes met his son's.

"I have no difficulty in understanding how this all began. The German people had every reason to feel ill-treated. The Treaty of Versailles dealt unfairly with the Fatherland. Few rational people in today's world would argue that fact. After the loss of the Great War our country was ground under the Allies' boots, and the imbalance of Versailles definitely needed to be addressed, but how far the other way should the pendulum swing before the German people accept that we have reached a balance with the rest of the world?"

Wilhelm shrugged and was about to respond when there was a knock and the waiter entered with a tray holding tankards. He waited until they had been set on the table between him and his father and the door closed behind the man before he spoke.

"We must trust in The Fuhrer to make those decisions for us. He has a clear view of what needs to be achieved for the Fatherland in order for it to take its proper place in the world.

Have you read Mein Kampf yet? My God Father, how can you still have doubts? He has proven himself again and again. In little more than a year the New Germany has corrected historic imbalances that have existed in Europe for centuries. Releasing thousands of subjugated German peoples and freeing many of those under corrupt foreign rule.

The German Eagle now flies over an empire larger than we could have ever imagined and it is all thanks to one man, our Fuhrer, Adolf Hitler. He has welcomed into the Reich, Austria, Czechoslovakia, Poland, Denmark, Norway, and now France. He has accomplished most of this without shedding even one drop of German blood. Yes, and now France knows the feel of a German boot and they felt it strike across the same table in the same rail car in which Germany faced the imposition of the crushing Allied reprisals of the Great War, a war Germany did not start and would not have lost if the Jews had not stabbed the Fatherland in the back.

How can any German question the Fuhrer's leadership now. He has proven the truth of his vision for the Fatherland. No real German can possibly question The Fuhrer's brilliant intuition with regard to his Military and Diplomatic policies."

The Count's expression didn't change, but he was analyzing his son's comments.

Indoctrinated or not, there is some truth in what the boy says. Our new leader, the Austrian Corporal, has certainly been blessed with luck. But even in a world that does not want war, appeasement will only hold sway for so long and any state will eventually take up arms if pushed too far.

It takes more than luck to win an extended war, and that is what this could so easily become. It would be disastrous if that should come to pass, and Germany's ability to fight is lessened over time through the attrition of men and materials brought about by a long war. Will Hitler know when enough is enough, or will he sink into the fog of megalomania and believe he can conquer the entire world?

If the vast majority of Germans continue to bow blindly to the Nazi propaganda machine, denied the openness of free thought, will they ever consider the use of a collective open mind and remove their support of a man, who now appears to most, as the Fatherland's redeeming messiah?

It seemed very unlikely that under the circumstances The Fuhrer would ever allow that to happen. It is hard for a man of war to look for peace; history had proven that over and over again: and this man looked every inch a man of war.

In many ways, like any good German, he would like to be able to share his young son's conviction that the New Germany was, under Hitler's leadership, destined for a wonderful future. Perhaps that would in fact come to pass; only time would tell.

For now, he would bide his time and hold his tongue. He would agree with his son and hope that they might both enjoy the meal they were about to share.

CHAPTER ELEVEN

- Berchtesgaden Bahnhof -

- July 31st 1940, 07:30 hours -

The morning arrived as a mirror image of the previous day.

Bright sunshine with a warm but fresh breeze ruffling the many Nazi banners adorning the impressive Bahnhof Berchtesgaden train station as Wilhelm walked with his father through the building and out to the street to where the Count's powerful factory-fresh and brilliantly polished black Mercedes-Benz 770 Series ll – W150 Cabriolet awaited.

His father noted with some displeasure that his Wehrmacht driver had been replaced along with his previous staff car.

His new vehicle came complete with a uniformed SS chauffer, and fender flags reflecting his new rank accompanied by SS runes plus a matched set of uniformed SS motorcycle outriders.

On the flip side of the coin, he also took note of the pride reflected in Wilhelm's eyes as his son took in the solid presence created by the beautiful vehicle, and as a result, he made no comment with regard to these changes in his official mode of transport as he said his goodbyes to his son and watched as his driver moved quickly to salute and open the door of the impressive vehicle for him.

* * * * *

- Bahnhof Berchtesgaden –

Wilhelm was a little early for his scheduled meeting with Joachim Peiper, managing to locate him in the conference car of the Reichsfuhrer's train at zero seven forty-five hours; however his premature arrival appeared to please rather than irritate the Hauptsturmfuhrer who he found cradling a steaming cup of coffee as he sat at a map table with some files spread out in front of him.

Joachim was immaculately dressed and appeared well-rested.

Upon spotting Wilhelm, Peiper waved his free hand in the direction of the credenza on the far side of the car.

"Fresh coffee over there, pour a cup and join me."

Wilhelm helped himself to a cup and filled it from the carafe, added sugar and cream and then carried it over to the table and sat across from Peiper who looked up and smiled.

"To start this off right Wilhelm, we will address each other with given names from this point on when we are alone. Now, the Reichsfuhrer has assigned you the responsibly of acting as his liaison officer with your father, the Count's, agency. Understand up front that your job will be to keep the Reichsfuhrer completely informed as to the progress and activity on all of the programs that fall under the leadership and control of that agency. You must ensure that you take this responsibility very seriously for I assure you the Reichsfuhrer will; you may take it as a given that he has already seen to it that there are checks and balances in place to guarantee that you represent him effectively and keep him fully informed at all times. Not that he has any doubt that you will perform this duty studiously I'm sure, but because these are trying times and he considers it an absolute necessity that he be kept well informed by his assigned staff. He will have other sources in this regard. Report everything, no matter how insignificant. Do you have any questions in that regard?"

Wilhelm tasted his coffee and set the cup down before shaking his head.

"No Hau…Joachim. You may rest assured the Reichsfuhrer will receive full and complete reports."

The other man raised a dismissive hand.

"Wilhelm, I recommended you for this assignment and you may believe me when I say that I would not have done so if I had even the slightest doubt as to your abilities or your loyalty to our cause. We SS are the chosen and we do not shirk from our duty. "

His eyes briefly held Wilhelm's for effect and evaluation and then he continued.

"While this assignment to your father's agency will be your primary concern, it will not require your full attention. You will simply be conducting a meeting with the Count once per week at which time, based on the orders he received this morning directly from the Reichsfuhrer, he will provide you with all the information you will need to formulate your reports. The remainder of your time will be spent working on other projects as chosen specifically by the Reichsfuhrer. Some of these will be projects that fall under your father's oversight and therefore will simplify your weekly reports in that you will be fully up to speed on them in a hands-on sense. What do you know about eugenics?"

Wilhelm blanched slightly.

"Very little really..."

Peiper laughed.

"Well you will soon be an expert in the field. How about the Lebensborn program?"

Wilhelm flushed and smiled.

"Well, I've heard a few rumours about that one."

Peiper nodded knowingly.

"Yes, well the Reichsfuhrer seems to feel that you should be involved in the administration of both of those projects and that you become a direct participant in the latter."

He bundled and held out the files that had been resting on the map table.

"Familiarize yourself with these... there is one more thing."

As Wilhelm took the files Peiper held out to him, his superior leaned back in his chair and opened the top center drawer of the table to withdraw two Adjutants' aluminum thread aiguillettes, which he dropped down on the top of the files.

"You may keep the files; they are your copies of the current situation. You now have the right to wear the aiguillette,and ensure that you do so at all times. The Reichsfuhrer will take note if you do not, and in consideration of the fact that you will be accompanying him and me to today's conference meetings which begin at nine, you have only one half hour to make yourself presentable."

He pointed at his own aiguillette and smiled.

"It runs from the second tunic button, over, around and under the left shoulder and back to the second button. You've been assigned a compartment on the train. My orderly will show you the way. If all has gone according to plan you will find your new orderly in your quarters awaiting your instructions. You'd better run along now; the Reichsfuhrer will expect us to be in place when a car arrives at the front of the station and it would be very bad form to be late on your first day. The Reichsfuhrer is much disciplined and expects the same of his staff. He is a fair man but not one a sensible officer would wish to disappoint or displease."

CHAPTER TWELVE

- Berchtesgaden -

Consisting of only three cars, the SS-Reichsfuhrer had only been provided with a relatively small motorcade for the short trip from the train station to the Obersalzberg complex which had been constructed around Hitler's much renovated Berghof home.

Two black SS clad motorcycles stood in front of the lead car which was manned by six members of his personal SS-bodyguard unit. This was followed by the Reichsfuhrer's chauffeured open green BMW staff car with the ostentatious 'SS-1' number plate and trailed by a tail car in which Wilhelm, Peiper and one other junior adjutant were to ride.

As the motorcade pulled out to begin the trip Peiper and Wilhelm rode in the back seat of the final car and the efficient Hauptsturmfuhrer did not hesitate to take advantage of the trip to further groom his new protégé for his future duties.

He talked and the young Obersturmfuhrer listened.

"Today you will accompany the Reichsfuhrer and me to the Berghof. Once we have arrived, you will be present for the initial ceremonies of greeting for the participants who in this particular session will consist of the members of the OKW High Command, the Navy High Command and the OKH General staff as well as recently promoted Reich Marshall Herman Goering representing the Luftwaffe and Reich Propaganda Minister Joseph Goebbels.

The Reichsfuhrer and I will be remaining for the first meeting of the day which will commence at 09:00. I do not know how long we will be spending with the Fuhrer today, but you will not be personally attending any of the meetings.

Once the initial ceremony of welcome is over you and your compatriot in the front seat, Obersturmfuhrer Helmut Muller, will instruct the driver to take this car to the SS Compound, *The Kaserne*

Once there you, with the assistance of your companion, will become familiar with the material in the files I gave you this morning, which I assume are within the briefcase at your feet."

Wilhelm nodded and Peiper continued, as the motorcade began to work its way out of the town and then upward towards the east for the two mile climb to the Obersalzberg compound, twelve hundred feet above and overlooking the town below.

"While you are in the presence of the Reichsfuhrer today, you will under no circumstances speak unless spoken to. If that should happen, which is highly unlikely under the circumstances, you will reply concisely and quickly. You will not initiate a conversation with anyone present. You are there to be seen, not heard. You will be notified later in the day when the Reichsfuhrer is about to leave and this driver, who will remain with the car, will bring you both back to take part in the return motorcade. At some point this evening I will find the time to review the files with you to ensure that you fully understand what is expected of you. Do you have any questions about how you will be expected to act when we arrive, or how you will spend the day until the motorcade leaves to return to the Reichsfuhrer's train?"

Wilhelm shook his head.

* * * * *

- Obersalzberg -

- July 31st 1940, 08:30 hours -

The Reichsfuhrer's motorcade outriders reached the first SS-guardhouse at what had been designated as the border of the exterior security zone which surrounded the massive Nazi Obersalzberg complex.

Here the road leading to the compound crossed the bridge

over the Ache Berchtesgaden River.

The lead car pulled up behind the motorcycles stopped at the barrier as an impeccably dressed SS-Officer stepped out of the guardhouse on the left side of the bridge approach.

The following two vehicles came to a stop in line while the driver of the first car exchanged salutes with the officer in charge and the two men conducted a brief verbal exchange.

The SS-Reichsfuhrer was both expected and readily recognized as he sat in the rear of the open green BMW behind the lead car.

As a result the examination of the motorcade was cursory and the barrier was lifted swiftly to allow their passage through.

A split second later the car containing Wilhelm crossed the bridge and slipped majestically beneath the bulk of the massive sign reading 'FUHRER, WIR DANKEN DIR' (FUHRER, WE THANK YOU), which ran from post to post above and across the roadway.

The lettering on the wooden sign was three feet high and the sign itself ran between the tops of two thick thirty foot high columns, one on either side of the roadway.

A few moments later the motorcade was again brought to a halt, this time at the main SS gatehouse, the 'Torhaus Berghof' which was situated on the road just below the Berghof itself.

This gatehouse, more elaborate than the first, was constructed of rock and timber with a closed solid wooden gate. It spanned the entire roadway between the mountainside and the cliff on the left.

This time the exchange between the SS guards and their supervising officer was anything but cursory.

In this instance, after the obligatory salutes had been exchanged, the papers of all passengers with the exception of the Reichsfuhrer himself were examined and their names were checked against a clipboard holding the names of those previously pre-screened for admittance into the inner security area of the compound.

Once the checks had been completed to the satisfaction of the officer in charge, the salutes were repeated and the gate was opened to admit the motorcade, which proceeded up the grade of the mountainside and then turned sharply right into the driveway that swept past the stairway leading upward to the Berghof itself.

Here it stopped and Himmler's entourage alighted, formed up and began to follow the Reichsfuhrer who led the way up the broad stairway. The drivers then pulled the vehicles away to make room for other motorcades which were now working their way up the mountainside from the town below.

Wilhelm, accompanied by the other junior adjutant, trailed the group. He did his best to keep his mouth from gaping as he took in the scenery.

It had been said in the nineteen thirty-eight edition of the English fashion magazine that the site of the Berghof commanded the fairest view in all of Europe. Wilhelm was no expert, but the lush greenness and thick forest framed by snow-capped mountains was certainly impressive.

They reached the top of the stairs and stepped into the entrance hall which was decorated with an array of cactus plants in pots. Here the party was greeted by one of the Fuhrer's aides and after a few moments, Muller nudged Wilhelm and nodded his head.

It was time for the two of them to leave the entourage.

As they climbed back aboard the car that had brought them up the mountain, at Wilhelm's request and after some consideration by Muller, the driver was instructed to make a short detour on the way to the 'Kaserne' SS headquarters, within the massive complex.

The compound had been closed to the public since nineteen thirty-six and Wilhelm wished for a brief round of sightseeing among the eighty buildings which encircled the Berghof and were contained within the inner security zone.

They found viewpoints that allowed Wilhelm to take in the scope of the compound, which in addition to the Fuhrer's home, contained several other villas and chalets owned by senior Nazi leaders as well as the infrastructure required for the massive compound's day to day operation.

Of note were the kindergarten, the huge greenhouse complex to serve Hitler's vegetarian diet and the humongous coal storage bunker which, Muller advised him, could hold up to ten thousand cubic meters or over thirty-five tons of coal to meet the power needs of the complex.

Muller had no wish to attract the undue attention of one of the many floating SS-squads of the Fuhrer's personal SS guard unit who irregularly patrolled the inner security area and he soon put an end to the sightseeing and advised the driver to take them directly to the Kaserne.

CHAPTER THIRTEEN

- The Kaserne –

- July 31ˢᵗ 1940, 09:20 hours –

The staff car pulled up in front of the impressive SS headquarters situated within the Obersalzberg complex.

Built in a rectangular shape with a large parade square at its centre, the Kaserne consisted of a barrack building, kitchen and mess hall, vehicle maintenance and storage building, gymnasium and staff Headquarters building.

Their transport pulled up in front of the Headquarters building, and Wilhelm and Helmut Muller stepped out and dismissed their driver.

Muller led the way inside and within a few moments the two of them were alone and comfortably ensconced inside an elaborately furnished reading room.

Despite the early hour, in preparation for and anticipation of several hours of review, they dispatched an SS-orderly to bring them a snack and a couple of beers.

Once they had received their refreshments they settled down side by side at a table near the window and Wilhelm took out of his briefcase the files which he handed to Muller, who began to review them.

In typical German style, some administrating bureaucrat had tediously mapped a history of both subjects, a copy of each which now resided in the two plump file folders.

Muller glanced briefly at both before beginning to speak.

"As the study of Eugenics predated that of Lebensborn, we will begin there.

I understand that you have only a smattering of understanding with regard to each so let us begin with a thorough foundation of a history of both, beginning with that of Eugenics."

Wilhelm nodded in agreement and Muller continued.

"Put simply, Eugenics is the study of, or belief in, the probability of improving the base characteristics of the Human species or of a specifically chosen sector of the Human population. This may be attempted in one of two ways, either by discouraging reproduction by persons having genetic defects - those that are presumed to have inheritable undesirable traits - regarded as Negative Eugenics or conversely, of encouraging reproduction by persons presumed to have inheritably desirable traits, or Positive Eugenics."

He glanced over at Wilhelm and took a bite out of his sausage and cheese sandwich then washed it down with a swig of beer before continuing.

"Any Questions?"

Wilhelm shook his head and Muller went on.

"It is of interest to note that the attraction for Eugenics is not a particularly German phenomenon. In fact there are strong followers of the subject among many races: the United States, America containing one of the largest groups, with a vociferous assemblage primarily centered in the state of California."

Wilhelm was a little taken aback and he arched his eyebrows as Muller went on.

"The formation of this approach to a specific type of racial purity has been with us for centuries, and its development is not difficult to understand. Many races have sought to create a standard of excellence within the confines of their specific genetic makeup. As examples of Positive and Negative Eugenics, we Germans, under our superior Nazi administration, have moved into the forefront of scientific research in this field as well as a plethora of others."

He looked up from his reading to meet Wilhelm's gaze.

"But then of course you already know that, since your father oversees all of our military and scientific research programs."

Wilhelm shrugged.

"I'm relatively new to it all I'm afraid. My father is extremely closed mouth about what he does."

Muller's features reflected his seriousness.

"Yes of course he is. How foolish of me. Most of his work is top secret. At any rate, let me move on here. Our scientists have leapfrogged ahead in Eugenics. They are currently studying the ability to genetically engineer human structure and offshoots of that program are currently probing the likelihood of the Reich's ability to create specifically genetically engineered Aryan human specimens outside of the normal requirements of natural sexual union.

It is an externally complex field of research and only a handful of our top scientists are currently involved at this point. It is only they who understand the potential of that field. But I can tell you that the concept of producing an endless supply of perfect male Aryan warriors is no longer just a dream for the party. It will soon be a reality."

A picture of an endless stream of tall muscular blond-haired, blue-eyed, supermen spewing forth from a factory formed in Wilhelm's mind and he marvelled at the thought.

"This is fantastic! No nation could stand against the Reich if we had such a capability."

Muller smile broadened.

"Yes, well we are not there yet. However, you will soon find yourself in the middle of the whole program. Give you a month and you will know as much as anyone in greater Germany about the prospects of our wondrous scientific achievements in this area. You will of course also see to it that the Reichsfuhrer is kept completely informed regarding all progress being made in this area of research."

Wilhelm could feel the excitement at the thought building within him and Muller gave him a few seconds to enjoy it before he moved on to the other file folder which, like its mate, was clearly marked in large red letters 'STRENGES GEHEIMMIS'

(TOP SECRET).

Muller opened the second folder and spread out the contents in front of him on the table.

"In the interim and as an adjunct to this new eugenically stimulated advancement in science toward the achievement of a much expanded Aryan race, you will also find yourself assisting in the administration of another facet of the whole concept of Eugenics: the 'Lebensborn Eingertragener Verein' (Registered Society Lebensborn Program). This program was initiated shortly after the passage of the Nuremberg Laws outlawing the intermarriage of Aryan Germans with Jews and all others deemed inferior races. It was founded by Reichsfuhrer-SS Himmler himself on December twelfth, nineteen thirty-five. To this day he takes a direct interest in its operation. The end goal of these combined efforts is to reverse decades of declining birthrates in the Fatherland and increase the Germanic/Nordic population of Germany to one hundred and twenty million. The Reichsfuhrer-SS has now requested that you be assigned to the administration and development of this programme in addition to your other duties."

Wilhelm nodded his understanding.

"What are the current aims and goals of this specific programme and how advanced is it at this point in time?"

Muller bent to the file.

"The goal of this society is to offer interested young girls deemed 'racially pure' the opportunity to help raise Germany's Aryan population by having one or more children safely, comfortably and in secret. Both the mother and father are tested for purity; blond hair and blue or green eyes are preferred and family lineage must be traced back for a minimum of three generations."

He paused to look up at Wilhelm.

"You are of course aware of the direct order to all SS and police personal to father as many children as possible to compensate for war casualties. This was issued in thirty-nine as the programme had by that time not produced the results anticipated and therefore required expansion. The mothers successfully impregnated are immediately taken under the wing of the SS and are cared for in every aspect by our organization until their child is born. All children produced by these liaisons come under the direct control of the SS organization and are placed in nurseries with regard to education and adoption by qualified Aryan families. Since inception, only forty percent of those females who have applied have successfully passed the strictly enforced racial purity test and have been granted admission to the programme.

Up until thirty-nine, fifty-seven percent of the mothers taking part were unmarried, it would appear that the percentage of unwed is rising and it is predicted that about seventy percent who participate this year will fall into that category.

We opened the first Lebensborn home in thirty-six in Steinhoering near Munich. Others in the Reich have followed and we are currently working to vastly broaden this programme to meet the needs of the expanding borders of the New Germany.

This particular programme is long-term, as it is estimated that it will take at least fifteen years for its progeny to begin to produce the anticipated results.

The need for large numbers is the goal and toward that end the Reichsfuhrer urgently wishes to expand the system into the newly conquered sphere now under the Reich's control.

That will mean increasing our administrative staff, which is where he sees a growing need for involvement by strong young officers who demonstrate your qualities and abilities with regard to the formation of a new, vital and strong Aryan race prepared to defend and govern a new and world-dominating Germanic Empire. Any questions so far?"

Wilhelm shook his head.

"No, I think I understand the basics, but as to the specifics of each assignment, that will obviously take some time in that it will require a hands on study of what had been accomplished so far in the development of each."

Muller gathered up the separate reports and placed them back within the file and closed it.

"Yes it will, and arrangements are already underway for you to spend as much time as you require with those in charge of each of them. The scientific developments with regard to the Eugenic and genetic advancements currently fall under the control of your father's offices while the Lebensborn programme is under the direct control of another arm of the SS. While both are important, the former is by far the most paramount.

It, when successful, will negate the necessity for the encouragement of the natural process of procreation to take place in an enhanced manner in order for us to reach the level of a racially pure population that we will require to govern our expanded territory, for it will create, in a single stroke, the volume of children that we must have to complete the Fuhrer's vision for the new Reich."

CHAPTER FOURTEEN

- Berlin –

- July 16th, 1940 –

On July sixteenth nineteen-forty, after the rapid and crushing defeat and occupation of France and the Low Countries and deeply disappointed at the lack of progress in his peace attempts directed at the English, Hitler issued 'Fuhrer Directive 16'.

This directive was for the invasion of Britain: 'Operation Sea Lion'. It specified the following conditions as being absolutely necessary: The Royal Air Force had to be driven to their knees, giving the Luftwaffe control of the skies over the invasion ports and demarcation target areas on the coast of Britain; the English channel had to be under the full control of the German Navy, using surface ships, U-boats and mines; and the English coast must be dominated by German heavy guns situated on the coast of France.

Upon learning of the Fuhrer's plans, the Italian Dictator Benito Mussolini promised to supply ten divisions and thirty squadrons of aircraft in support of such an invasion.

Despite having secretly issued Directive 16, Hitler, on July nineteenth, nineteen-forty while delivering a Victory Speech at the Kroll Opera House which lasted for over two hours (at which time Hitler promoted twelve new Field Marshals), The Fuhrer extended yet another olive branch to England. He made a public 'appeal to reason' aimed at the British at the end of that speech.

At this time Hitler still strongly believed that it was imperative that he convince the British to join with Germany in a future fight against Soviet Bolshevism.

A basic necessity in his plans for the New Reich would

require him to move east against other countries in order to gain the 'Lebensraum' (Living Space) he would need for his plan of an expanded Germany.

That meant he would eventually have to attack Russia and he was determined not to put himself in the position of having to fight a two-front war.

Before an attack on Russia, he desperately needed to have a treaty in place with the English to ensure the security of his new western front.

Hitler wanted, and still believed he might manage to bring about a treaty with Britain. Joachim Von Ribbentrop, his Foreign Minister and The Great War fighter Ace and early party member, Herman Goring, were at the time both deeply involved in separate negotiations with the English to reach that end.

* * * * *

- Obersalzberg –

- July 1940 –

The secret Nazi Military Planning Conference held at the Fuhrer's Berghof home at the end of July in nineteen-forty was purported to be for discussions on Operation Sea Lion.

The initial plan for this invasion had taken place earlier in the year and had been stimulated by a request from Hitler to the Kriegsmarine (German Navy) for an examination as to the possibility of landing troops in England.

At that time Grand Admiral Erich Raeder had assigned his Operations Officer, Kapitan (Captain) Hans Reinicke to the task.

The Captain's report was prepared in under a week and it set out four specific requirements for success in such an endeavour.

Those were: the elimination of the ability of the Royal Navy forces to defend the landings or their approach, control of the skies over the invasion points by the German air force, destruction of all Royal Navy in the coastal zone and the ability to assure the defence against any British submarine operations against the landing craft.

This first report on the topic was followed in December nineteen thirty-nine by the German Army's own study which had also sought input from both the Kriegsmarine and the Luftwaffe (German Air Force). The Army report was not an encouraging document.

It openly noted the many problems involved and thereby gave more weight to the necessity of meeting the four pre-requirements that had been stated in the original Kriegsmarine document, if such an invasion was to have any hope of succeeding.

To the surprise of most of those in attendance at the Berghof Military Conference on the thirty first day of July, mainly consisting of Germany's highest military leaders, Adolf Hitler had, for good reasons begun to have some doubts about the advisability of Operation Sea Lion and was already considering shifting the sights of his Panzers.

At the meeting it was the Grand Admiral who spoke first.

Preparations for the invasion were well advanced. The required material and equipment had been gathered as planned. The conversion of the troop-carrying barges would be completed by the first of September.

It all sounded very good up to that point, but then the other shoe fell.

The quantity of merchant shipping required was unequal to the task. This was due to mines and the losses sustained in the taking of Norway. The Allies had air superiority over the channel. It would be better to delay the operation until the following May.

Hitler's face clouded. Although he had his own doubts, this was not what he'd expected to hear.

He immediately took the floor, raising his voice slightly, as he told them in no uncertain terms that a delay of that length would allow England to expand her army and take in mounds of supplies from America, and the way things seemed to be heading, possibly the Soviets.

He made it abundantly clear to all in attendance that he would not wait for May. The invasion was to take place on or begin on September the fifteenth and no later.

Over the next twenty-four hours the Fuhrer struggled with the obvious complications that revolved around the chances of a successful completion of Operation Sea Lion.

On September the fifteenth, he issued another Directive in support of his decision to go ahead as planned and shortly followed that with one placing the decision entirely on Goring's shoulders, ordering the Luftwaffe Leader to prepare for the invasion by removing all the obstacles by way of a concentrated air offensive.

A self-assured Goring, appointed Reichsmarschall only a month before, had eagerly accepted the challenge and 'Operation Eagle' was launched with that aim in mind.

The Reichsmarschall assured the Fuhrer that the Luftwaffe could force the English to their knees and therein to the negotiating table negating the need for a mass invasion, and that this would be accomplished within two weeks.

* * * * *

- Port of Kiel –

- August 2nd, 1940 – 15:20 hours –

As soon as U-62 had completed docking at Kiel at 15:20 hours on August second, nineteen-forty, the band struck up and the cheers rose from the onlookers lining the dock, many of whom, despite the season, were jubilant young women clutching bouquets of flowers.

Kriegsmarine Konteradmiral (Commodore Admiral) Karl Donitz and his entourage of support staff stood at the foot of the gangplank awaiting the crew of the U-boat, dressed in full uniform and led by their officers, to form up in ranks. Once this was completed, salutes were exchanged and the award ceremony commenced, accompanied by the muted sounds of a naval march.

While this was not an unusual response to the arrival of a submarine returning from a successful patrol, only the crew's radio operator, the communications officer and the Captain were aware of what specific medal presentations were scheduled to take place.

It surprised no one present when Donitz approached and spoke with the Captain to present a medal. However, Oberfahn-rich zur See Eric von Stauffer was taken completely by surprise when Donitz next stopped in front of him.

The Konteradmiral smiled broadly as their eyes met and then he turned away briefly to accept the first of two small boxes being held out to him by an adjutant before turning back to face Eric again.

"So I finally get to meet in the flesh the young man I've been hearing so much about."

Eric stood stiffly at attention as the adjutant responded.

"Yes Admiral, this is von Stauffer."

Eric's surprise was quickly replaced by a warm flood of pride as Donitz, still smiling, opened the first box and removed the Iron Cross second class.

Donitz handed the box back to his adjutant, before pinning the medal into place on the lower left side of Eric's brass-buttoned midnight blue double-breasted uniform jacket.

Eric was still struggling to accept what had just taken place as the Admiral retrieved the second box from his aide and reached with his left hand to lift Eric's corresponding hand and turned it palm upward in order to pass the box to him.

He then took Eric's right hand in his own and shook it firmly.

"I congratulate you on your promotion, 'Oberleutnant zur See' (Lieutenant Junior Grade) Von Stauffer. You will be receiving new orders tomorrow, and I expect big things from you in the future."

He then released Eric's hand and saluted. Eric, his mind reeling, managed, if stiffly, to return the salute.

Moments later the official party departed and once the crew had been dismissed, Eric found himself surrounded by his proud crewmembers, several of whom then promptly lifted him up onto their shoulders and began to pass him about as they congratulated him en masse.

The spectacle took a while, but finally, flushed and riding an adrenalin-high, he found himself deposited back onto the surface of the dock.

CHAPTER FIFTEEN

- Kiel -

At 08:30 hours the next day Eric, who had been celebrating his promotion with the other officers from U-62 until the wee hours of the morning, and had then found it impossible to sleep, dragged himself into a cold shower as a first step in an attempt to make himself presentable for his scheduled 09:00 hour appointment for the receipt of new orders.

More than anything else, it was due to his tender years that he was able to present himself to the Officer of the Day at the appointed hour, if not bright and bushy-tailed at least clean and properly uniformed with his new badges of rank in place.

Fifteen minutes later he found himself back out on the pavement next to the parade square with his new orders and travel documents in his hand.

He was surprised, confused and disappointed. Not because he did not know what his new assignment was. It was stated very clearly. He had been seconded and was ordered to report within two days to something called the 'Buro der Wissenschaftliche Forschung' at the Kaiser Wilhelm Institute in Berlin.

What was immediately clear to Eric was the fact that he was not going to get what he had hoped for; the Captaincy of his own sub.

When hesitatingly questioned, the Officer of the day had been of absolutely no help in determining exactly what this organization was, or what it did. Nor did he have any idea as to why a U-boat Officer would be assigned to it by way of secondment.

In short order and somewhat exasperated by Eric's line of questioning the Duty Officer had pointed out that he "did not personally draw up new orders, but simply passed them on" and suggested that if the 'Oberleutnant zur See' wished for more information, he might want to nip down the hall and question the Konteradmiral on the matter, face to face.

At that point he saluted Eric, received one in return and promptly showed him out of the office.

Of course, the Officer of the Day's last suggestion didn't even bear consideration, not if one valued his chances for future promotion.

Mystified as to what his new assignment would entail he paused to gather his thoughts for a few seconds in an attempt to sort them out. Getting nowhere, he shrugged his shoulders and hurried back to his rooms where he could find some privacy and an opportunity to think things through while getting himself organized for his upcoming trip to Berlin.

* * * * *

- Berlin –

At 08:00 hours on August fourth, nineteen-forty, as per his orders, a still mystified Eric reported for duty at the outer reception center of the 'Buro der Wissenschaftliche Forschung' at the Kaiser Wilhelm Institute in Berlin.

A willowy dark-haired receptionist in her mid-twenties, wearing a high-necked but formfitting and superbly filled out blouse and thereby making her of immediate interest to Eric, who was new in town and attuned to his need for future prospects, glanced at his orders briefly and then exchanged smiles with the handsome young U-boat Officer before directing him to take a seat in the waiting area.

"Herr Professor Keller is expecting you. He will be with you shortly."

Eric managed to catch her eye several times during his brief wait and by the time an interconnecting doorway to the reception area on his right opened to admit the squat figure of a balding middle-aged man wrapped in a white lab coat, he was fairly confident that that it would be worthwhile for him to take the time to speak to her again at the next opportunity.

As the man approached him he stood and saluted.

"Heil Hitler!"

The professor's round face tilted upward as he raised his right hand slightly in return and then lowered and extended it toward Eric.

"Ah yes our U-boat expert; very good to have you joining us."

Eric took the pudgy proffered hand and shook it briefly and then with a slight smile, Keller spun on his heel and started back toward the doorway he had used to enter the waiting area and Eric dropped into step behind him as the other man's words drifted back to him.

"I've got a meeting to attend in a half-hour, but I'm sure you have some questions to ask, so let's go to my office where we can talk privately over a nice cup of coffee before I introduce you to the other members of our little Military Research and Development Oversight Committee."

He waved Eric through the door into the adjoining hallway and then closed the door behind them and took the lead down the broad, brightly lit hallway which continued ahead into the distance.

In the hopes that he would gain some idea as to what his future duties might entail Eric searched for any signage on the outside of the several closed doorways arranged along both sides of the hallway as they passed. Unfortunately he only found numbers, absolutely nothing to indicate what might be going on behind those doors.

They passed several people as they walked. The age groups varied as did the dress.

For the most part those in uniform appeared middle aged and reflected badges of rank much higher than his, while those dressed in civilian clothes and lab coats appeared younger. Uniforms definitely dominated and this didn't surprise him in view of the changes that had come about within the New Germany over the past few years, but perhaps a third of those who crossed their path were civilians, dressed in the same fashion as the professor he was following, although some simply wore business suits.

Those in uniform were all male and divided about equally between the SS and Wehrmacht. They had yet to pass anyone in a Kriegsmarine or Luftwaffe uniform.

Those in civilian dress, considerably younger than their military counterparts, were for the most part female and although displeased at being unable to determine much from his surroundings in relation to what his future might hold with regard to his assigned duties, he was definitely pleased at this obviously enhanced prospect for future perspective female companionship.

Keller turned right at the intersection of another hallway and then pulled out a ring of keys and selected one before inserting it to unlock a numbered doorway leading off to the left. He pushed the door open and stood aside waving Eric into a small outer office which held a reception area with a single desk at the far end and several straight -backed wooden chairs arranged at right angles along one wall.

Following Eric inside, he pulled the door closed behind him then smiled and glanced at the young woman sitting on the far side of the desk who was diligently working at the keys of a typewriter.

"My secretary, Fraulein Karina Hoffmann, this is Oberleutnant zur See, Eric von Stauffer, who will be joining our military advisory team."

They exchanged smiles before he and the professor stepped past the desk and entered Keller's office through a doorway located behind and to one side of her.

CHAPTER SIXTEEN

- Hitler's Berlin –

- September 3rd, 1940 –

On September third, nineteen-forty at Hitler's direction the operational orders for Sea Lion were issued. A caveat to those orders was the inclusion of a reference to the fact that the final decision to go ahead with the invasion would take place ten days prior to its execution.

The tentative date for the attack itself was now scheduled to take place on September twenty-first nineteen-forty.

* * * * *

- London –

- September 7th, 1940 -

The British High Command reached the conclusion that a German invasion was likely imminent and accordingly issued the 'Cromwell' order, a general invasion warning.

On the same day, the Germans altered their bombing tactics, and sent a major daytime raid against, not the airfields of the RAF (Royal Air Force) as had been the practice to date, but the city of London itself.

They did this at the direction of Hitler who, in agreement with Goring's suggestion, had decided that such a change in tactics would force the British to commit its so far strategically hoarded reserves of fighter aircraft, to the protection of the city, thereby hopefully setting them up as targets for the Luftwaffe, whose aim was their total destruction.

In the afternoon of that day, three hundred German bombers escorted by six hundred fighters attacked the London dock area. The switch in tactics took the British by complete surprise and the attack was immediately followed up by a second flight of two hundred and fifty bombers who had no difficulty in finding their target in the dark, due to the still blazing fires which had resulted from the first attack and had clearly marked it.

The Germans were ecstatic with their accomplishment considering it a decisive success in the ongoing battle for air supremacy.

* * * * *

- Berlin –

- September 10th, 1940 –

Hitler, while more than pleased with the recent successes experienced by the Luftwaffe with regard to the Battle of Britain, reached the decision that they had still been unable to gain air superiority in the skies over the English Channel. In consequence, he postponed his decision on the launch of Operation Sea Lion until the fourteenth of September, which in view of the earlier caveat, meant that the invasion itself was now tentatively set to go ahead on September twenty-fourth, nineteen-forty.

* * * * *

- Berlin -

- September 11, 1940 -

On this date Goring was beside himself with glee as the results came in from the day's bomber raids over London.

As icing on the cake, a later strike on the Spitfire fighter aircraft factory situated in Southampton also proved highly effective and Buckingham Palace had also been hit by a bomb, although reportedly, no royal family member had been injured.

He and Hitler discussed the numbers after the raids. Over the past twenty-four hours the Germans had lost twenty-nine planes to twenty-five for the British. It was an acceptable trade-off for the Germans who at this time had the larger air force.

* * * * *

- Berlin –

- September 14/15, 1940 –

On September fourteenth, Hitler came to the determination that Goring needed only about four or five days of co-operating weather to allow him to complete the job he had set for his Luftwaffe. He put off the invasion decision once again, this time to September fifteenth. Once again, due to the caveat, that would schedule the new tentative invasion date to take place on September twenty-seventh.

The Fuhrer believed that the RAF has almost been destroyed.

On the attack on the fifteenth, German bomber pilots, who have been told that the English had fewer than three hundred fighters left in total, found themselves facing more than that number on the first raid of the day alone. As a result, morale among German bomber pilots began to plunge as they watched, from a ringside seat, a good number of their comrades being seemingly effortlessly shot out of the sky.

* * * * *

- Berlin –

- September 17th, 1940 –

On this day, a frustrated Adolf Hitler concluded that the Luftwaffe had not achieved air supremacy over the channel, and that the Kriegsmarine was unable to command the waters of the English Channel.

He postponed Operation Sea Lion indefinitely.

His immediate staff, who had fully expected The Fuhrer to lash out at the leaders of both arms of the military forces who had let him down in an open display of displeasure at this turn of events, was surprised to find Adolf Hitler generally apathetic about the situation.

While the Fuhrer said little, those in the map room around him took note of the glint in his eyes as Hitler moved his gaze over the map on the table in front of him.

Without further comment, his scrutiny had turned away from the British Isles and begun to shift eastward before resting briefly on the lands newly conquered and now subjugated to the Nazi Reich and then move on, further to the east.

* * * * *

- The von Stauffer Ancestral Estate –

- Castle von Stauffer - Lake Konstanz – Germany –

- September 18th 1940, 10:00 hours –

At forty years of age and despite having given birth to four children, two of whom had arrived within minutes of each other, the Countess, Erika von Stauffer was still a very beautiful woman.

At the moment she was efficiently, if rather frantically overseeing the transformation of her country estate, Castle von Stauffer, in preparation for the upcoming family weekend and the guests who would be attending as a result.

She'd been very short with her husband when he'd called midweek on such short notice to advise her of his plans. Her displeasure at the audacity of his suggestion, however, had quickly dissipated.

The Countess was an individual who under normal circumstances absolutely loved entertaining. She also prided herself on her reputation as a gracious hostess and in consideration of the fact that her entire family would be taking part in the weekend event, began to see it as a possible opportunity for her to arrange for the interaction between some suitable male prospects and her two, as yet unmarried daughters.

She had no more than hung up the phone before she'd found she was warming to the idea and within the hour had sprung into action. The challenge of pulling off a social event of this magnitude at Lake Konstanz, under wartime conditions and on incredibly short notice had quickly taken precedence over her initial displeasure and she was now in full control of bringing it to successful fruition.

CHAPTER SEVENTEEN

- Wartime Berlin –

For Eric, the past six weeks had been full of surprises, not the least of which was finding out that the man in charge of the vast enterprise to which he had been seconded, was none other than his father.

Prior to his transfer, Eric had been aware that the Count had been reactivated in rank at the specific request of the Fuhrer, but he had not been made aware of what precise assignment of duties that had entailed. He had simply been informed that his father's position was of a secret nature and not to be discussed outside the family.

Eric was not much of a writer and although he spoke with his mother and father fairly regularly by telephone, any further information about his father's responsibilities since his reactivation had not been forthcoming for the simple fact that such knowledge could only be provided to him securely by way of a face to face meeting and he had been granted no leave since that time.

When he was taken to be introduced to the 'Aufseher', 'Buro der Wissenschaftliche Forschung' toward the end of his first day of his secondment to that organization and found himself being escorted into the large, window-filled corner office of that personage he found himself facing his father, dressed in an SS-Oberstgruppenfuhrer uniform, across a massive desk. His mouth dropped open and he was momentarily at a loss for words.

A twinkle of mirth filling his eyes, the Count had waited until the door had closed behind his secretary before he rose from his chair and smiled over at his eldest son.

"Do close your mouth and sit down Eric; we have some things to discuss. Would you care for tea? I was about to have some sent in. Oh and before you conclude that it was I who arranged for your secondment here, away from your precious U-boats, I want to make it clear to you that although your mother is extremely happy about it and I can say without hesitation that I am not in the slightest displeased, I had nothing to do with the actual decision resulting in your transfer."

Eric nodded and settled into one of the comfortably upholstered chairs facing his father, and the Count sat back down and lifted the lid off the silver cigarette box on the right side of the desk.

He bent toward the contents and Eric shook his head and took out one of his cigarillos instead and then leaned forward as his father placed a cigarette from the box between his lips before replacing the box top and picking up the matching lighter to light them both up.

His father sucked in a deep drag and then leaned back into his chair as he exhaled.

"You should know too that your brother has recently been selected as one of the SS-Reichsfuhrer Himmler's adjutants and that one of his current duties is to act as the intermediary between Herr Himmler and me with regard to what takes place here. As a result, I now see a good deal of Wilhelm, as will you, I'm sure."

Eric had spent some time with his father in the office that first day and they'd dined together that night, at which time the Count had shared with him the information he had received earlier in the day with regard to the Fuhrer's decision to indefinitely postpone Operation Sea Lion. It was a decision that, at the time, although he had not expressed it as such to Eric, the Count believed was destined to deeply affect the future of their entire family.

The next morning Eric found himself immersed in his new duties which turned out to entail his overseeing of the operational end of research and development for new U-boat design.

While it was far from what he had expected to find himself doing, it did appear that it would be interesting work and his disappointment at leaving active duty on U-boats was blunted somewhat when he considered the fringe benefits of his posting by way of available female companionship which seemed certain to outshine his previous experience of weeks at sea aboard a sub without so much as an opportunity to get so much as a sniff of a skirt.

The fact that he and his father could expect to spend some time with his older brother also promised to make the secondment easier for him to accept.

* * * * *

- Road Trip-

Within an hour of speaking with her husband in Berlin by phone, the Countess Erika von Stauffer had arranged for both her daughters to attend the weekend festivities.

While this had been absolutely paramount for her in view of the need to find them both suitable husbands, it had not been a forgone conclusion that it could be accomplished. Germany was at war and both of her girls held important positions within the New Reich.

Pulling them away from those responsibilities on such short notice had meant going directly to their superiors, something Erika, a woman always to be reckoned with, did without hesitation and with immediate success. She had after all been an early Party member and her family held high social prominence within Nazi Germany.

Within hours the two girls had left Berlin together choosing to drive down to the castle in Gabriella's much prized nineteen thirty-seven Horch 853 A 'Spezialroadster' (Sport Cabriolet), which had been a present from her parents on her nineteenth birthday.

Each vehicle of this make and model had begun life as a rolling 853 Horch chassis, boasting a straight eight engine producing 120 horsepower. All roadsters created from this particular chassis were specifically tailored to the needs of the individual customer.

No two were the same.

The Count had chosen the coach building firm of Erdmann & Rossi to create the body for the car. After several months, the firm had supplied a breathtakingly beautiful, low-slung two-toned black over silver two-seater roadster body.

The resulting partnership of chassis and body produced a one-of-a-kind sports car, a supremely elegant vehicle, imposing and majestic in nature, coupled to a drive line that could deliver speeds of up to one hundred and thirty-five kilometres per hour.

Three hours into the trip, top down and with Gabriella in her element, *meaning right foot buried to the floorboards*, and pushing the powerful car to the limit, they exited a tunnel and careened past a parked Volkspolizei unit which immediately pulled out behind them to give pursuit.

Ursula turned slightly in the passenger seat to look over at her younger sister in that annoying hindsight way Gabriella, based on a great deal of previous experience, had fully expected. She anticipated what her older sister would say and she was not disappointed.

"I did warn you, didn't I?"

Gabriella tossed her long blond braids in distain and kept the accelerator to the floor.

The colour drained out of Ursula's face.

One did not even consider disobeying an authority figure in the New Germany and she could not believe her sister was even contemplating anything but instant obedience.

"My God Gabriella, you know we have speed limits now due to our need to conserve fuel. If I've told you once, I've told you a hundred times! You're speeding. Now take your foot off the gas and pull over!"

Gabriella ignored her sister completely. Her eyes were on her rear-view mirror and after a few moments her lips shifted into a determined smile

"We have nothing to worry about. They're driving a Mercedes 260 D. It's a four cylinder diesel for Heaven's sake. My car will leave them in the dust. Don't look back; we'll just pretend we didn't see them."

Ursula's mouth fell open in disbelief but she did as she had been asked and kept her head straight to the front. Within minutes the police car had disappeared from the mirror and Gabriella's smile turned to one of complete satisfaction.

"There, you see, nothing to worry about."

Ursula, shifting slightly upward off her seat, turned to look behind them.

The wind whipping over the top of the windshield of the racing vehicle threatened to tear at the neatly pinned up braids of golden tresses nestled atop her head in a plaited chignon and pull them loose. She lifted a hand to hold it in place as she let her eyes sweep the empty road behind them.

When she turned back and dropped down into her seat she shook her head slowly.

"I'll never understand you. You'd think you were raised over a beer hall. Have you absolutely no sense of propriety or responsibility?"

Gabriella eased off the accelerator slightly, threw back her head, tossed her braids and laughed heartily. When she'd finished she beamed a broad smile over at her sister.

"Not if I can avoid it big sister, not if I can avoid it. Life is too damn short. We're approaching Mannheim. I don't know about you but I'm famished. Let's just put this unfortunate little episode behind us and turn our attention to finding a spot for lunch"

CHAPTER EIGHTEEN

- Anti-Semitism -

Mannheim is an old German city located in the Rhineland, the area of Germany that borders France at the confluence of the Rhine and Neckar rivers just downstream along the Neckar from the city of Heidelberg.

The Rhineland has been historically an industrial area of importance to Germany from the point of view of both military significance and economic wellbeing. Under the terms of the Treaty of Versailles, created after the Great War, the Rhineland had been classified as a de-militarised zone in order to create a military-free or buffer area between France and Germany. The French army occupied the left bank of the Rhine according to peace terms and maintained that occupation until nineteen-thirty. During that period many of Mannheim's most impressive homes were built for the officers of the French garrison.

Though Germany controlled the area in both a political and economic sense the vast majority of Germans found it humiliating and unconscionable that, according to the treaty, they were forbidden to place their own troops on German soil.

Adolf Hitler detested the Treaty of Versailles and everything it stood for. He had every intention of ignoring it in any way he could. Following his orders, on March the seventh, nineteen thirty-six, three Wehrmacht Battalions had crossed the bridges over the Rhine River with instructions to re-occupy the de-militarized zone. The French had every right to prevent such action and Hitler was far from sure that he would get away with it.

His orders to the marching troops had reflected that doubt in that they were instructed to immediately and peacefully evacuate should there be any military response from the French Armed Forces.

France took no military action. She cried foul to the world through diplomatic channels but had no desire whatsoever to physically face off with the Germans.

Hitler had won the day without firing a shot and was absolutely overjoyed at the meek French response.

Mannheim is unusual among German cities due to the fact that the streets are laid out in a grid pattern which is not the norm in Germany and as such has been nicknamed 'die Quadratestadt' (City of Squares).

The grid pattern came as a result of the rebuilding of the city after it was almost completely levelled by the French army during the Thirty Years War in the early sixteen hundreds.

Mannheim is no stranger to the sufferings of war.

When the Great War had broken out in nineteen-fourteen the city's many industrial plants had played a key role in Germany's war economy and on May twenty-seventh, nineteen fifteen Mannheim had become the first civilian settlement behind the battle lines to be bombed by air. The aircraft were French and their target was the BASF plant. This bombing operation was to set a precedent for the years to come.

The small restaurant Gabriella had in mind for lunch was one she had stopped at once before. The tiny building housing it was tucked away between two larger structures in the old area of town along the bank of the Neckar.

When they pulled up in front of the restaurant they found that the door and several of the windows on the ancient building, facing onto the street, had been boarded up.

Two upper windows, which still held glass, were supporting large signs reading 'Deutsche! Wehrt Euch! Kauft nicht bei Juden!' (Germans! Defend Yourselves! Do not buy from Jews!).

Such signs were not new to either of the girls. They had seen plenty of their like in Berlin preceding the destruction and desecration of Jewish properties on 'die Kristallnacht' (Crystal

Night) which took place on November ninth/tenth of nineteen thirty-eight, resulting in hundreds of Jewish homes, hospitals, schools and Synagogues being ransacked, damaged and set on fire, while the police stood by and watched.

Both women were also well aware of the new laws, initially restricting activities and finally removing Citizenship for all German Jews that had been brought into being since the Nazi's rise to power. Anti-Jewish sentiment was of course not localized to Germany; however, it had an especially large following in the Baden Region of the country of which Mannheim was a part.

Gabriella sighed and looked over at Ursula.

"I had no idea the owner was Jewish. I thought he had served with some distinction with the Wehrmacht in the Great War."

Ursula shrugged and shifted her eyes back to the front of the boarded up restaurant.

"You know the Jews, they will lie about anything."

Although the two of them were disappointed to find the restaurant closed, it was not because of the signs in the windows nor the closure of the restaurant per se. After all, it had obviously been a Jewish establishment, and any good German could easily understand and accept its demise as an obvious necessity. But now they would have to make other plans for lunch.

It was quickly decided that they would deal with this inconvenience by paying a visit to a distant aunt who was, as a result of inheritance, a very large stockholder in the huge industrial concern of BASF.

BASF had been founded in eighteen sixty-five using funds garnered from the principals who had set up the gasworks and street lighting for the town council in eighteen sixty-one.

A by-product of the gasworks had been tar, which had then been used in the production of dyes. BASF had been incorporated for the purpose of manufacturing other chemicals, mainly soda and acids, which were needed for dye production.

The BASF plant was not built in Mannheim itself, but on the

opposite side of the Rhine River at Ludwigshafen so that any air pollution caused by the factory would not cause bother to the citizens of Mannheim. A year later the dye production itself had also moved out of the city and over to the BASF property in Ludwigshafen.

Through several patents held by BASF in relation to the chemical processes they had developed over the years and the monopoly they therefore held in the field, the company had grown exponentially and on December twenty-fifth, nineteen twenty five BASF, Bayer, Hoechst and three other companies had founded IG Farben.

BASF was the nominal survivor in that all shares were exchanged for BASF shares prior to the merger. At this time coatings, fuels and rubber were added to the company's product line.

As did many German industrialists, IG Farben supported and cooperated with the Nazi regime from its inception and by nineteen-forty was profiting handsomely from government guaranteed volumes and prices.

A deeper and more sinister arrangement between the company and the SS, with regard to the use of slave labour in their factories, which was already in the works but was still to come to fruition, coupled with the fact that IG Farben was producing the chemical Zyklon B (which was to play a huge part in the operation of concentration camps), was still on the horizon.

Aunt Hannelore, their father's oldest sister, was a Baroness. She was seventy years old, had been at birth very well off in her own right and was thrice a widow who had married well on each occasion.

She currently lived on her own in an ancient, rambling mansion with considerable grounds that backed onto the banks of the Rhine River.

The estate was located in an old upscale area of Mannheim, consisting of huge ostentatious homes, all of which dated back centuries and reflected generations of old money in their massive gated and fenced park-like settings.

While considered by others of her upper class society as living alone, she in fact had several servants and it was one of these, the gateman to be exact, who responded to the girls' arrival at the huge wrought-iron gates at the front of the property which provided the only opening in the tall, thick, brick wall that surrounded the entire estate.

This elderly gentleman, a family retainer since birth, greeted them politely and asked them to wait while he used the gatehouse phone to announce their arrival to the main house staff, after which he promptly returned to advise them that their aunt was at home and would receive them.

He opened the gates and waited until Gabriella had driven through, then pulled them closed again and watched as they swept up the driveway between borders of two hundred year old oaks until the sleek sports car rounded the first bend in the cobble-stone drive and disappeared from sight.

Gabriella and Ursula pulled up under the expansive Porte Couchere at the front door and were received by the Butler and a uniformed maid who stood just behind him.

The butler greeted them and then inquired politely as to the purpose of their visit.

Upon learning that they were simply paying a brief visit as they passed through, he dismissed the maid with a nod and then welcomed them into the house.

When he had closed the door behind them he led the way down the wide marble-floored hallway and into the first room on the right, pausing at the entrance to announce them.

The Baroness didn't rise from her large and well-upholstered armchair as they entered the room, but did set her knitting aside and offer a genuine smile as she waved her hand in the direction of the couches beneath the big floor to ceiling windows overlooking the front drive and gardens.

"Ursula and Gabriella! What a wonderful surprise."

CHAPTER NINTEEN

- Afternoon Tea -

The Baroness's clear blue eyes took in her nieces' dress, which differed in style considerably.

Ursula had joined the Nazi party upon graduation and had continued on in the Hitler Youth 'Bund Deutscher Madel' (League of German Maidens) or BDM when, in nineteen thirty-eight, it had initiated the 'Glaube und Schonheit' (Belief and Beauty) programme for older girls aged seventeen to twenty-years. At age twenty-one she had joined the Nazi party and within a short period of time had benefited from both the social position of the family and her mother's early party membership. This resulted in her rapid promotion within the local leadership of the BDM and within a few months she was taken on as a paid assistant to Jutta Rudiger.

Rudiger, a trained psychologist, had become enamoured with the Nazi movement while in university and had joined the 'Nationalsozialistischer Deutscher Studentenbund' (National Socialist German Students League) in the nineteen twenties.

She worked at the Institute for Occupational Research in Dusseldorf and became active in the leadership of the BDM and in climbing through the rank structure was chosen in nineteen thirty-five to become BDM Leader in the Ruhr-Lower Rhine region.

She was subsequently appointed Leader of the BDM and joined the Nazi party in November of nineteen thirty-seven, receiving the title of 'Reichsrefererntin des BDM' signifying, as was strict Nazi policy, a subordination to male leadership.

In this particular case, that of the overall Nazi Youth Leader, Reichsjugendfuhrer Baldur von Schirach.

Ursula, articulate by nature and carefully indoctrinated in the

Nazi beliefs throughout her teen years was also nobody's fool.

Women in leadership roles of any kind in Hitler's Germany were figureheads and held their posts due to a gender-inspired necessity only. They towed the party line, or their tenure was short-lived.

The Nazi party line in relation to the role of women in the New Germany was clear. Support the Party. Support the State. Support the Fuhrer. Marry young. Serve your husband. Have as many children as possible.

Ursula was an assistant to Jutta Rudiger, whose mandate was to lead the female youth of Germany toward the Party's goals for womanhood. In general, women were not expected to work once they had reached a childbearing age. As housewives and mothers, their lives were controlled. They were not expected to wear make-up or trousers. Hair was not to be dyed, perms were frowned upon. Only flat shoes were to be worn. Dieting was not recommended. They were to strive for a well-built figure, with wide hips for the ease of childbearing.

Ursula was of course an anomaly. She was a member of an aristocracy that did not really fit into Hitler's overall view of the New Germany, but that had historically played an important role in Germany and had therefore been inherited by the Nazi party. This was something they had chosen to maintain as a political necessity.

She was a young woman employed in a figurehead leadership position and she worked as such for the State. She was both satisfied and comfortable in her situation and wished to remain where she was until she was married and ready to raise a family. Consequently she always dressed in a manner acceptable to the party, severely and simply, in this case, a grey skirt reaching well below the knee, a double-breasted black jacket over an open-necked white shirt and functional flat black shoes.

Gabriella was another story altogether.

Unlike her sister, Gabriella had from birth shown a bubbly, spontaneous personality. She had also exhibited a somewhat self-centred but outgoing and full of life style as she grew older, whereas Ursula had always made every decision only after careful consideration as to what it would mean to both herself and others, and with the addition of a great deal of consultation accompanied by the added delay of much inner-mulling. Gabriella tended to live for the moment, rarely considering any personal consequences that might result from her actions and had no thought for their effect on others. She had always been primarily attuned to what 'seemed like a good idea at the time'.

In her late teens, her membership in the Hitler Youth organization had helped to somewhat curtail Gabriella's impetuous wild streak by way of indoctrination and discipline; however it certainly was not the 'be all' or 'end all' of the entire problem.

A prime example of this was the result of the eighth Nazi party rally, 'Reichsparteitag der Ehre' (Rally of Honour) held in Nuremberg in nineteen thirty-six at which the then seventeen year old Gabriella , at the time being on a 'Landjahr'(the mandatory service every Hitler Youth member was required to complete in the agricultural sector), was in attendance.

These yearly gatherings were held with a specific celebratory purpose in mind. In this case it was the remilitarization of the Rhineland that had taken place in March of nineteen thirty-six. The primary point of holding the Nuremberg Rallies was to drive home the personality cult of The Fuhrer. They served to portray Hitler as Germany's saviour. The gathered masses, all of the party faithful, listened to Hitler's speeches, marched past and swore loyalty to the cause and its leader.

In the year that Gabriella attended, the camp sites where the girls and boys of the Hitler Youth were housed had been laid out side by side and separated by gender of course. Prior to her joining the camp, Gabriella had formed a friendship with a very handsome, muscular and broad-shouldered, if not aristocratic boy of sixteen while the two of them were fulfilling their Landjahr requirement and were jointly assigned to assist with the harvest on the nearby farm.

As a result Gabriella was one of the nine hundred girls attending the rally who came away from it pregnant.

The massive number of pregnancies resulted in the party forbidding camping to Hitler Youth groups who attended future rallies.

Unlike the majority of the other eight hundred and ninety-nine girls who'd found themselves expecting, Gabriella would suffer no ill effects or any embarrassment over the unfortunate affair, nor would her family.

Instead, Gabriella had been sent off to Aunt Hannelore for an extended visit. Ten months later she had returned home healthy, some thought wonderfully so in fact, and no worse for wear. Upon birth, the baby had gone by way of adoption to a well-connected couple, the wife of which was unable to conceive. Gabriella had not requested to, nor would she have been allowed to see the child again.

Although Gabriella was now twenty years old, she hadn't as yet achieved what her parents, who loved her dearly but often despaired at her ill-conceived decisions and conduct, referred to as a reasonable level of 'maturity'. This attitude of a devil may care, 'you only live once' approach to life had given her mother a great deal of difficulty. It had made the job of securing proper employment for her youngest daughter after the age of eighteen, at which time Gabriella would had been obligated to leave the Hitler Youth programme, She'd had to find work within a fitting field and acceptable to the restrictive guidelines for women in the New Germany.

Although, as far as her mother was concerned this was to be a short-term problem because her main objective was to marry Gabriella off as soon as possible to a suitably-positioned and strong enough man who could bring her to heel and provide for her the lifestyle she deserved. Short term or not, it had not been an easy task.

Luckily the BDM had chosen to initiate an extended period of membership for Girls aged seventeen to twenty one, and this new segment of Hitler Youth, called the 'Belief and Beauty' organization, had required leaders.

Gabriella's mother took advantage of the situation and sprang into action, seeing to it that her youngest daughter immediately stepped into just such a position. She had hoped this would occupy any free time Gabriella might have while completing her nursing school programme at the largest hospital in Berlin.

Her parents, due to her father's military career, were now spending the majority of their time residing in the capital at the family's large, centrally-located mansion. This enabled them to keep close track of their wayward daughter's extracurricular activities while she attended school and performed her duties in the Hitler Youth. On most weekends, the parents with the girls in tow, travelled to their ancestral castle at Lake Konstanz.

It was hoped by her mother and father that this arrangement would allow them and her older sister an opportunity to keep a watchful eye over Gabriella while serving to keep their youngest daughter too occupied to find time for the commission of any further indiscretions.

All had gone well for several months and then Gabriella began to balk at the training, not because she found it difficult for she was in every way bright and her upbeat and outgoing nature guaranteed her acceptance and welcome at every level, but she found it mundane and unfulfilling.

Once again her mother had stepped into the breach, managing to find her a placement to help fill the growing staffing needs for the Nazi programmes aimed at seeing all Germans gainfully employed in the service of the state.

The Nazi state liked to portray German women as wholesome homemakers and mothers, dressed in traditional costumes.

Foreign clothing designers were considered to be decadent and un-German, as were modern hairstyles.

When Gabriella attended her nurses' training classes she dressed in relatively simple clothing.

She stretched the parameters just a little. Perhaps her designer skirts were somewhat shorter than what was considered acceptable and her peasant blouses carried a little too much ornamentation and occasionally placed on display a larger expanse of her natural beauty than was the norm.

When she fulfilled her duties in 'Belief and Beauty' she wore a uniform, although it was a tailor-made uniform, and it fit her like a glove.

When she was not taking classes and not in her uniform however, Gabriella dressed in the latest European style and typically considered the opinions of others be damned.

Her aunt had always had a soft spot for Gabriella, and although Hannelore did take note of her niece's stylish formfitting dress featuring an above the knee hemline and deeply plunging bodice, she balanced that with the obviously expensive material that had been used in its construction and the quality of the workmanship which was clearly demonstrated in the garment.

Hannelore was certainly well past the age where she could realistically wear such a costume.

However, had she been even twenty years younger she would have, without doubt, seriously considered doing so.

Gabriella's dress brought to the forefront the difference between the two sisters when it came to their individual personalities, reminding Hannelore of Gabriella's robust propensity with regard to the physical enjoyment readily available from members of the opposite sex, something that had made itself known years before when she had suddenly arrived as an extended houseguest.

Hannelore, who had been of a somewhat similar nature in her youth, had at the time of Gabriella's stay taken the opportunity to educate her young niece in all facets of birth control with a view to preventing any future unwanted pregnancies and their resulting trials and tribulations.

To the best of her knowledge, her niece had put these into practice with a good deal of success.

CHAPTER TWENTY

- Unproductive Citizens -

Hitler was convinced that two factions had played a large part in the defeat of Germany in the Great War: Bolshevism and National Jewry. He believed in eugenics.

He envisioned Germany as an entirely Aryan society bereft of any peoples who were inferior or unfit. He decreed that Germany had to be cleansed of any citizen who was deemed by the State to be unsupportive of his party's political views, unproductive, hereditarily of a lesser worth, racially impure, or foreign.

The second thrust of Hitler's plan to have all Germans fully and gainfully employed within the New Germany could not be, as in the first thrust, accomplished by economic stimulation and job creation or be dealt with by way of reclassification of the manner in which such statistics were gathered. This second push by the Nazis was a two-pronged approach designed to tackle an entirely different set of problems.

It was designed to deal with two specific areas of concern to the new government: the drain upon the State caused by those who were either too old or were physically or mentally disabled to the point where they could not likely ever be expected to labour gainfully in the interest of the State and, those who were not considered by the party as to be racially pure and, therefore fell into the category of the sub-human.

The attack on these groups was propagandized as diligently as the first thrust toward unemployment had been, but the actual practical application of the systems and laws needed to manage it were, of necessity, hidden as far as possible from the German people and from the world.

The individual parts of what was planned as a two-pronged

attack were shaped differently, structured to deal with each area of concern in its own unique manner.

The old and disabled were to be addressed as a separate problem from the racially impure. Those in the first category could not work productively for the State, but the latter group, the sub-human's, could and should do so by way of relative enslavement. They could be worked until they died through manual labour, which benefited the State.

Dealing with these two particular areas of the economic situation regarding the non-producing segments within the New Germany could not be handled in the same manner as had those which applied to people fit for employment but who simply lacked a job to go to.

The Nazi Party's plans for dealing with these problems could not be openly discussed with their own citizenry, nor could they be proudly broadcast to the rest of the world, as had been done while addressing the situation of general unemployment. Hitler recognized that his party's answers to these problems would not, at least initially, be palatable to the German masses and would therefore have to be handled with a good deal of finesse if they were to succeed over the long-term as envisioned.

To ensure this goal was realised as quickly as physically possible, the party took several steps as soon as it came into power. Propaganda was the first of these steps. The effective and well financed Nazi party's propaganda machine was headed by Dr. Joseph Goebbels who joined the party in nineteen twenty-four.

The diminutive five foot four inch Minister was disabled by a crippled foot, wore a brace, a special shoe and limped. He had been rejected for military service in the Great War. His size and disability led to a deep personal sense of physical inferiority, but that was counterbalanced by his abilities as a speaker and his absolute and devotional enthusiasm for both the Nazi Party and Adolf Hitler.

This brought him to early prominence within the party and resulted in his being appointed to oversee the task of building

Nazi support in Berlin in nineteen twenty-six. He was extremely good at this job and in nineteen twenty-eight he was one of the Nazis elected to the Reichstag.

In nineteen twenty-nine he was given overall charge of the party's propaganda machine where he once again excelled.

When Hitler was appointed Chancellor of Germany in nineteen thirty-three he promptly appointed Goebbels to the post of Minister of Propaganda and Enlightenment.

Well-educated and with a quick mind, Goebbels relied on his intelligence and quick wit to overcome his physical shortcomings but never lost the 'small man' chip on his shoulder.

He worshiped Hitler, but had a caustic tongue for others and did not fit in well with the other Hitler political hangers-on who formed The Fuhrer's inner circle.

This might have posed a political problem for him if it had not been the case that every individual member of that inner circle owed his position to, and directly reported to Hitler who was a strong believer in a *divide and control* system for his immediate subordinates which he felt would ensure his autocratic control of all phases of the country's future development.

Each of them therefore had their own personal agenda.

As individuals they feverishly strove to endear themselves to Hitler on a continuing basis in hopes of solidifying their lofty positions within the New Germany and receiving the party leader's support for whatever personal aims or goals they held. Any interaction between them was inevitably based upon the need for a spur of the moment, self-serving and symbiotic liaison which was unlikely to be supported by any sincere affection or respect on the part of the individuals involved. Such cooperation between them was therefore rare and when it did come about, was more often than not, short-lived.

This vying for Hitler's attention and support was a game played by all those within the inner political circle and with his education, intelligence and quick mind Goebbels - despite the problem of being a committed skirt-chaser - *which at one point brought about a sharp rebuke from Hitler* - was good at the game. He was perhaps, over the long term, the most successful of the bunch at maintaining Hitler's ear.

Propaganda was the first card played in dealing with the physically and mentally handicapped, who were considered by the party as non-productive and a drain on the State economy, as was the need to cleanse Germany of its non-Aryan population and increase the birth rate of Aryan Germans.

Once the Nazis came to power in Germany, every form of media and education was state controlled.

For example, a textbook would contain a mathematical question for German students something like: 'If the construction of a Lunatic asylum costs six million marks, how many houses for working German people could be built instead of an asylum if each house cost fifteen thousand marks to build?'.

Goebbels's propaganda ministry controlled what material the radio played, everything the newspapers reported and what plays, books or movies were available to the public. This was in addition to controlling what all children were taught from their first day of school until they completed their education and the teachings and ideologies of any youth club to which a child belonged, in this case a mandated programme under the Hitler Youth organization. The Nazis loved posters and every one they put out had a party theme.

The radio played Party-approved music only and the 'news reports' portrayed only 'facts' that towed the Nazi line. Movies, books and plays were vetted before release and all contained a party theme, at times subliminal, but for the most part flaunted with a flavour of nationalistic pride.

In the New Germany all forms of media and education portrayed Hitler as the saviour of the German people, and non-Aryans as subhuman and unworthy of being called German. The disabled were categorized as a drain on the economy and unworthy of life; Jews as unclean, dishonest and disloyal and as a race breeding like rats that carried plague and disease and were a cancer-like growth destined to pollute a pure Germany.

Carefully staged propaganda created the impression of Hitler as that of a God-like personage, a man whom all could trust to know exactly what was best for the citizens of a resurrected Fatherland.

The second step Hitler took toward the cleansing of Germany of the unproductive or inferior segments of the population went hand in hand with the extensive propaganda campaign and consisted of the passage of several laws.

On July thirty-first of nineteen thirty-three the so called 'Nuremberg Laws' were announced to Germans. One of these was the 'Gesetz zur Vechutung erbkranken Nachwuchses' (Law for the Prevention of Genetically Diseased Offspring).

At the time the idea of preventing hereditary disease through sterilization was not one that was particularly unique to Germany, nor was it particularly unpalatable to the German people. Nazi propaganda had been hammering at this specific solution to the problem for some time and earlier support for it, based on eugenics, was spread worldwide.

Before Germany adopted this law, the United States, believing as did many other countries that the human race would be vastly improved if future births were restricted to only those who were free of unhealthy inherited characteristics, led the world in forced sterilizations, having over the previous twenty years completed the sterilization of tens of thousands of American citizens against their will.

In the case of the Nazis, the selection of subjects for this programme was by law to be based on a medical diagnosis of feeblemindedness.

The methods used in the sterilizations themselves ranged from vasectomies and ligations to x-ray treatments. Most of those affected were Aryan Germans. The programme was not aimed at specific racial groups although both homosexuals and gypsies fell under the process in that their chosen lifestyles were considered as deviant. Although they did not meet the criteria from the point of view of mental illness, by way of a special order a substantial number of young, visibly mixed-race citizens, for the most part the progeny of French colonial troops who had been stationed in the Rhineland during the demilitarization of that area, also suffered the fate of forced sterilization.

Always concerned about the maintenance of the good opinion of its citizens, and ever politically perspicacious, the Nazis showcased the sterilization programme as legally balanced and fair by setting up 'Hereditary Health Courts' to make the individual selections for sterilization.

Each of these consisted of two doctors and a judge. They went so far as to create special appeal courts that could overturn decisions in the interest of the State.

The State, however, was not particularly interested in reversing any decision and few appeals were considered and even less granted.

Another of the Nuremberg Laws, the 'Marital Health Law' banned sexual union between the 'hereditarily healthy' and persons genetically unfit. Another, the 'Blood Protection Law', criminalized not only marriage, but sexual relations between Jews and non-Jewish Germans.

After in-depth planning over the late spring and summer months of nineteen thirty-nine a further stage in the process of cleansing Germany of non-productive citizens was advanced. This proposal was aimed at the termination of disabled children by way of what was termed 'euthanasia'.

CHAPTER TWENTY-ONE

- Nazification of the Medical Profession -

On August eighteenth nineteen thirty-nine the Reich Ministry of the Interior sent out a decree which required all medical personnel working in greater Germany to complete a report to the government of any newborn infants and children of three years or less who were suffering from severe mental or physical disabilities. Based primarily on how this particular form was presented, it gave the impression that the information forwarded was destined for use as the basis of statistical analysis.

In reality its purpose was to form a master list of those children who the Nazi system considered as of no value and therefore a present and future economic burden to the New Reich.

Upon coming to power, Hitler immediately strove for the complete Nazification of all German professions and organizations which he saw as the only efficient way to gain and maintain the absolute control he deemed necessary for the swift rebirth of Germany as he envisioned it.

By nineteen thirty-seven his efforts in this regard had born fruit to an amazing degree. Professional Educators showed the best return by that date; almost one hundred percent of them had become party members and now expounded the party line. The Nazification of that profession owed much to the fact the educators were for the most part public employees and if they wanted to work they had to become a party member.

Interestingly, the second most Nazified group was that of the medical profession. By thirty-seven, forty-five percent of doctors were members of the Nazi Party and many of these also belonged to the SS or affiliated organizations.

This strong support for the Nazi Party from the medical

profession came about at a time when German medical science led the world.

Research in the country was underway for wondrous new medical treatments for the future, but the very progressive German medical community was already at the forefront in most fields, including those of disease prevention.

Why did they, most of whom were self-employed, eagerly embrace Nazi ideology and goals?

The international eugenic love affair played a large part in their eagerness to help the Nazis. Eugenics had a very strong following in the German medical profession and as a result its general support of the theories fit hand in glove with the Nazi view of the necessity of amassing a strong, pure Aryan race for a revitalized Germany.

The opportunity to take part in a well-funded, State backed, move into the cutting edge of the medical science whose aim it was to become the cornerstone of a hereditarily strong and disease free future society tempted many. Public Health authorities who were eager to legally protect, support and extend a free hand to those doctors who furthered their Party's aims and were prepared and eager to back them with unlimited research and development funds created an elite god-like group within an already vaunted and respected profession.

They flocked to it in droves.

In early October of nineteen thirty-nine the German medical community was instructed to suggest to parents of disabled children that they admit those children to one of several newly designated 'paediatric clinics' within greater Germany.

Children admitted into these institutions, which were manned by carefully chosen and committed medical staff, very quickly succumbed to overdoses or starvation. Relatives would shortly thereafter receive an urn containing ashes taken from a communal pile cleaned from the crematory ovens accompanied by a false death certificate giving the cause of death as some serious medical condition.

Part and parcel with this programme was the decision to move on the unfit adult population.

Concerned as to a negative public backlash to any formal law promulgated with regard to this plan, Hitler instead chose to personally issue a decree empowering physicians to grant a 'mercy death' to all institutionalized (private and public) patients considered incurable. On that day, the doctors involved, having been given by the State the power of life and death, did indeed become God.

The decree was a thinly veiled order for Germany to be 'cleansed' of all the handicapped and mentally ill which a political party in a position of absolute power considered defective genetically and a destructive drain upon the State economy.

Hitler had the decree backdated to September first, nineteen thirty-nine, the day Germany invaded Poland. His reasons for doing so had been articulated years before, when in nineteen thirty-five he'd expressed the view that a programme of euthanasia of the unfit would be more easily acceptable to the masses if it was carried out under conditions of war.

He'd gone on to explain that when at war the value of life tends to be diminished and the death of others becomes less traumatic to the individual citizen.

In addition the stresses of war would make it easier to keep such a programme secret and if it did happen to come to public notice over time it would by then most likely find general acceptance since as a consequence of such action medical staff and facilities would have been freed up for the care of those valiant men injured fighting for the Fatherland.

The code name for the programme was 'Operation T-4', which referred to the address of the Berlin Chancellery offices where the administration office, initiating and overseeing the programme, was headquartered.

Doctors envisioned, created and ran Operation T-4. Hitler's personal physician, Dr. Karl Brant headed the programme.

He was assisted by Philip Bouhler, Hitler's Chancellery chief.

Having proved their worth in the earlier programme with regard to children, questionnaires, which appeared to be required for statistical purposes only and related to the ability of patients to work productively in the future based on their current physical and mental disabilities were sent from the Ministry of the Interior to all German asylums, extended care facilities and nursing homes.

Completed forms were then forwarded to 'Review Commissions' staffed by Physicians, primarily psychiatrists, whose job it was to evaluate them. This task was massive and the individual doctors were immediately presented with a deluge of completed questionnaires which they were expected to process rapidly.

The programme was to complete its task as quickly as was humanly possible. Patients were almost never examined personally by the evaluating physicians. They read the short questionnaire and marked it in one of three ways. "+" noted in red ink meant 'death'. "" in blue ink meant 'life', and "?" meant additional assessment required.

In general, the German mind tends to be conscientious and efficient. These doctors knew what task had been assigned to them by the Nazi Government and they worked diligently and competently toward that end without compunction. They became an industrious part of the struggle to create a stronger and healthier Germany, and in so doing they used massive quantities of red ink.

Once a patient's questionnaire was marked in red, immediate arrangements were made for him or her to be transported to the nearest of six 'Treatment Centres" in military-grey buses whose windows had been painted over so that the cargo could not be observed during transport.

These centers had been set up in Brandenburg, Sonnenstein, Bernburg, Hartheim, Grafeneck and Hadamar, using various buildings, psychiatric hospitals, castles, even a former prison. From inception to nineteen-forty, death was administered to the patients by way of lethal injection. In nineteen-forty a more efficient and sophisticated method of killing was adopted using carbon monoxide poisoning delivered through what appeared to be normal showerheads.

The same process of delivering a false death certificate, along with an urn of communal ashes taken from the attached crematory, to the next of kin which had been successfully used after the euthanasia of children, was employed in this programme.

* * * * *

- Tea in Mannheim –

The conversation in the estate's brightly sunlit tearoom consisted primarily of an attempt by Aunt Hannelore to be brought up to date on the current situation with the von Stauffer arm of the family. It was punctuated by a steady parade of tasty snacks and a second pot of tea.

Once that had been satisfactorily completed, Gabriella and Ursula politely inquired about the situation of their aunt in view of the conditions of war that now existed. Hannelore, who rarely left her mansion and led a fairly sheltered life professed to little change in her day to day activities, the one exception being her interest in the state of affairs with the Jews which had come up as a result of Gabriella's earlier comment regarding the inconvenience of finding the restaurant closed and their planned stop for lunch spoiled.

Hannelore, an early member of the Nazi party who firmly believed that the removal of all Jews from Germany would be a positive step and one long overdue, immediately picked up on the topic, expanding on it.

"Ah yes, the matter of the Jews seems to be well in hand, especially here in the Baden region. I was at a function not too long ago, a small diner hosted by the Mayor. The Gauleiter (Governor) of the Baden Region was the guest of honour. Since the

French capitulation, he has also been named the Governor of the French region of Alsace. He spoke on the Jewish situation. He has been of late under a great deal of pressure from the locals here in Mannheim to take decisive action toward the expulsion of the remainder of this inferior race. He brought with him a guest speaker, a very intelligent and well-spoken SS-Hauptsturmfuhrer (Captain) by the name of Adolf Eichmann.

He's been recently transferred, taking charge of the Prague office of Jewish Emigration working under that dashing Gruppenfuhrer, head of the RSHA, Reinhard Heydrich. Apparently the magnitude of the Jewish situation we suffered here before the Fuhrer's expansion of our borders eastward was just the tip of the iceberg and we have now inherited millions more of them. Getting rid of the pestilence has become a huge problem as no other country, quite understandably of course, wants any part of them."

Ursula nodded.

"Well, we certainly can't blame them for that; they would be a drain on any country's economy."

Hannelore smiled and set her teacup down onto the table beside her.

"Herr Eichmann went on to say that more resources and manpower have been put into place to deal with them. Eichmann has come up with a wonderful plan to relocate the lot of them to the Island of Madagascar. The Governor later spoke briefly and told us that while he was on an official visit, as a result of his new responsibility in Alsace France, he was advised that the Gurs Interment Camp in south-western France, used to house Spanish refugees during their civil war was nearly empty. He is going to suggest it be used to temporarily house our Jews who have not left the country of their own volition until their permanent resettlement can be accomplished."

Gabriella glanced at her watch and stubbed out her cigarette.

"Yes, well, that sounds like an excellent suggestion if you ask me, but on that note I'm afraid Ursula and I should get on our way, that is if we if we want to make it back home to Lake Konstanz before dark"

CHAPTER TWENTY-TWO

- Adolf Eichmann -

- Jewish Emigration and Resettlement -

Adolf Eichmann joined the SS in April of nineteen thirty-two. In nineteen thrifty-three he was promoted to Scharfuhrer (Squad Leader) and assigned to duty as part of the administrative staff of Dachau, the first German concentration camp.

He performed well in his task and in nineteen thirty-four when he requested a transfer to the SS – Sicherheitsdienst (Security Service) or SD, his request was granted. In short order he requested another transfer resulting in his joining the 'Jews Section' at its Berlin Headquarters where he very happily settled in.

In nineteen thirty-five, a thriving Eichmann was promoted to the rank of Hauptschiarfuhrer (Head Squad Leader) and in nineteen thirty-seven commissioned as an officer with the rank of SS-Untersturmfuher (Second Lieutenant).

At the start of the war, Eichmann was again promoted, this time to the rank of SS-Hauptsturmfuhrer (Captain).

In December of nineteen thirty-nine he joined the 'Reichssicherheritshauptamt' (Reich Main Security Office) or RSHA and was assigned to head RSHA 'Referat IV B4 a sub-department which dealt with Jewish Affairs and Evacuation, reporting directly to Heinrich Muller.

Up to this time the Nazi plan for dealing with the Jews had been a haphazard affair.

In a nutshell, they considered the Jews as a sub-human race, subversive and unfit for life in the New Reich.

They wanted the Jews out of German territory. They'd

made that fact abundantly clear well before they came to power in nineteen thirty-three and taken office, by conducting a massive anti-Jewish propaganda campaign intended to unite the German people behind the State policy of a cleansing of the Jews from German society.

Initially the Nazis pushed for emigration; however they had no intention of allowing the Jews to take their wealth with them when they left German soil, a fact which made the move unpalatable to most of those targeted. In order to increase the pressure, the Nazi regime began to work toward the ideal of making the day to day life for Jews in Germany as unpleasant as they possible could.

They passed laws and took action behind the scenes between April of thirty-three and the start of the Second World War that would, for all intents and purposes, make Jews non-citizens and strip them of all their rights.

This process began in early April of nineteen thirty-three when the party began calling for a boycott of Jewish shops and businesses, while unleashing the SA (Brown-shirts), the Nazis' private army to harass Jewish business, painting them with the white Star of David and marking them with 'Jude' or 'Juden' accompanied by racist comments.

On April eleventh, the Nazis issued a decree that defined a non-Aryan as anyone descended from a non-Aryan, especially Jewish parents or grandparents. On September twenty-ninth of thirty-three, Jews were prohibited from holding land; on October fourth, from being newspaper editors. On January twenty-fourth nineteen thirty-four Jews were banned from membership in the German Labour Front (In Nazi Germany, the Labour Front represented all workers and employers).

If you were not a member you could not employ people, nor could you be employed.

On May seventeenth of that year Jews were disallowed national health insurance, and on July twenty-second they were prohibited from becoming lawyers.

In nineteen thirty-five the Nuremberg Race Laws against Jews were decreed.

In thirty-six the Jews got a bit of a break. Germany was hosting the Olympic Games that year and wanted to encourage attendance at the event which they intended to use to build a positive international reputation for the New Reich under Hitler. Propaganda against, and active persecution of the Jews was temporarily placed on the back burner.

In January of nineteen thirty-seven, Jews were disallowed child allowances and tax deductions and banned from several professions. These included accounting, dentistry and teaching,

In November of that year the 'Der ewige Jude' (The eternal Jew) traveling exhibit opened in Munich. The Exhibit's purpose was to further expand the propaganda campaign against the Jewish race. As its title suggested, it was based upon the popular fable concerning the Jew who ridiculed and / or physically abused Jesus while he was being transported to the cross and as a result was thereafter damned to wander the world in perpetuity, abandoned and reviled by all who crossed his path. The Nazis chose to use this theme as a general basis for the good God-fearing races of the world to vilify all Jews.

Advertised as a 'Degenerate Art Exhibit', it first appeared in the library of the German Museum in Munich and ran until the end of January nineteen thirty-eight. From there it moved to Vienna, running from August through to October before moving to Berlin for a run from November to the end of January nineteen thirty-nine.

Consisting of photographs and text depicting Jews in the worst possible light and making use of any and all historically negative connotations with regard to their appearance, dress or activities was to make the Jewish people appear as foreign or untrustworthy, money-grubbing and disease-ridden.

Police reports indicated a distinct rise in anti-Semitic activity, including increased violence against the Jews in the cities where the exhibition was held.

The Party considered the exhibit a resounding success and Goebbels was so pleased with the results that he immediately commissioned the making of a movie with an identical theme.

In April of thirty-eight Aryan ownership of Jewish businesses determined to be acting as a front for the real owner was prohibited.

Jews were required to register all their wealth and property and in June of that year all Jewish businesses were required to register with the State.

Needless to say, by this point *the writing had quite definitely and very literally, been on the wall* for some time and many Jews had decided to leave Germany, with or without their wealth.

Word had inevitably slipped out through the German borders and in July of thirty-eight the United States and France convened a League of Nations conference to address the problem. Thirty-two countries attended and there was much wiping of eyes and ringing of hands but none of the States present extended an offer to accept any Jewish refugees. The conference result was used by the Nazis to bolster their claims that Jews were a plague on all mankind and unwelcome worldwide.

In June of that year the Nazis made it illegal for Jews to trade and to supply numerous services. Jewish doctors were prohibited from practicing medicine.

All Jews over fifteen years of age were ordered to carry identity cards and to present them to police on demand.

In August of thirty-eight an ill-disguised Nazi group destroyed the Jewish Synagogue at Nuremberg. They also decreed that all Jews must add an additional name on all legal documents including passports. Women would add 'Sarah' and men 'Israel'. September saw Jews prohibited from practicing as lawyers and August brought about the custom of stamping a large red 'J' on all Jewish passports.

After the Nazis had occupied the Sudetenland in October of thirty-eight, they arrested approximately seventeen thousand Jews of Polish extraction who were living in Germany and transported them to the Polish border.

The Polish government refused them entry and the Germans simply abandoned them, leaving them to fend for themselves. In November, using the excuse of the assassination of a third secretary at the German Embassy in Paris by a deported Polish Jew, the Nazis unleashed 'Kristallnacht' (The Night of the Broken Glass), a night during which Jewish businesses, religious structures and homes were attacked in a wholesale wave of destruction while police watched and refused to intervene.

After this the Nazis promptly fined the Jewish community one billion marks for collateral damages caused during the mêlée.

That was also the month Jewish students were expelled from all German non-Jewish schools.

December saw the passing of a law that required the Aryanization of all remaining Jewish businesses and the appointment by Hitler of Herman Goring to head a group to deal with what was now being classed as the 'Jewish Question' by way of emigration and evacuation.

In January of nineteen thirty-nine, Goring ordered SS 'Gruppenfuhrer' (Group Leader) Reinhard Heydrich, Himmler's right-hand man, to accelerate the emigration of the Jews.

In February all Jews were required to turn over to the State all silver and gold items they possessed. In March the Nazi's overran Czechoslovakia and a month later the new Slovakian government passed its own version of the Nuremberg laws. In May a ship loaded with Jewish refugees was refused permission to land in Cuba and the United States and other countries and had no choice but to return toEurope. In July German Jews were forbidden to hold any government job and Adolf Eichmann was chosen as the Director of the Prague Office of Jewish Emigration.

In August of nineteen-forty Eichmann produced his solution to dealing with the Jews, his 'Reichssicherheitshauptamt Madagascar Project' (Reich Main Security Office: Madagascar Project), a plan for Jewish forced deportation to the island of Madagascar.

CHAPTER TWENTY-THREE

- Gurs Internment Camp -

- Gestapo -

The French government constructed the Gurs camp near the Spanish border during the Spanish civil war. Built in nineteen thirty-nine and staffed by the French militarily, it was hastily build to house the mass of refugees streaming into France to escape retribution from the winning Fascist Falange under the leadership of Francisco Franco.

The camp had not been designed to serve as a long -term containment centre. It was roughly built out of thin wood planks and had no insulation against the weather, running water or toilet facilities.

Before the second world began the camp had morphed from its original purpose into a concentration camp being used to house suspected German fifth columnists and French political prisoners.

At the time of the French capitulation to Germany it was nearly empty.

Robert Heinrich Wagner, Governor of Baden and a Hitler supporter from the early days was given the extra responsibility of Alsace when that portion of a conquered France came under German control.

Aware of the rapidly growing numbers of homeless, penniless Jews and the need to temporarily house them before their resettlement could be accomplished he immediately saw the potential of Gurs for that purpose. Using it would allow him to cleanse his state of Jews and get them off German soil and at the same time force the French to look after them until they could be otherwise dealt with.

He immediately forwarded such a proposal to Berlin.

* * * * *

When he came to power, Hitler knew from the election results that his stated vision for The Third Reich had the support of the majority of Germans, but he also realized that the party had its dissidents, many of whom would, if given the opportunity, work to create the downfall of his dictatorial power. He also knew that parts of that vision, parts that he had for political reasons held back from the public due to the intended methods of how they would be implemented, would also have dissenters, once they had been introduced.

He had no intention of allowing this type of dissention to become effectively organized or grow vocal among the masses of the German people. To prevent it he created two new organizations intended to eradicate such movements at the source. The first of these was an education system which strictly taught the Nazi Party line and involved a mandatory political indoctrination of all children between ten and twenty-one years of age.

This was combined with absolute State controlled censorship backed by a propaganda machine the likes and success of which had never been known to man.

The second organization structured to control dissenters was the establishment of the 'Geheime Staatspolizei' (Secret State Police) or 'Gestapo' which took place shortly after Hitler became Chancellor and named his staunch supporter Herman Goring to the position of Interior Minister of Prussia which placed him at the head of the biggest state police agency in Germany.

Goring was no policeman but he was a savvy politician and in short order he had separated the intelligence and political sections from the main police force and promptly expanded their ranks by way of employing a large contingent of Nazi sympathizers.

He then merged the two on April twenty-sixth, nineteen thirty-three into a single organization which he named the 'Gestapo'.

Those who had ridden Hitler's coattails into high political office continually connived against each other in attempts to gain further influence with Hitler and through that influence, more personal power within the party. In any country that has such an organization, the man who controls the secret police is a man controlling a great deal of power and in a dictatorship he is likely a man who also holds the power of life and death in his hands.

One of Goring's fellow ministers in the new government was Wilhelm Frick, the Reich Interior Minister, who was lobbying to centralize control of all of Germany's police forces.

This was no easy task since historically the control of police forces throughout the various states that made up the country had been local in nature.

Goring had no particular interest in who controlled the regular police, but he did not want to lose control of the Gestapo in his large state of Prussia. A power struggled ensued between the two men and Goring used his influence with Hitler to receive permission to have his newly created Prussian Gestapo become a separate entity from all other police agencies within Prussia.

In so doing he removed it from the control of Frick's Ministry.

He also personally took over the leadership of this new secret intelligence and political force.

Taking advantage of his success in pulling off an end run around Frick, Goring then urged Hitler to consider expanding his Gestapo, to transform it from just a Prussian state force into a German federal agency with countrywide authority and responsibility.

He didn't get a 'yes' from Hitler, but then in consideration of all the infighting and active power struggles going on around the man, one rarely did.

Hitler had also not said no, so Goring decided to give it a try.

Frick was not confident about taking on Goring on his own so, as was often the case in these power struggles, he looked around in the Nazi hierarchy for a strong ally and since Bavaria was the next largest state in Germany after Prussia he decided to pal up to Heinrich Himmler the police chief in Bavaria, a man who happened to distrust Goring.

Frick approached Heydrich who was Himmler's number two with a suggestion that they join forces against Goring.

Himmler, lower on the totem pole than Goring, kept himself in the background initially, testing the waters carefully as he allowed Heydrich and Frick to formulate a plan to circumvent Goring's intention to expand the Gestapo outward from its Prussian roots. Once a plan was formulated and presented to him by Heydrich, who felt it had a good chance of success, Himmler, fully supported by Frick, began to take over all state police forces in Germany.

In a matter of months he found himself in control of them all with the exception of Goring's Prussian state police and the Prussian Gestapo.

Goring found himself swiftly outmanoeuvred by the seemingly unassuming but wily Himmler whose first step on taking control of each state was to mimic Goring by separating out the political and intelligence police units from the main force and placing them under his direct control.

In accomplishing this, Himmler had managed to shift the balance of power among Hitler's inner circle enough to put him into a position where Goring had to recognize his growing support from the Fuhrer and the resulting increased influence within the hierarchy of the New Germany.

Needless to say this caused a heightened dislike and distrust between the two men which might well have continued to fester and build if it had not been the case that an even more dangerous threat to the control of the Nazi Party from within the core group around Hitler began to assert itself.

The threat coming to a head was the massively growing

strength in Germany of the 'Sturm Abteilung' (Storm Troopers) or SA, and a growing tendency by its leader Ernst Rohm to try to influence Hitler's personal views of how a renewed Germany should be constituted.

CHAPTER TWENTY-FOUR

- Sturm Abteilung (SA) –

- Night of the Long Knives –

Without the support of the SA, Hitler and the Nazi Party would not have come to power in Germany, but by nineteen thirty-four what had been an asset for over a decade had become a definite liability.

The beginnings of what had morphed into the SA by thirty-four took place after the end of the Great War. The precursor of this organization started at that time with the formation, by many German ex-soldiers, of the 'Freikorps' (Free Corps), a voluntary paramilitary organization.

Shortly after the war, in nineteen twenty, the newly formed German Workers' Party, the forerunner of the Nazi party, found itself in need of a militia group it could call its own which would be capable of providing protection at party meetings against the hecklers and dissenters from the other political parties. Some of the Freikorps members who supported the Nazi platform, calling themselves the 'Turn-und Sportabteilung' (Sport and Gymnastic Division) chose to take up this gauntlet and they promptly joined the Nazi Party and accepted the responsibility of keeping order at future meetings. One of these men was an ex-Bavarian Army Captain named Ernst Rohm.

On November fourth of nineteen twenty-one the Nazi Party held a large meeting at which the usual demonstrators attempting to disrupt the programme were soundly thrashed and removed by this new force.

That success marked them as worthy of their acceptance within the party and they were renamed the SA and provided with uniforms consisting of brown shirts with the party swastika armband on the left sleeve, khaki trousers, brown belt and boots as well as a brown peaked cap trimmed in red.

When Hitler was arrested and imprisoned after the failed Munich Putsch the government of the day prohibited the SA organization as an entity. The prohibition was circumvented immediately by way of a name change. The SA simply became the 'Frontbann' and at Hitler's order Ernst Rohm became its leader and was given a free hand to reorganize and expand the organization.

When Hitler was released from prison on December twentieth, nineteen twenty-four he eased back into his leadership role and began to solidify his base. Hitler and Rohm had become close friends by April of nineteen twenty-five, and it was then that he gave Rohm the authority to reorganize and expand the SA. In February of twenty-five the Party felt confident enough to drop the Frontbann name and restore the paramilitary force to its original SA designation.

Between February and April of that year Hitler found himself displeased with the direction in which Rohm was taking the organization.

They disagreed as to the long term goals of the SA, which Hitler considered being paramilitary in nature and Rohm saw as morphing into becoming the main German military force.

As a result Rohm left the SA on May first of nineteen twenty-five and went into retirement. In nineteen twenty-eight he accepted a position as a military advisor to Bolivia and was given the rank of Lieutenant Colonel.

By nineteen-thirty Hitler had advanced his political agenda considerably and as his popularity grew, the Party's need for the SA diminished and their lawless street-fighter mentality began to become an embarrassment.

Hitler took direct control of the organization in order to bring it under control and made a call to Bolivia to ask his old comrade and friend Rohm to return to Germany and become his

Chief of Staff of the SA. Rohm eagerly took up the position in January of nineteen thirty-one.

Rohm, a homosexual, brought with him the radical social ideas that had caused the earlier break with Hitler's views regarding the direction the organization should take, but he had learned his lesson and was now more guarded as to these policies. He immediately replaced the top leaders of the SA with his own friends, most of whom shared his sexual orientation. By this time the SA had grown to a compliment of one million men and the black uniformed SS or 'Schutzstaffel' (Protection Squadron), formed from volunteers from within the SA had been created under Himmler's command as a separate entity to serve as Hitler's personal bodyguard.

Hitler had his hands full during this period and was content to allow Rohm, who reported directly to him, a relatively free hand with the SA. The day he declared himself as Fuhrer of Germany, he made the SA Auxiliary Police and used them to rapidly take over all government offices and place them under the control of the Nazi Party.

Shortly after that time, all political parties other than the Nazis were declared illegal and any dissenters were locked away in concentration camps. From that point on Hitler had little need to call on the SA for other than ceremonial matters and he rarely needed them to assist the party in enforcing its political aims.

The honeymoon period between Hitler and Rohm was not destined to last for long.

Rohm was a staunch left-winger and kept pushing for what he called a 'Second Revolution'. He wanted Hitler to break up the old estates and share the land with the lower classes, and to nationalize all large corporations.

Big business had supported Hitler's rise to power as had the large landowners and members of the Aristocracy who also held most of the top military positions within the German army. By nineteen thirty-three Rohm started to make noises about merging the SA with the much smaller German army, the obvious intention was to become the leader of the combined force. Toward that end in nineteen thirty-four he sent a message to the Minister of defence Werner von Blomberg demanding that this amalgamation take place immediately.

These were groups that Hitler had taken pains not to alienate and this rash move by Rohm drew the attention of the others within the Fuhrer's inner circle who had all become very aware of Rohm's growing power and influence over Hitler and were eager to bring him down.

Von Blomberg, already personally concerned about the SA leader's growing sway within the New Reich, instantly approached Goring and Himmler with the contents of Rohm's message.

Goring and Himmler, shaken by Rohm's demand and what it would mean to their own positions of influence with Hitler immediately dismissed their differences, buried the hatchet and agreed to work together to convince Hitler to dump Rohm.

After a short meeting during which Goring agreed to hand over to Himmler the full control of the Gestapo, Himmler directed his right-hand man Reinhard Heydrich to compile a report for presentation to Hitler that would provide evidence that Ernst Rohm was plotting to use his SA - which now numbered two million men - to perform a coup and take personal control of the Nazi Party.

In Berlin on April twentieth nineteen thirty-four Goring transferred full authority over the Prussian Gestapo to an over-joyed Himmler.

Two days later Himmler named Heydrich, who reported directly to him, to head of the Gestapo.

For Himmler, Heydrich proved to be an ideal choice to lead the new agency.

In short order he placed into his boss's hands a mendacious and very damning report on the activities of Ernst Rohm.

Himmler, with Goring, Heydrich and Minister of Defence von Blomberg, who had by this time become fiercely loyal to

Hitler and had aided in harnessing support for the Fuhrer from the army leadership in support, presented the report to Hitler.

This was at a time when the Fuhrer, who was becoming aware of Rohm's public statements with regard to his far left socialist cries for a 'Second Revolution', thereby alienating several groups of people Hitler needed for support was receptive to the suggestion from the group that it was time for his old friend Rohm to go.

Von Blomberg played a large part in the resulting planning and operation of 'The Night of the Long Knives', which involved the arrest of nearly one thousand persons including all the leaders of the SA as well as several other political opponents, by the SS and Gestapo which took place beginning on the night of June twenty-ninth and lasted until July second of nineteen thirty-four.

Official records of the number of men executed as a result vary but Himmler saw to it that Rohm and all the leaders of the SA met their deaths.

The SS and Gestapo under the leadership of Himmler and Heydrich took advantage of the situation to dispose of any and all others whom they considered to be disloyal to Hitler or the party by way of summarily executing or confining them in concentration camps.

The killings, executions and internments were made legal by Hitler on July thirteenth when he made a speech to the Reichstag in the Knoll Opera House in which he stated that the cleansing had been necessitated as an act of self-defence by the SS and Gestapo against an act of treason against the state.

He took full responsibility for what took place saying that he as Fuhrer was the supreme judge of the German people and therein above the law and as such had every right to order the SS and Gestapo to take action to prevent the attempted putsch.

The operation had gone like clockwork. Hitler was extremely pleased with the result which left the SA under the leadership of Victor Lutz who was ineffectual and completely under Hitler's thumb.

The organization itself quickly dwindled from three million to just over one million men and from this point on young German men did not select the SA but chose to join the regular army or Himmler's independent SS which were both rapidly growing in size and stature.

The swift action had also served to impress upon the German people that no one, not even those holding high office could ever again assume that they were safe from arrest or summary execution by members of Himmler's Gestapo.

On July third von Blomberg publically expressed his appreciation for Adolf Hitler's decisiveness in executing the measures to put down the treasonous plans of the SA organization before it could destroy the new Germany.

Seventeen days after Hindenburg's death on August second, the cabinet ordered a plebiscite to be held for the German people on August nineteenth, nineteen thirty-four for the purpose of approving the combination of the offices of Chancellor (head of government) and President (Head of state) into a single office to be known as 'Fuhrer und Reichkanzler' (Leader and Chancellor).

The vote was eighty-nine point nine percent in favour and on the next day at the urging of Defence Minister von Blomberg supported by General Walther von Reichenau, the cabinet decreed a law that the oath of allegiance required from all members of the military and all German civil
servants would change from an oath to the 'Volk und Vaterland' (People and Fatherland) to one of personal allegiance to Adolf Hitler.

CHAPTER TWENTY-FIVE

Anhalter Bahnhof – Berlin

- September 21st 1940, 17:30 hours –

On the twenty-first of September the male members of the von Stauffer family found themselves together at the hectic main train station with the aim of boarding the Count's private railcars.

For weeks the rail-yards had been abuzz with activity, going from eighty-four departing and arriving trains per day pre-war to the current numbers which were in excess of two hundred per day.

Most of these were military transports disguised as regularly scheduled civilian units with newly fitted blackout blinds in place.

The noise level of the constantly arriving and departing trains made it impossible for conversation and the men who had been joined by Doctor Baron Heinrich Von Kliest in preparation for the weekend trip to the ancestral home on Lake Konstanz which had been hurriedly arranged at the insistence of the Count, made no attempt to speak to each other as they quickly made their way to the rear of the train to which the Count's private cars had been attached.

The first of the luxurious coaches had been built shortly after the turn of the century to meet the unique specifications of the then Count, Diedrich Von Stauffer, the current Count's father.

It had been custom built and richly appointed, encompassing observation platform, full kitchen, dining room, secretary's room, observation lounge and servants' quarters in addition to a large self-contained combination bedroom and study suite.

In the early thirties it had been modernized and updated both structurally and internally to facilitate use with the new, more powerful engines and revised standard travelling speeds of the modern German railway system.

At that time the Count had also ordered from the original coach builder, Henschel and Sons Company who had in nineteen thirty-five designed the new 'Streamliner' type locomotives for the German State Railway, a second private coach to be built to the same style and size of the original but consisting internally of only large and luxuriously appointed self-contained sleeping compartments.

These provided room, when coupled to the original coach, for the sleeping comfort of his growing family whenever they traveled by rail. This second coach was now always attached in tandem to the original.

It would take the train pulling the family's two private railcars approximately seven hours to reach Castle von Stauffer, situated above Lake Konstanz in Austria on the Rhine River in close proximity to the German, Austrian and Swiss borders.

The Count led the others into the family's main car which was coupled between the custom built sleeping car and the caboose at the end of the train. The small party climbed up onto the observation deck at the rear of the carriage and from there made their way into the observation lounge where he invited them to partake of the well-stocked bar and an array of freshly prepared dishes of bread, cheeses and cold cuts arranged on a side table.

A white-jacketed, uniformed SS steward approached the Count and bent close to speak briefly in his ear and then left the compartment. The Count excused himself and followed the man into the adjoining dining room, closing the door behind him.

An army sergeant, holding a set of earphones in his left hand and wearing a leather strap around his neck that ran down to support an unwieldy black rectangular box resting against the front of his body at waist level, stood waiting.

The top of the suspended instrument held several switches and dials and an attached brown cord ran from one side of the box to a wand-like device which the man held in his right hand.

His gaze met the Count's eyes.

"There are no listening devices to be found Herr Oberstgruppenfuhrer."

The Count nodded

"Thank you Otto, I appreciate your taking the time. Now please enjoy the rest of your weekend."

The sergeant's boot heels came together smartly as he bobbed his head and began to remove the earphones and instrument which he hurriedly placed into the custom made case sitting open on the large dining table.

Leaving him to the task, von Stauffer spun around and opened the door leading back into to the observation lounge and stepped through, closing it behind him.

He found his sons and the Baron, drinks in hand, seated in the comfortable overstuffed chairs arranged at the rear of the room. He waited for a break in the conversation before speaking.

"Wilhelm, would you be good enough to join me in my compartment. I need to discuss something with you, if Heinrich and Eric can spare you for a few moments"

The Baron and his oldest son turned to face the Count and Eric, who couldn't pass up a chance of a light-hearted jibe, smiled.

"By all means Father, take him from us. It will give Heinrich and me a chance to speak of something other than the wonders of the SS."

All of them, including his youngest son, well aware of Wilhelm's tendency to both dominate conversation and expound on the greatness of the SS whenever the opportunity arose, broke into laughter and Wilhelm got up and followed his father out of the lounge through the dining room, and down the hallway past the adjoining kitchen to the Count's private rooms.

Once inside with the door closed the Oberstgruppenfuhrer waved his son into an armchair beside the small desk and chair that served the Count as a private workspace when on the move, then he turned the desk chair to face Wilhelm and sat down.

A quizzical expression formed on his son's features as the

Count quietly studied his son for a few seconds. He was about to speak when his father raised his hand to dissuade him, and then broke the silence.

"Bear with me for a moment please, Wilhelm. I'm concerned that what I have to ask you may seem strange or of little importance to you under the circumstances and I want you to stop and take the time to very carefully consider your responses before you make them. I say this in part because of our past differences of opinion, but primarily because your answer to my question will have immediate and very definite future long-term consequences not only for our family but also the entire German nation. Please keep an open mind and treat what I am about to ask you as serious and worthy of careful thought and the application of a good deal of honesty."

Wilhelm could not dispute that he and his father had experienced disagreements over the changes brought about by the Nazi rise to power and some of the policies resulting from Hitler's new vision of Germany.

While these had been at the time relatively serious they had been short-lived and had never caused him to lose either respect or admiration for his father.

He was therefore both puzzled and concerned about what situation could have arisen that could possibly bring about the serious manner in which his father was now addressing him.

He felt his previous light-heartedness drain away and he shifted uncomfortably in his chair.

"All right Dad. You've got my full attention. Fire away."

The Count fixed his eyes on his son as he spoke.

"Exactly where does your strongest loyalty lie - with your family and the future of Germany or with the SS?"

The question took him completely by surprise and Wilhelm placed his hands together and raised the tips to rest against his lips.

He allowed the question to reverberate around in his mind while considering it carefully and then lowered his hands slowly and replied.

"I'm not sure what you are asking. Both you and I are honour bound by way of oath to the Fuhrer. I'm not sure that my loyalties, as you have expressed it, can be divided, that they are not one and the same. I am loyal to the SS and I have sworn an oath of loyalty to Adolf Hitler, who is the future of Germany and of course I am loyal to my family."

The Count shook his head.

"I did not ask you where your loyalties lie. I am well aware of what they are and to whom.

I asked you specifically, where your strongest loyalty lies, and yes, I want you to separate the wheat from the chaff and force yourself to choose only that which is most important to you.

I understand that it may not be an easy choice but I must ask you to make it and then provide me with an honest answer. I am going to return to your brother and our guest and will leave you to think on what I've said. When you have an answer for me please join us in the lounge."

CHAPTER TWENTY-SIX

– A Tough Question –

As the Count opened the door leading into the observation lounge he felt the initial lurch as the engine began to pull forward and picked up the slack in the car couplings as it began to increase speed. He briefly rested his right hand against the door frame for support against the pull and took the opportunity to check the watch on his left wrist.

Amazingly they were pulling out on time. It would appear that even the hectic increase in traffic to allow for the many new military trains leaving and arriving at the station would not be allowed to interfere with the reputation of the Deutches Reichbahn (German National Railway) with regard to meeting their scheduled departure and arrival times.

The initial shifting of the car as the train began to move was brief and once it had passed he stepped through the doorway into the lounge to join the Baron and his eldest son.

His SS steward, who had been waiting for his return to the car reached for a bottle on the sideboard and poured a drink for the Count and then moved to hand it to him as he was crossing the room.

* * * * *

The train was leaving the outskirts of Berlin and rapidly picking up speed by the time Wilhelm entered the observation lounge. The Count looked up from where he was sitting and eagerly searched for some sign in his son's features that would give him a clue as to what his answer would be.

He found none and felt a twinge of unease in the pit of his

stomach. A sense of helplessness filled him.

Where had the oh-so-transparent boy of a few years ago gone? How could they have changed him so much, made him so guarded and unreadable?

He and his brother had been physically so much alike as young boys. Even today Eric retained those early boyish good looks, but Wilhelm, always the more serious of the two, while still handsome, clearly reflected a more sombre and somehow threatening presence.

I am not even sure that I really know who he is any more. I may not be an overly religious man, but I pray to you now God, please give me back my son!

The tension between father and son was apparent to both the Baron and Eric, and the conversation dribbled off as they looked over to study the other two men in an attempt to ascertain its source.

All eyes on him, Wilhelm shifted his eyes to meet his father's. He held them for a few seconds, taking the time to be sure that he had no lingering doubts and then he spoke three words.

"Family and Germany."

The Count, who had been unconsciously holding his breath, released it and nodded before he stood up and moved over to Wilhelm.

He was not a man easily given to blatant public signs of affection and Wilhelm was initially taken aback when his father threw his arms around him and hugged him firmly.

The surprise of it passed quickly and he raised his own arms as he openly welcomed his father's embrace.

* * * * *

The train was four hours out of Berlin and running at full speed. Darkness had fallen by the time they had completed the evening meal.

The fact that Eric and the Baron were still wondering what had taken place between the Count and his eldest son earlier in the evening served to dampen what probably would have been a more steady and casual conversational exchange between the four of them. Neither of them felt comfortable in raising the issue.

The Count was aware of their unease, but extremely pleased with Wilhelm's answer to his question and considering it a private matter between him and his youngest son saw no need to address it.

When the dishes had been cleared, he dismissed his steward for the evening and led the others into the observation lounge for Port and cigars.

When they had settled into well stuffed armchairs they lit up and the count raised his glass in toast.

"Let's drink to the future of the Fatherland, gentlemen."

They drank and the Count set his glass down and let his eyes move from man to man before speaking.

"What we discuss here tonight will remain in this room. It may well prove to be the most important conversation each of us ever has."

He let the words sink in before he continued.

"I know that all of you are wondering why I arranged for this weekend away together on such short notice, and you have probably reached your own conclusion as to the reason. However, until now there were only two men in this room who know the truth of it and I am one of them. The other is our good friend the Baron. What we decide here tonight, and over the remainder of the weekend may well
determine the future of Germany."

Again he paused for effect before speaking.

"On September seventeenth Adolf Hitler made the decision to postpone the invasion of England indefinitely. He is now going to turn his attention to the east, and he will eventually attack Russia.

In my opinion and that of many others, including most of his staff officers, in so doing he has destined us to once again fight a two front war that Germany probably cannot win. While this is admittedly a worst case scenario, since no one can predict the future, it is factually based and reasonable when viewed from what has historically been the case."

Wilhelm opened his mouth to speak but the Count held up his hand for silence.

"Please hear me out before you respond."

Wilhelm's mouth closed but he was obviously displeased.

The Count continued.

"Some of those others, who are far more knowledgeable and informed than I, have come to the unfortunate conclusion that this war will become drawn out as was the last, to become one of attrition in both men and weapons. If Germany had been allowed to take advantage of our more modern military machine to fight a short war while at optimal strength, after either defeating or reaching a peace treaty with England, we may well have been successful in defeating Russia. We have not invaded England, nor have we managed to bring them to a peace agreement and therefore we do not have a secure western front. Instead we have left the English their stronghold and with it a jumping off point from which they will be able to directly attack us in Europe. This is precisely what they will do, and they will do it with the support of their empire and that of the United States of America.

When we break our treaty with Russia they will join in the war against us, just as happened in the Great War. For a second time in history we will face the enemy on both the Western and Eastern fronts. Germany has neither the overwhelming manpower nor military might which would be required to win an extended war under those circumstances.

I am convinced that the men, who are in the best position to judge and have prophesied this result, are right in their thinking, and so is the Baron.

We have given the matter a great deal of thought and we have come up with an idea of how to deal with the probable outcome of such a military struggle in a manner that will allow Germany to rise like a phoenix from the ashes of a beaten and destroyed county, for that is what the Fatherland will become before this war is finished. The world will not allow Germany to sue for peace a second time around. No, this time Germany will be obliterated and occupied before our enemies are satisfied."

The Count paused to let his words sink in. He picked up his glass and took a drink.

Tension had built in the room to the point that it could be felt by all of them.

"Wilhelm, Eric, do you wish to question the validity of what I have said so far?"

Eric was following his own train of thought, rolling his father's words around in his head as he drew on his cigar. Wilhelm, his drink forgotten and his cigar smouldering untouched in his ashtray sat erect in his chair. He was the first to speak.

"Father we, all of us here, have sworn an oath of loyalty to the Fuhrer, as have those to whom you refer as others. I may be wrong, but I get the impression that what you are about to suggest could be the foundation of what may well be considered a breach of that oath at best and treason against the Fatherland at worst."

The Count shook his head and placed his glass back down on the table.

"Then you would be wrong Wilhelm. What I am about to suggest is merely a sensible approach to what may possibly be the failure of Germany to win this war.

A fall-back plan if you like and one that will in no way conflict with your oath of allegiance and one that certainly could not be considered by any reasonable person as treason against the Fatherland."

CHAPTER TWENTY-SEVEN

- A Fall-back Plan -

After several seconds of silence Eric broke in.

"Father, you ask us to accept your appraisal of Germany's chances to win this war. In the same breath you say that no one can predict the future. Are we to take it on faith alone then?"

Again the Count shook his head.

"Not at all.

Neither of you are currently informed enough to do that, but I hope that you will be by the time this weekend is over. You will find that we have a much diversified array of eminent gentlemen visiting us at the castle this weekend.

They will, I hope, be able to answer any questions you and Wilhelm may have about the probable outcome of a two-front war."

Wilhelm seemed to relax a little, his back losing its stiffness as he settled back into his chair.

"Assuming that after the weekend we agree with the assessment you indicate Father, what is it exactly that you have in mind that would give us what you refer to as a fall-back plan?"

The Count let his eyes meet the Baron's briefly before answering.

"Well it isn't all that easy to explain, but very simply we have come up with a strategy to use science to accomplish what we believe this war will not."

He held the rapt attention of both sons at this point.

"As you know the Fuhrer has put me in charge of all new military and scientific developments. I report directly tohim and am aware of everything that we are currently working on.

I have every intention of doing all I can to see to it that

Germany is provided with the newest and best weapons our scientists and engineers can produce with a view to preventing the necessity of a long term and debilitating war which I believe we will lose. If however we are correct in our assessment and we do in fact lose the war I want us to be in a position to recover from that destructive result. In order to ensure that we can do that I intend to concurrently set up the infrastructure that will guarantee us the ability to regain a position of world domination in the future should we suffer defeat. With the support of a few individuals I believe I can accomplish this over a reasonable period of time, certainly not within the timeframe of the current war, but in the foreseeable future. The Baron would be better able to explain the science behind it to you than I could."

Doctor Baron Heinrich von Kliest who currently held the rank of SS-Sturmbannfuhrer (Major) was not only the man who had, in their estimation, saved their father's life and to whom they therefore owed a priceless debt of thanks; he was also a friend and in practical terms considered as a member of the family.

The von Stauffer boys had grown up with Heinrich as a neighbour and he had been very much treated as a respected older brother, always around in those early years to save their skins and offer sage advice whenever it became necessary.

The Count was very much aware that they had been in awe of the Baron as children and now as adults both trusted him implicitly. He knew they would take whatever the Baron had to say as the God's truth.

Both boys now turned to face him directly, waiting for him to speak.

The Major finished his cigar and ground the stub out in his ash tray and then took a deep breath.

"Well, where do I start?"

He looked at Wilhelm.

"You know a fair amount about eugenics and the concept of cloning by now, Wilhelm. We are miles ahead of everyone in the development of this field and I am currently working under your father and solely dedicated to its enhancement. We are very close to perfecting it and when we do we will be able to produce military manpower, vastly superior manpower I might add, in numbers that will ensure our ability to put boots on the ground - in numbers that will be capable of overcoming any enemy.

Through eugenics we will accomplish the development of a military and scientific community that will outshine anything seen in generations and Germany will produce scientists and engineers that will be far superior to any in the world.

As your father has suggested, we will be aiming for world domination over the long term. It will take at least fifteen to twenty years for us to accomplish what we have set out to do, but with the financial and administrative support we have under our wartime conditions everything we will need to complete the task has been made available to us and is there for the taking. Given the will and the determination of those loyal to the Fatherland, we will be able to continue producing the world's finest minds in all areas of endeavour. There will be no limit to our expertise and our Aryan race will naturally evolve into a position of world domination. A new Reich will come into being without the need for war or bloodshed. It will rise from the fire and destruction of a broken Germany like a phoenix from the ashes. Humankind will be saved and a new Germany will lead a cleansed Aryan-populated world."

The Count smiled and lifted his glass.

"Let us drink to the Fourth Reich."

- Part Two -

CHAPTER TWENTY-EIGHT

- Castle von Stauffer –

On September twenty-first nineteen forty, Gabriella and Ursula von Stauffer were on the last leg of their autobahn trip from Berlin to the family ancestral castle located on Lake Constance in the Bavarian Alps.

As it had been since the start of the war when fuel rationing had been initiated, non-military traffic was sparse on the autobahn and any military traffic using the roads normally travelled by night leaving the road system unencumbered during daylight hours.

The vast majority of military transport, both human and material, moved by train. As a result the von Stauffer daughters found themselves on a surprisingly empty freeway.

The dashboard clock on Gabriella's Horch 853 convertible showed eight and the sun was just beginning to slip behind the mountains on the west side of the autobahn as the black-over-silver two-seater roadster raced through the southern tip of the lush and fertile Rhine valley landscape.

Despite the approach of evening, the blissfully warm temperature was holding.

* * * * *

- How Hitler viewed the British -

At the end of the Great War, Hitler, after fighting in the trenches, saw the British in simple terms.

The English were Germany's enemy.

During the nineteen-twenties he began to change his opinion. The change happened over time and began shortly after the war when the British opposed the French occupation of the German Ruhr in nineteen twenty-three.

This simple act, although ineffectual in the end, nevertheless caused Adolf to reassess his earlier impression of the British.

They had been ferocious enemies during war but now, unlike the French, seemed inclined to treat Germany with respect, demonstrating a fair and honourable approach to their old enemy now that the peace had been signed.

He spent some time researching German/English, French/English and German/French historic relationships and over time concluded that both counties had been politically at odds with France far more often than they had been with each other.

In *Mein Kampf* and its sequel *'Zweites Buch'* (Second Book) which was written in nineteen twenty-eight and was in rough manuscript form, unedited and unpublished until after his death, Hitler vehemently criticized the pre Great War German government in nineteen-fourteen for striving to offer challenge to the British Colonial Empire of the time.

In Hitler's mind such a challenge was a needless and foolish endeavour which only served to alienate the English, who by this point in his life he considered to be a like race to that of the Germans.

In his mind the British were an *Aryan* race whose friendshipcould have been won diplomatically had Germany not undermined the relationship by threatening the far flung British

Empire.

He made it clear in his writings that should he ever come to power in Germany and face another war, he would not repeat the same mistake, nor would he challenge the British superiority on the seas.

Both books clearly expressed that he fully expected the British, when made aware of his intentions, to willingly ally with Germany in a war against France and Russia.

* * * * *

The deep-throated purr issuing from the powerful engine of the Horch filled their ears as Gabriella and Ursula swept past the vineyards, apple, pear, and hop farms that had been cut out from among the natural flora within the bird-filled riparian forests of the rich valley which consisted mainly of silver willow, alder and ash.

The classy little car flew through the turns as it wound its way through the bottom of the valley between the rolling foothills of the Austrian Alps.

Both young women were enjoying the invigorating thrill provided by the balmy breeze as it whipped through their hair.

Their nostrils welcomed the memorable scents given off by the lush fresh growth mingled with that of the thick, rich newly-turned loam of the valley floor as it whisked over the top of the split windshield.

* * * * *

- Treaty of Versailles –

The Treaty of Versailles, signed by the Germans after their resounding defeat in the Great War, placed stringent restrictions on the size and content of the German Navy for the foreseeable future.

It stipulated that Germany's naval fleet would consist of a maximum of six pre-dreadnought battleships, six cruisers, twelve destroyers and twelve torpedo boats.

Germany was forbidden both aircraft carriers and full-sized battleships.

The treaty did allow for the Germans to replace its pre-dreadnought battleships as it saw fit but this had to be accomplished through the building of vessels displacing a maximum of ten thousand long tons.

To replace these pre-dreadnoughts the Germans immediately designed what they called the 'Panzerschiffe' (Armoured Ships). The allies later referred to these as Pocket Battleships.

These vessels were specifically designed to be both faster than their stronger enemies and stronger than their faster enemies. The German navy envisioned this class of warship as fulfilling the capability of use as a dedicated offensive commercial raider in times of war.

The startling successes of the U-boats during the Great War were dully noted by the allies when they drew up the Treaty of Versailles, which prohibited the vanquished Germans from having any submarines whatsoever after nineteen-eighteen.

In the period after the Great War and before the Second World War the Germans took every possible diplomatic opportunity to portray to the rest of the world that the treaty restrictions imposed by the allies with regard to the stipulated allowable German military levels in their armed forces were both harsh and unjust.

Germany took the position that this situation needed to be remedied and that such remedy should take one of two paths.

Either all the other states of Europe should disarm down to the German levels or Germany should be allowed to rearm to the level of the other European states.

This position on the part of the Germans found considerable fertile ground in Britain where, since nineteen-nineteen, there was much guilt over what had been considered excessively severe terms placed on the defeated Germans at the end of the conflict, these terms having been inflicted primarily as a direct result of demands made by the French.

Germany's repeated pleas for a *fair* revaluation of those terms leading to an equality of arms among the nations of Europe rapidly received considerable support in England.

This reconsideration of the fairness of the terms of the treaty on the part of the British came at a time when the German public at large and every subsequently elected government after the Great War in the new democratic German Weimar Republic, was obdurately opposed to the terms of Versailles.

From the British perspective, Germany was and had always been the strongest power in Europe.

The unrest caused in Germany by the excessively ruthless terms of the treaty ran counter to the British concept of fair play. With a view to ensuring future peace it made sense to the British Government to support adjustments in the treaty terms that were, in hindsight, considered by their own people as unjust.

The resounding victory of Hitler and the Fascist Nazi Party in Germany's national elections in nineteen thirty-three sent a jolt of electricity crackling through the British government benches.

The English were only too aware that the callous terms of the treaty and the years of diplomatic dithering involved in attempting to bring about much needed adjustments in its contents had played no small part in the creation of that decisive democratic choice on the part of the German populace.

Who was Hitler?

What did he and his Nazi Party stand for?

What might this change at the highest level in Germany mean for Britain's future?

Hitler's book, 'Mein Kampf' (My Struggle) suddenly became required reading for the illustrious gentlemen residing in the well-padded seats of the British Parliament and there was much ado and enquiring discussion in those hallowed chambers.

As a result, Royal Marine General Sir Maurice Hankey, Chief

of the committee of Imperial Defence, was dispatched to Germany on a diplomatic fact-finding mission in August of nineteen thirty-three.

Upon his return to England he provided an overview of Hitler that, simply broken down, posed two questions.

Was the new leader of Germany a mainstream learned statesman, who, not unlike many others who had preceded him throughout the history of the world, had matured, mellowed and shifted away over time from his early radical political positions; or did he retain the opinions he expressed in *Mein Kampf* to this very day and would he do as he had written, cloak himself in diplomacy and disguise his true aims in flowery discourse while achieving the time-frame required to build his military machine to a level where he could safely reveal his true colours to the world and confidently make his move to take Poland by conquest?

Which of the two was it?

This question remained unanswered and the resulting indecision was destined to affect all British foreign policy towards Germany until nineteen thirty-nine.

After the Great War left a world demanding peace, attempts to avoid further major wars were discussed during two International conferences on naval strength which took place in the late twenties and early thirties, the first in Washington and the second in London.

These imposed cuts on military ship production worldwide.

The Great Depression following these conferences also slowed or cancelled new military construction, resulting in a collapse of a good deal of England's shipbuilding industry.

Britain found itself in the position of being both unable to afford or to secure builders to maintain its massive navy, the world's largest at the time.

Finding itself in this situation, the United Kingdom actively promoted these conferences aimed at reducing world fleets, knowing full well that they could not compete with several of the other nations when it came to the production of new ships or have any hope of maintaining their current balance of sea power. Of specific concern to the British was the Versailles treaty's allowance of Germany to build more *Panzerschiffe*, what they referred to as the pocket battleships.

The Admiralty considered these new designs to be outstanding and if allowed to be mass produced, very likely to tip the balance of sea power worldwide. In an attempt to forestall further construction by Germany of this type of ship, the British Admiralty wanted to get into a position of reopening the treaty specifications with the aim of negating this design. They therefore made public announcements in both nineteen thirty-two and thirty-three to the effect that they were of the opinion that Germany was entitled to some relaxation in the naval restrictions as laid down by the treaty.

The World Disarmament Conference opened in Geneva, Switzerland in February of nineteen thirty-two. The British immediately pushed their agenda to reopen the terms of the treaty, ostensibly playing the part of conciliator between France, who wanted no part of such a suggestion and Germany who actively lobbied for this very opportunity.

It was obvious at the outset that all three parties to this tug-of-war were acting purely in their own self-interest.

Neither the French, who wanted no changes nor the Germans who were demanding 'Gleichberechtigung' (Equal Status), were interested in any form of compromise offered up by the English who were gung ho to open up discussions with the aim of stopping the Germans from building any additional pocket battleships.

Frustrated with the hopelessness of the negotiations, Germany walked out of the conference in September of nineteen thirty-two.

At this time the Weimar Republic of Germany was a democracy, but the writing was on the wall in regard to the massive following Hitler and the Nazis had built up and it appeared to all that if something didn't occur before the next

German Federal election, the Nazi Party was headed for a victory.

The British wanted no part of that scenario.

They were desperate to have the conference decide to give the Germans what they wanted.

This, they felt, would serve to provide a feather in the cap of the current German government with a hopeful view to strengthening its popularity with the nationalistic citizens of that country before the next election. In so doing the British hoped it would take the wind out of the sails of Adolf Hitler and his Nazi Party.

They were determined to get the Germans back to the table.

Over the next few months the British hammered away at France both at the table and in the backrooms, applying all the diplomatic pressure they could.

They were finally triumphant in December of nineteen thirty-two when all delegates participating voted on the British-sponsored resolution that provided *equality of rights and security for all nations.*

It was the best the Brits could do, allowing the Germans the right to re-arm beyond the treaty limitations. It brought the Germans back to the table but left the new limits of such a change up to further negotiations.

The question remained: would it be enough to satisfy the German people and serve to shore up the current Weimar Republic's government against the onslaught of the burgeoning Nazi's popularity?

CHAPTER TWENTY-NINE

-A Time for Reflection-

The two von-Stauffer daughters experienced little need or desire for conversation since leaving their aunt's mansion.

Despite Ursula's concern as to the speed at which Gabriella drove, she recognized that their time on the road would soon be over and for the sake of her own sanity, she'd forced herself to accept the fact that her sister's driving habits were not about to change. That done she'd determined to endure the status quo and not allow Gabriella's wild driving habits to spoil the remainder of the trip for her.

They were close to the Castle at Lake Constance now.

Located on the north side of the lake near the Swiss border a short distance from the city of Friedrichshafen, the massive castle was where they'd grown up, and every mile passing below the singing wheels of the speeding roadster brought with it an increase in the sights and smells that took them back to their childhood.

Each was lost in the encompassing individual enjoyment of the ride to the extent that it was enough to simply appreciate the significance of the familiar surroundings.

Despite the sinking sun, they still had some time left before dusk would settle over the valley floor.

They were about to start the climb upwards toward the castle situated above the big freshwater lake, third largest in Central Europe.

Lake Constance was almost thirteen hundred feet above sea level. Castle von Stauffer stood one hundred feet above the sparkling blue body of water, the estate's curtilage overlooking and running down to the shore and pristine waters of the lake.

By the time the powerful little roadster finished its climb and with a little luck they would arrive to find the last rays of the sun still shining over the large, nineteenth century structure.

* * * * *

- Fall Weiss -

Germany's invasion of Poland 'Fall Weiss' (Case White), began on September the first, nineteen thirty-nine.

The attack against the Polish State resulted in the start of the Second World War two days later, when Great Britain and France finally indicated that they intended to fulfill their obligations under their individual treaties with Poland and subsequently declared war on Germany.

The German campaign against Poland got off to a good start and progressed at a timely pace.

When, as earlier agreed, the Russians, without warning, attacked Poland from the east in support of the Nazis on September seventeenth, there was little doubt as to what the end result of the conflict would be.

By October sixth the invasion was over and the country of Poland, now divided between the German and Russian attackers, ceased to exist.

Hitler had always hoped and believed that France and the United Kingdom would not go to war over Poland.

He was of the opinion that even if the two countries didn't eventually choose to repudiate their treaties with the Polish Government as a result of his diplomatic pressure, (which he felt was probable); they would simply posture and vocalize their displeasure at Germany's aggression.

Neither France nor England wanted another war.

Hitler was confident that they would not be prepared to back up their words of condemnation by going so far as to actually involve themselves militarily.

On September third, nineteen thirty-nine when the two countries declared war on Germany after the Nazis had launched their invasion against Poland, Hitler was of the opinion that France and England would quickly decide to acquiesce once the Polish State had been successfully conquered.

He was convinced they would accept the *fait accompli* and quickly move to seek peace with Germany.

With that in mind he made an offer of peace to both the French and British on the sixth of October nineteen thirty-nine, shortly after the Poles had been vanquished.

* * * * *

- Reflection -

SS-Oberstgruppenfuhrer Count Karl von Stauffer, his two sons and their guest, family friend, Dr. Baron Heinrich von Kliest, were traveling by train from Berlin to Castle von Stauffer at Lake Constance in the Bavarian Alps.

Shortly after dinner the men moved out onto the covered observation platform of the Count's rear-most private railcar. They settled into the comfortable overstuffed chairs arranged in a semi-circle at the back of the platform with their cigars and brandy close at hand.

Night had settled over the rapidly moving train, but under bright moonlight, the passing terrain was still clearly visible.

The temperature was dropping slowly but the residual warmth remaining after a sunny day radiated upward from the land and had far from dissipated. It was both comfortable and exhilarating to be able to view the passing countryside on a warm evening under a full moon and cloudless skies.

The requirement of drawn blackout blinds on the rail cars, mandated by war, had prevented such a vista from the inside of the train and the observation platform was both less claustrophobic and reflective of the wartime conditions under which they were travelling.

On three occasions since leaving Berlin they had been shunted onto sidings to allow the passage of military goods trains moving north, two of which consisted of nothing behind their engines but strings of flatcars carrying tanks, large wheeled mounted guns and armoured cars. These trains had all been provided with specialized anti-aircraft cars and squads of soldiers who perched in groups along the length of each train.

The train pulling the Count's private cars had also been forced to halt several times at small country stations, all of which had been festooned with brightly coloured Nazi banners and nationalistic posters.

Here they had been boarded by teams of SS and Gestapo members who routinely checked papers and travel documents.

The Count's private cars were well known to those in charge of these inspections and for the most part their occupants had been spared such personal scrutiny, although a cursory check of the two units had occurred on one occasion thus far during the trip.

Any residue of stress clinging to those traveling in the cars after the hectic pace of Berlin was quickly lulled by the rhythmic clacking of the wheels and the sense of being warmly embraced by the rich, earthy smell of the lush growth which abounded as they followed the rails past the suburbs and small stations and began to move through the southern portion of the Rhine valley toward their destination at Lake Constance.

The occasional spotting of a country farmhouse framed in shadow on the far side of a producing field further served to draw the men's minds toward things other than the waging of war.

Conversation was general and muted and became less and less necessary as they found themselves relaxing and ready to take advantage of the opportunity to enjoy the excellent cigars and brandy which served very well to complement the simple peacefulness of the passing countryside and the likely expectation and enjoyment of a restful evening ahead.

* * * * *

- Case White -

In case his supposition with regard to the allies likelihood to attempt to secure a diplomatic peace with Germany proved correct, Hitler, now in high spirits and chaffing at the bit, was in no mood to simply wait patiently for the French and British responses to his peace offers.

On October ninth, just three days after he had extended his two olive branches, he circulated his 'Fuhrer-Anweisung Number Six' (Fuhrer-Directive Number Six) which was to be Germany's military answer to a negative response from those countries should they decline to make their way to the peace table with Germany.

Up to this point things had been definitely going Hitler's way.

On October tenth, nineteen thirty-nine the British refused the Fuhrer's offer of peace. On October twelfth the French followed suit.

This response to his offers of peace initiated Hitler's first examination of a prewar plan that had been drawn up for a possible invasion of the Lowland Countries and France.

This plan, code named 'Fall Gelb' (Case Yellow), was presented to Hitler on October the nineteenth, nineteen thirty-nine by 'Generalstabschef des Heeres' (Chief of Staff of the German Army) Franz Halder.

Hitler had hoped and striven for a peaceful, non-military solution to the current declaration of war, particularly on the part of the British, who he saw as potential allies against his planned, eventual attack on Russia.

He was however, also prepared to take on the French if necessary, and of course that meant first overrunning the Lowland Counties and eventually dealing with British forces, if any, who happened to be on the European Continent at the time of such conflict.

Hitler had a vision for Germany and part of that vision was the garnering of 'Lebensraum' (Living Space) to allow for the expansion of a new German Fatherland.

As he envisioned it, this conquest for territorial expansion would be primarily wrought from the countries of Eastern Europe.

The taking of the territory in Poland was just the beginning of that planned eventual territorial expansion, but it was far from the end. He had Russia in his sights.

He did not want to find himself having to fight a two-front war and he desperately wanted the United Kingdom as his ally when he took on the Russians.

In order to avoid a two-front war on European soil, he wanted the French, whom he considered decadent and in decline, under German occupation before he went to war with the Russians.

Hitler's *Fuhrer-Directive Number six* was based on a desire to begin to deal with Western Europe in a manner that would concurrently bring France under the German boot and convince the English that allying with a militarily-superior Germany against *Bolshevik* Russia was the only way to go.

The plan recognized that Germany was not militarily ready to sweep westward in one fell swoop. It reflected the understanding that it would take Germany several more years to reach the military strength needed to consider taking on a long-term commitment with a view to successfully conquering Western Europe prior to waging the planned war against the Russians.

As it stood, Germany was at war with France and Great Britain.

If Hitler could not drive an immediate wedge between the French and English through diplomacy, he had to discourage them from joining forces in Europe and attacking him until Germany had the military superiority required to safely commit to a long-term conflict to subjugate the countries to his west.

If he wished to achieve his eastern goal for *Lebensraum*, he could not stand idly by and allow the Allies to build up a large force on his western border.

With this in mind, *Fuhrer-Directive Number six* outlined limited objectives aimed at preventing the current situation in the west to worsen.

The directive therefore ordered that a conquest of the Low Countries and as much territory in Northern France as possible was to be executed as quickly as feasible.

This was deemed necessary to prevent the French from occupying the Low Countries and then using them for airbases that could threaten the vital German Ruhr industrial area, thereby bringing the war to German soil.

Hitler wanted this accomplished quickly. He envisioned such an invasion to commence within a few weeks.

His Generals, who were still licking their wounds after the campaign in Poland, were stunned by such a suggestion.

Their equipment was battered, their troops exhausted. The motorized units had to be repaired, ammunition stocks were low, and the men needed rest.

It would take time to recover and transport men and materials from the east to a new western front.

A frustrated and impatient Hitler acquiesced but warned his generals that the current situation was unacceptable and ready or not, the German army would have to take immediate action if the Allies showed any indication that they were about to go on the offensive and made any move to occupy the Lowland Countries.

And so began what the British called the 'Sitzkreig' (Sitting War), a play on the anglicized word 'Blitzkreig' (Lightning War).

The English had coined the word *Blitzkreig* to describe the newly introduced German form of attack through the use of a concentrated motorized force. This new method of attack was made up of a combined force which included artillery, tanks, infantry, engineers and air power.

These various units were trained to work in conjunction with each other and were applied in overwhelming strength. They had proved extremely effective in decimating enemy defensive lines and pushing far beyond, demonstrating little or no concern for the defence of their own flanks.

The application of this *Blitzkreig* attack against static lines of defence had repeatedly left the attacked forces in shattered disarray as the Germans swiftly moved the front ahead keeping it rolling in a continuous forward surge.

CHAPTER THIRTY

- Preparation -

The Countess, Erika von Stauffer, had slept poorly the night before, what with plans for the weekend guests and activities swirling around in her mind. Under the circumstances that was to be expected, but her lack of a solid sleep had in no way slowed her down.

While the majority of the junior staff was obviously somewhat frazzled around the edges, the Castle von Stauffer matriarch was anything but.

Calm, cool and collected, she moved quickly from room to room issuing an instruction here, rearranging there. Her demeanour was serene, but all working about her expected and received a scrutiny that was as keen and exhaustive as it was relatively unobtrusive.

Initially the guest list had been somewhat of a problem, what with the Count uncharacteristically providing several invitations, prior to consulting her. However, after an hour spent at her writing desk she had managed to balance it satisfactorily with a view to equity of the sexes, the younger and older generations and in relation to the station and social position of those who would be invited to stay over at the castle for the entire weekend.

After all, being invited to drop in for a swim or dinner was one thing, staying the entire weekend as a houseguest was quite another.

* * * * *

- Master Race -

After the Great War the Germans were a beaten and down-trodden people.

A large part of the Nazi party's propaganda machine was aimed at fostering a nationalistic frenzy within the population of the Fatherland.

Himmler, among others within the party, strove to create a culture of German *superiority of being* with a view to elevating the common German citizen up out of the doldrums and raise a sense of intense national pride in the German people.

All their efforts were directed in hopes of preparing them for acceptance of the inevitability of the war to come.

The Nazis believed that formation of the persona of the all-powerful *'Aryan male'* would go a long way toward accomplishing this goal.

With this aim in mind the 'Lebensborn' (Fountain of life) programme in Nazi Germany was formed on December twelfth, nineteen thirty-five. It was the brainchild of SS-Reichsfuhrer Heinrich Himmler.

The founding of *Lebensborn* was not seen as the be-all and end-all in the move to create the so called *Master Race*. Rather it was the taking of the first step toward that end by putting into action an original concept formed by the Reichsfuhrer himself. It was the first step of an elaborate approach to help achieve a given goal.

The specific objective of the *Lebensborn* programme was to expand Germany's dwindling birthrate through prevention of abortion which was common (as high as eight hundred thousand per year since the end of the Great War), and help to ensure that a future German Fatherland would be populated by, what the Nazis considered to be a true and pure *Aryan* race.

The concepts upon which this programme was based had been around for eons.

At the time of the Nazi rise to power in Germany, a form of selective breeding was being advocated on a worldwide basis due to the general beliefs of the international eugenics movement.

This faction which had come to the fore in the late eighteen hundreds had, since that time, been bolstered by recent developments in the new scientific disciplines of psychology and sociology.

In a nutshell, those advocating the application of *eugenics*, (the practice of improving the genetic makeup of any given population), throughout the world were promoting the theory that the use of selective breeding could and would improve the quality of the human race.

They were pushing the idea that by using science one could improve any given population simply by carefully selecting its breeding pairs on a wholesale basis with a view to removing bad genetic traits in favour of good ones.

They maintained that if any given living creature were to have its breeding stock chosen carefully the resulting progeny would be thoroughbreds, or in the case of humans, the perfect man and woman.

The proponents believed that with the new developments in scientific research into the area of eugenics they were now in a position to produce a list of solid physical standards that could form the basis and ensure success in any such program.

These included such things as hair colour, head size, facial features, eye colour and size and physical structure of the genitalia as sufficient markers to determine a given subject's value in the desired procreation cycle from a genetic point of view.

Such ideas were not new to the world in nineteen thirty-three when Hitler and his party came to power, but in addition to the recent developments in the field of eugenics, the Nazi researchers into this field had chosen to super-impose over the new science available, the Greek ancient notions on selective breeding as expressed by Plato.

It was Plato (429 - 347 BC), the Classical Greek philosopher and mathematician, who had set out five criteria for children who were to be 'Bred to become the Philosopher Kings and Guardians of the Greek Republic':

1. *The race of the Guardians is to be 'pure'.*

2. *The children will be put into the rearing pen and turned over to nurses. The mothers will nurse the babies, but will not know which one is theirs.*

3. *Children of inferior parents and defective children will be put out of sight in secrecy as is befitting.*

4. *Male and female guardian children will be educated as both philosophers and warriors.*

5. *Children will be taken on horseback to witness battles and have their taste of blood like puppies.*

In the Greek Republic of Plato's time it was policy that children should be produced for the good of the state, not for the sake of personal satisfaction. It was deemed necessary that this process should be undertaken for a specific period of time which was tied to the ages of the parents. Children conceived by women over forty or men over fifty were to be aborted or abandoned to die.

These same philosophies were shared by the Nazi hierarchy.

The Greek's aim was the selective breeding of their future leaders within a structured timeframe. The Nazis also shared this target.

By the time Adolf Hitler came to power this concept was well represented in all corners of the world. Unfortunately such an approach to selective breeding, if seriously entertained, had to become a two-sided coin.

The other side of that coin was simple and a forgone conclusion.

If you needed to breed those whom you considered best to improve a given race of people then it quite obviously followed that you did not want to breed the rejects.

The concept was that you chose a specific base, which constituted a superior genetic pool to utilize for your breeding stock and you would thereafter propagate from that pool only.

The question then became, where did you find the stock you intended to emulate and who were the *rejects* and how did you stop them from breeding?

For the Nazis the answers to those questions appeared obvious.

Their gene pool would come from the archetypal superior race, that being the decedents of the people of Atlantis, the *Aryan race.* By selectively breeding from this gene pool the Nazis would be able to create their 'Master Race'. To eliminate the bad genetic pool, the *rejects*, they would simply have to remove them from German territory.

While the interest in genetics and breeding a better human was spread throughout the world, it goes without saying that it was a minority point of view; after all it was a blatant suggestion that certain members of the human race play God.

The popular base for those advocating selective breeding was located primarily in the developed world, in the USA, England and Germany.

At the time of Hitler's rise these countries were considered Christian Democracies, whose citizens were not likely to support a government which had determined to play God.

When Hitler became Chancellor he quickly turned Germany into a dictatorship.

What citizens living under a strong autocratic dictatorship support or do not support, rarely matters and Nazi Germany was as strong and autocratic a dictatorship as the world had ever seen.

For the Germans the *Lebensborn* programme was the first step toward achieving the *Master Race.* It was intended that it would create the Aryan gene pool from which the Third Reich would breed all future Germans.

Himmler was committed to the concept and as his power grew within the hierarchy of the Nazi party so did the authority of his SS and their degree of influence over the average German citizen.

The SS-Reichsfuhrer's strongest supporter for the programme was Joseph Goebbels, the propaganda minister. The two of them worked hand in glove, one to structure and enforce and the other to sell the Nazi vision of Germany as the world's *Master Race* to all German citizens.

In a speech to the Wehrmacht in January of nineteen thirty-seven Himmler articulated the SS doctrine:

"We have an ideological enemy…Bolshevism lead by International Jewry and Free Masons. All states and peoples who are ruled or are under strong Jewish-Free Mason influence will eventually be hostile to Germany and create a danger for us. Bolshevism is an organization of sub-humans, it is the absolute foundation of Jewish rule, it is the exact opposite of all which the Aryan peoples love, cherish and value. It is a diabolic outlook because it appeals to the lowest and meanest instincts of humanity and turns those instincts into a religion. Its goal is the destruction of the white man.

We are more valuable than the others who may now and always outnumber us. We are more valuable because our blood enables us to be more inventive than others, to lead our people better than the others, because we have better soldiers, better statesmen, a higher culture, a better character."

The same year *Lebensborn* came into being, the *Nuremberg Laws* were proclaimed.

These laws were aimed at dealing with the *rejects* which the Nazis determined should include; Jews, Poles, the mentally retarded, the mentally ill, those politically and philosophically at odds with the Nazi Party's platform, Gypsies, those of mixed race, those whose religion was considered as nonconformist, all physically disabled and elderly who were non-productive, people of colour and sexual deviants.

CHAPTER THIRTY-ONE

- Daughters Arrive -

Erika was in the process of passing through the busy kitchen where dinner was being prepared, when the tall, slight form of the aged butler appeared as an apparition at her elbow to announce that 'The Ladies Ursula and Gabriella had just arrived by motor'.

Erika lifted an eyebrow at the use of the titles but held the gesture only briefly and then turned her wrist to glance at her watch.

"Late. They will be hard pressed to be properly dressed for dinner."

The butler managed a brief, knowing smile which threatened to shatter his deeply lined and dry, parchment-like features and then nodded sagely.

"Yes Countess, I suggested they go on up to their rooms straightaway and prepare. They did express the hope that you might find time to go up to see them, if time allows."

* * * * *

- Kriegsmarine -

With full knowledge that the German Navy's surface strength fell far short of hoping to stand up against the guns of the far superior, both in numbers and armament, British fleet, Germany's Admiral Raeder was looking forward to the completion of the extensive German naval building programme, scheduled for completion by nineteen forty-five under the 'Z Plan'.

He'd made it clear to Adolf Hitler that the opening of hostilities with the British before completion of that massive construction phase would, in short order, doom the German Navy to inevitable decimation.

Doenitz who had been promoted to Commodore and commander of U-boats on January twenty-eighth nineteen thirty-nine had a more realistic reading on Hitler's plans and determined early on that war was likely imminent and would certainly take place before the 'Z' programme could be completed.

Confident that the outbreak of war would come in less than a year and based on the stipulation in plan 'Z' that would thereby shift production away from the surface fleet and into U-boat construction, he determined that the only effective naval force the Germans would have to use against the British when war came, would be his U-boats.

He chose to adopt a positive twist on Raeder's fatalistic take on the situation. Still convinced that if he had enough of the new type 'VII' U-boats under his command he could defeat the British Navy by conducting a *commercial* U-boat war against their maritime fleets, he threw himself into training his crews in his new tactics. When war broke out on September first, nineteen thirty-nine he immediately began a diplomatically sheathed struggle both against Raeder, for a larger part of the naval budget for his submarines and Hitler, who was pushing him to attack the English Naval fleet rather than the targets Doenitz desired, those being the British tankers and freighters which carried the lifeblood of the island nation, and would pour out of Canada and the USA.

* * * * *

- The Right People –

Due to the distance of Castle von Stauffer from Berlin, where the majority of the weekend guests resided, the Countess Erika von Stauffer considered this Friday evening to be the calm before the storm.

No one was expected to arrive before morning, although those traveling by train and who had left Berlin in the early evening, as had the Count and his three companions, could be expected to reach the family estate between two and three in the morning after having slept on the trip.

Those travelling by car would begin to arrive in the afternoon or early evening of the next day.

Dinner on the night of September twenty-first, held at nine in the evening was to be a small affair, just the Countess and her two daughters. Due to the number in attendance it would be held in the smaller of the two formal dining areas, where a seating of up to ten could be easily managed in the white marble floored thirty by forty foot high-ceilinged room.

* * * * *

- Sitzkreig –

The *Fall Gelb* plan for the invasion of France and Low Countries presented to Hitler by General Halder was very similar in content to the *Schlieffen* plan which the Germans had intended to execute during the initial phase of the Great War in nineteen-fourteen.

Both plans envisioned a surprise attack through the middle of Belgium.

The *Schlieffen* plan had as it goal a decisive victory based on the rapid encirclement of the French Army. Halder's plan intended a similar frontal attack and was projected to cost half a million German casualties with a minimal goal of pushing the defending troops back to a line on the River Somme.

The plan determined that at the completion of action the entire German strength for nineteen-forty would be expended and that a full attack against the French would have to be left until nineteen forty-two when men and materials in sufficient numbers would again be available to allow a continuation of the battle.

Hitler was not impressed.

The Fuhrer's first reaction was to decide to attack immediately, prepared for battle or not, before the Allies could reinforce the battle lines.

His generals formed a combined front, carefully working to convince a very vocal and perturbed Hitler from taking such a step. They repeatedly pled serious concerns.

They needed better weather or the tanks would bog down, it took time to transport sufficient motorized equipment from the east to the west. Battle damage suffered during the taking of Poland would have to be repaired or equipment would surely break down before the battle could be won. The troops would have to rest and resupply before another large battle. The available store of ammunition and weapons was not sufficient for such a large campaign, it would have to be built up and that would take time.

Hitler, frustrated beyond belief, lashed out at them and although he was beginning to consider them a group of far-too-timorous warriors, he nevertheless saw some of the logic in their arguments.

Postponement after postponement of the launch of *Fall Gelb* followed.

The Fuhrer also strongly disliked Halder's plan for the invasion. He spent hours going over it, trying to find some way to make improvements. The generals, desperate to delay the attack in any way they could, played into this dissatisfaction accepting Hitler's suggestion of including secondary attacks further south.

The plan would have to be adjusted and that would take time.

On November the eleventh Hitler again postponed so this could be done.

A revised plan was presented by Halder on October twenty-ninth nineteen thirty-nine and to appease The Fuhrer, it included a plan for an attack on the Netherlands. Hitler was still unhappy with it, but he was unable to envision exactly what needed to be changed.

The Commander of *Army Group A*, General Gerd von Rundstedt, also found the plan lacking but unlike Hitler he knew exactly what the problem was. The plan was unworkable because it simply did not follow the principles of the 'Bewegungskrieg' (Manoeuvre Warfare). It presupposed that a breakthrough had to be made in order that an encirclement and decimation of the enemy forces resulted. In such a scenario the point chosen for the main thrust by the current plan was the wrong selection.

Von Rundstedt was supported in this evaluation of the plan by his Chief of Staff, General Erich von Manstein. The two men put their heads together and reached the decision that the only logical place where such a breakthrough could be successfully made was in the region of *Sedan.*

Under the plan *Sedan* was located in the sector of battle line that von Rundstedt's army group faced.

Von Rundstedt ordered von Manstein to prepare an alternative plan proposing such a change in the location for the delivery of the main thrust of the initial attack and pushed for a strengthening of *Army Group A* at the expense of *Group B* whose placement on the battle line was further to the north.

* * * * *

– Sober Second Thought –

Following a carefully planned agenda Count von Stauffer excused himself and retired to bed after a second brandy and cigar, leaving the Baron and his two sons to enjoy the privacy of the observation platform at the rear of the car.

He was certain that both his boys, but particularly Wilhelm, would be weighing his earlier words and would in all likelihood take advantage of such an opportunity to confide in the Baron any concerns or questions they might have.

Fully confident that Dr. Baron Heinrich von Kliest would be more than capable of responding to any apprehension raised by either, he gratefully slipped into his bed and switched off the light.

* * * * *

- Denmark and Norway -

When war broke out on September the first, nineteen thirty-nine Sweden, Norway, Denmark and Finland jointly announced their intention to remain neutral in the conflict.

The decision to do this was primarily based on Norwegian foreign policy.

The Norwegians had maintained their neutrality during the Great War and it had served them well. As a result of that experience, when the Nazis came to power in nineteen thirty-three, neutrality in a time of war had become firm foreign policy for the Norwegians.

In addition to previous experience this stance was based on three main factors: fiscal austerity on the part of the conservative government; pacifism on the part of the Norwegian Labour Party; and a doctrine of neutrality that had already proven that it could keep the country out of a major war.

Toward the end of the thirties pressure from several groups within Norway had begun to influence national thinking. The military and right-wing groups, as well as the King had begun to question pacifism as the proper path to follow.

Mainstream politicians began to take note when the populace picked up on this theme and as a result in the late thirties the government voted to increase the military to the extent that it was determined the cost would force them to assume a national debt.

It was of course a long-term proposition and it had been initiated far too late to make any real difference in Norway's military strength at the time Germany went to war on September first of nineteen thirty-nine.

Hence the Norwegians decided to plead neutrality in the conflict.

Hitler was of the opinion that such a state of neutrality on the part of the Scandinavian countries was in the best interest of Germany, because it would allow for trade between the Scandinavian states and Germany to continue without hindrance for the foreseeable future.

This trade was very important to Germany who imported six million tons of Swedish iron ore a year, fifty percent of which was moved by way of the Norwegian ice-free port of Narvik.

These ore ships travelled along the *Leads*, the passage among islands down along the Norwegian west coast which, if considered a neutral zone, also made it nearly impossible to form a successful naval blockade against Germany in time of war.

Germany responded to these nations by declaring to respect their territorial integrity but warned that it expected the Nordic States to maintain irreproachable neutrality, indicating that Germany would not accept infringement of their stated neutrality by any third power.

As the successful German conquest of Poland was wrapping up in September of nineteen thirty-nine Hitler and Admiral Raeder began to consider the German Navy's position in the event that France and Britain would not succumb to diplomacy and seek peace with Germany.

If that did not come to pass Hitler felt that France could be taken in a land war in a very short period of time.

Raeder agreed with that position but was of the opinion that a blockade of Britain might become necessary to bring the English to the peace treaty table and in that event he suggested that Germany would do well to seek out northern bases, other than those in the Black Sea, from which the Luftwaffe, Kriegsmarine and more importantly the U-boats could operate against Britain.

Raeder pointed out that this would have to be done in order to prevent the much more powerful English surface fleet from using their superior numbers to effectively close the current German northern route out of the Black Sea.

This route ran between the Shetland Islands and Norway and the English were quite capable of successfully blockading it.

Raeder's staff determined that the best bets for northern U-boat placement would be the Norwegian ports of Trondheim and Narvik.

He made the unlikely suggestion to Hitler that diplomatic pressure applied by Germany and her ally, Russia, might be sufficient to accomplish this without military intervention.

Germany's immediate need for the continuation of Norwegian neutrality made such an idea impractical.

Raeder approached the Chief of Staff of the Army with the proposition of taking the ports by military force.

He did this at a time when the army was licking its wounds after what it considered a narrow escape in Poland and was striving to deter Hitler from opening an immediate offensive in the west against the allies in France.

His response from the army, who wanted no part of an additional Scandinavian battle, was far from positive - difficult terrain, long supply lines, etc.

In their view, if such an operation were to be undertaken, preparation would demand that all war materials would immediately have to go into army manufacture.

That would mean a halt in the production of U-boats.

The main purpose of such an invasion was to gain operational control of the bases in question in order to use them as U-boat home ports. If, in order to accomplish that end, Germany would have to immediately stop U-boat production in favour of Army production in order to procure the equipment needed to successfully occupy the ports, there would be by that time due to the halt in production, insufficient U-boat numbers available to properly man them, therein negating the whole point of the operation.

Hitler, riding high, was again displeased by the position taken by the Army. This was not the first time he'd found the Army's leaders wanting when they had been presented with an invasion plan. As a result he decided that the Army High Command should be all but excluded from any future planning with regard to a possible operation in Norway.

The Norwegian Government, who had absolutely no desire to go to war with the British, realized that if Hitler decided to turn his forces west in order to use military force to bring France and England to the treaty table, Norway would be at immediate risk.

This was due to its geographic location. Should Hitler make such a decision the Norwegians were convinced that they would find themselves in the position of not only having to protect their neutrality but of likely having to fight to maintain the freedom and independence of their country.

On October ninth, nineteen thirty-nine Hitler reaffirmed to his military staff his earlier stated intention of launching an offensive in the west.

In Directive Number Six, issued on that day, he ordered the army to prepare an offensive to attack the northern flank of the Western Front with the intention of destroying a large part of the French and Allied force and taking as much territory as possible in Belgium, the Netherlands and northern France.

They were ordered to secure the Belgian coast and northern France to garner favourable bases for a future air and sea war against Great Britain, should that become necessary.

On October tenth, thirty-nine Admiral Raeder told The Fuhrer that the taking of the coast of Belgium would offer no advantage to the German U-boat fleet and once again pushed his ideas for the taking of bases on the Norwegian coast.

Hitler felt that the Luftwaffe operating on its own could do the job of bringing the British to their knees at the peace table; they could do this quickly and without the need for U-boat intervention. But he indicated to Raeder that he would give the matter of procurement of Norwegian basis for the U-boats his careful consideration.

The Fuhrer, by now completely preoccupied with planning for the impending invasion of France and the Low Countries, code named 'Fall Gelb' (Case Yellow), did not however find any time to give Norway another thought.

Raeder was also busy planning for the invasion on the western front and he didn't bring the matter of Norway up again until November the twenty-fifth, nineteen thirty-nine.

On that date he informed his staff that he was concerned that when the Germans attacked the Netherlands the British would immediately land a force on the Norwegian coast with the intent of securing the ports. On the twenty-seventh of November he followed that up with the observation that anticipated attacks on the British Isles brought about by the invasion would mean the German Navy would inevitably be called upon to blockade the British ports.

This, he postulated, would necessitate the intercept of ships sailing from Norway, which would be extremely difficult due to the fact that the majority of such incursions would have to take place within Norwegian territorial waters.

He was concerned enough about this requirement that he brought the matter up with Hitler during a military Conference held on December the eighth.

Between September of thirty-nine and April of nineteen-forty several incidents had taken place in Norwegian waters that seriously strained the Norwegian's ability to credibly sustain their claim to neutrality.

Despite this fact the Norwegians had somehow managed to negotiate firm trade treaties with both the Germans and the British.

All well and good, however by this time it was becoming very plain to all three parties involved that both Germany and Great Britain had a building, strategic military interest in finding some way of denying access to Norway to their enemy.

On October ninth of nineteenth thirty-nine Hitler's mind was not on Norway; it was on other things. He was casting his eyes to the west.

The British were putting increasing pressure on the Norwegian government to divert more and more of their maritime merchant fleet to the transport of English goods in order to free up their own merchant navy for other tasks. They were also pushing for the Norwegians to join a trade blockade against Germany.

Norway was rapidly becoming a bone of contention in the three-way struggle, with Germany on one end of the bone and the United Kingdom on the other.

Of the two, Germany was keeping the lowest profile, seemingly still in strong support of Norwegian neutrality.

CHAPTER THIRTY-TWO

- Irons in the Fire -

The Countess, Erika von Stauffer, confident in her arrangements for the weekend despite the short notice she had been given and her husband's uncharacteristic involvement in the specifics of part of the guest list had moved the remaining minor concerns about the next two days to the back of her mind.

She had other irons in the fire to deal with over the evening, all of them relating to taking firm steps to marry off her daughters to worthy partners before they lost their bloom.

She sat in the small lounge adjoining the dining room, cocktail in hand, and let out a soft sigh as she glanced at her watch.

Three minutes after nine, late as usual. What was wrong with young people these days?

* * * * *

- The Manstein Plan -

Von Manstein closeted himself in Koblenz, Germany and began to work on improving the invasion plan for France. By coincidence Generalleutnant Heinz Guderian, Commander of XIX Army Corps, an elite Nazi armoured formation, was also in Koblenz.

Guderian was a pioneer in the development of stratagem and deployment methods of armoured warfare and the strongest proponent of the use of tanks and mechanization in the Wehrmacht.

When the two men happened to accidentally cross paths,

von Manstein, who was struggling with the plan, took the opportunity to invite Guderian to have an informal look at what was proposed and offer any advice he might have to improve the plan.

As it stood the initial thrust remained a northerly attack striking out from Sedan toward the rear of the bulk of the allied troops stationed in Belgium.

Guderian quickly grasped the situation presented with a new and informed set of eyes (Guderian had spent time in the area during the Great War) and in short order made a suggestion for a change in the battle plan that von Manstein would never have considered if left to his own devices.

Guderian supported the general plan but not the initial thrust.

The mechanized armour expert proposed that the forces poised for attack from Sedan should be made up of not only his XIX Army Corps but should also contain the vast majority of the other armoured forces that had been made available for the western theatre of war. In addition he indicated that in his view this massive concentration of armour should strike out to the west, not the north, with the goal of cutting a rapid, profound and autonomous penetration deep across enemy territory with the goal of reaching the English channel.

Von Manstein was shocked at the very suggestion of the armour acting on its own in a wild sweep across allied territory all the way to the channel without infantry support.

Guderian then suggested that such a move could very well serve to cause a strategic collapse of the enemy in the rear of their line, as it easily and methodically destroyed anything in its path.

It would cut their supply and communication lines and such a brazen move would most certainly take the enemy by complete surprise.

It would in his view also completely avoid the carnage of a full frontal attack on the enemy, thereby bringing the projected German casualty count down immeasurably.

The tactics proposed by Guderian were not new. He had been a supporter of such independent and swift applications of armour for years.

The German General Staff however, had been at best luke-warm to such use of armour, leaning more toward using the strong mechanized forces parcelled out as parts of large troop formations, primarily for support and to be kept in reserve to rapidly respond to any weak areas in the line of battle.

Germany's senior generals were of the old school and still planning by using tactics applicable to the Great War. What Guderian was suggesting was a very modern and unusual approach to mechanized warfare.

Von Manstein, who had been at a loss as to changes, was won over by Guderian's arguments and between October thirty-first, nineteen thirty-nine and January of nineteen-forty he forwarded seven memoranda to the *OKH* (Army High Command), all of which were based on Guderian's concept of battle.

Although von Manstein had kept Guderian's name out of the documents because he knew the mere mention of it would raise a red flag with his superiors, each proposal was rejected in turn and not a single one of his documents was forwarded to Adolf Hitler.

On January twenty-seventh, nineteen-forty the *OKH,* having had enough of his plans, transferred von Manstein from his position as Chief of Staff for Army Group A to the command of an Army Corps in Prussia.

He was to take up his new command in Stettin on February ninth, nineteen-forty.

It was an obvious step taken by Halder to sideline von Manstein and remove him from planning but it backfired when von Manstein's staff, several of whom were completely incensed by what had been done to their boss, brought the matter to Hitler's attention on February second.

As fate would have it, Hitler had been busy trying to improve the plan on his own and at one point, having no knowledge whatsoever of von Manstein's work, he had suggested that perhaps the main thrust of the battle should come from the area of Sedan. At that time he had been persuaded that such a move would be far too risky and he allowed the Generals to talk him out of it.

Now he had the latest von Manstein revised plan in his hands and he liked it.

In fact, he liked it very much. Why it even suggested that the first major thrust of the attack should be made from the area of Sedan.

On February seventeenth Hitler held a conference. Those summoned to attend were: Generals von Manstein, Schmundt (Army Chief of Personnel) and Jodl (Chief of Operations for the *OKW*).

Hitler was uncharacteristically laid-back throughout the meeting which centered on his copy of the latest von Manstein plan. He listened quietly to all opinions and discussion, and when it had all played out he sat back and calmly told all present that he approved of the plan as it stood. There would be no more discussion or revision made.

While Hitler had recognized the value of a breakthrough at Sedan from a simple tactical sense, he cherished its flamboyance and risk. Von Manstein had sold it well, leaving the Fuhrer with the impression that it was a risk but if the armoured Units were successful in reaching the English Channel they would have completely encircled the allied forces who would then be cut off in Belgium and locked into a pocket from which there was no easy escape.

The majority of Hitler's Generals wanted no part of the plan. They harangued Halder en masse demanding that he refuse to carry it out.

Halder was tired of arguing with Hitler. He knew Hitler would not entertain any further delays. This was the plan that he wanted and this was the plan that would be followed.

Halder saw it as one argument too many and knew full well that it was one he could not win.

He stood his ground and put his views plainly out for anyone who continued to complain. Germany's situation was tenuous as best. While this plan had only a slim chance of reaching a decisive victory for the Fatherland, taking no action in the long term would bring certain defeat.

There was no turning back. It was to be *Blitzkreig*.

Launched on May tenth, nineteen-forty it was over by June twenty-second of that year. It took Germany approximately six weeks to defeat Belgium, Holland Luxembourg and the French, whose army at the time was considered by some, to be the best in the world.

On the day the invasion started Winston Churchill replaced Chamberlain (Peace in our Time) as Prime Minister of Great Britain.

CHAPTER THIRTY-THREE

- Sisters -

Ursula tapped lightly on her sister's bedroom door, opened it and stepped inside. Crossing the small entry hall and then moving into the massive bedroom proper she turned to enter the doorway on her right.

She found Gabriella in the spacious room next to her en-suite bathroom, seated in front of her make up mirror.

Gabriella, in the process of putting on her lipstick, saw her sister reflected in the huge mirror and raised her free hand in acknowledgement before returning to the task at hand.

Ursula crossed the room and dropped down onto the beautiful brocade fainting-couch which rested against the far wall just below the large top floor window which was opened out to reveal the shimmering pools and extensive array of carefully groomed garden areas terracing downward toward the valley and sparkling lake below.

She absently arranged her skirt before she spoke.

"All ready to beard the lioness in her den dear sister?"

Gabriela pursed her lips and formed them into an 'O' and then clamped them down on a tissue to blot before she responded, raising the pitch of her voice and lifting her head upward to stretch her neck in a practiced mimic of their mother.

"I know these are new times and many view the old practices as out of date, but I have a duty to…etc…etc…etc"

Despite herself Ursula had to smile.

"Yes, I wonder who she'll have lined up for us this time?"

Gabriella put her lipstick back into its holder and placed it on her dressing table among the other beauty supplies spread across its surface.

"I have no idea, but you may rest assured that they will all have either old money or a prominent position within the Party and probably both."

Ursula nodded and lifted her wrist to tap the face of her watch.

"And we are already late for diner. Definitely not a good start to the weekend from Mother's point of view I'm sure."

* * * * *

- War at Sea-

As was the case in Germany prior to and after Hitler and the Nazis came to power, the leaders of the navies of the world had, before, throughout and after the Great War, suffered from a continuing in-house debate at the highest levels.

This ongoing debate involved two factions.

The first of these factions, consisting primarily of older officers of very high rank, was of the unshakable belief that during a period of war, naval vessels should, at all times, be configured in a group and centered on a battleship.

This combined grouping, which in the case of the German navy, was referred to as 'Entscheidunggschlacht', would then be used for battle on the high seas as a *balanced fleet* in horrific combat of decisive annihilation, where the best man would win by destroying the enemy's fleet.

The faction opposing this position, consisting primarily of younger officers of medium to high rank believed their opponent's position was archaic and wasteful, both from a practical and military point of view.

To these officers, the concept of a single massive battle between foes was no way to win a war.

They had the foresight to recognize that a new approach was needed to win a war in the modern world, which in the case of the

Germans would likely be fought against Britain, at the time the world's largest sea power.

That new approach would require the construction of a naval force designed to fight a war of 'guerre de course' (War of Chase).

To accomplish this they advocated building cruisers and submarines, which would then, operating independently, seek out and annihilate the enemy's merchant fleets, therein cutting off the supply line from North America that the British Isles could not live without.

In compliance with the Versailles Treaty restrictions the first major warship to be built by the Germans after the war was the cruiser Emden.

This was followed by the construction of three additional light cruisers, Konigsberg, Karlsruhe and Koln and two additional ships, modified versions of that 'K' class of cruiser, the Leipzig and the Nurnberg.

While the treaty did forbid the Germans naval aircraft and submarines, it did not prohibit the Germans from researching and designing submarines, nor did it ban the training of submarine crews. Both of these activities continued after the Great War, submariners being trained in both Spain and Russia.

* * * * *

– Discussion –

Wilhelm was the first to break the silence that had prevailed on the covered observation platform.

"Heinrich, why is father advocating this plan? The Fuhrer has clearly demonstrated his capacity to deal with both Germany's foreign affairs and military conquests successfully. We not only swore an oath to support him but he has proven himself repeatedly."

The Baron, who had been slowly warming his brandy glass with his hands, raised it to his mouth and took a swallow before answering

"I'm not qualified to comment on what led to the current situation from a military point of view, other than to say that our experience in the 'Great War' (World War One) clearly demonstrated to us that a long-running two-front war for Germany is unwinnable."

He paused before continuing.

"I would like to say however, that your question seems to be suggesting that what I, your father and the many others who support a fall-back plan for the future are proposing is in some way disloyal to The Fuhrer. Nothing could be further from the truth."

Wilhelm raised an eyebrow and opened his mouth to speak but the Baron cut him off with a raised hand.

"I, for one, am currently doing and will continue to do everything I can to support the Government and our leader in the days to come. So will all the others who are supporting the plan your father outlined.

Hitler is a very capable man and he has to date, as you have so eloquently expressed - proven his worth. He may very well lead Germany successfully to achievement of the utopian world position he foresees and predicts.

None of the men involved in this fall-back plan will do anything to jeopardize what The Fuhrer envisions; quite the contrary. But we are all intelligent men who have taken the time to use sober second thought and we have all learned, from years of experience, of the need to plan for all eventualities.

To us it would be foolish not to step back and take a careful look at the road ahead, and that, quite simply, is exactly what we are doing."

Eric looked from the Baron to his brother and back.

"Is the Fuhrer aware of this back-up plan? Is he in support of it?"

Dr. von Kliest downed the remains of his glass and took a drag from his cigar before he looked up to respond.

"Is it being done at his explicit direction? The answer to that is not a simple yes or no."

Wilhelm frowned thoughtfully.

"Could you be a little more specific?"

The Baron shifted slightly in his well-upholstered chair.

"The weekend retreat to the castle has been arranged for just that purpose.

The people you meet there will honestly and directly answer any of your questions much better than I can. I can tell you that I am in full agreement with the aims of the group and support its proposed direction without qualification, and I will say one more thing before we retire. Something I would like you to consider carefully."

He rose and stepped to the railing, resting his hands on it as he leaned out to watch the peaceful countryside pass under the bright light of the moon.

"When The Fuhrer asked your father to retake his commission, he gave him a reason for doing so. I am certainly not as eloquent as he, but I will attempt to paraphrase what he told your father."

The Baron took a few seconds to formulate the words in his mind and the two brothers sat on the edge of their chairs watching him, their breathing shallow with anticipation.

"The Fuhrer told your father that he, Adolf Hitler, was destined by God to lead Germany into a new era, but that he was only one man.

The challenge he had taken up was complex beyond belief and he would of necessity have to rely on others to properly carry out the specifics of his vision.

He stated that men were human and men made mistakes and that each would all die in his time.

He wanted your father back in uniform so that he could have a man in place who he could trust to take on the responsibility for overseeing and directing the continuing research and development that the New Reich required to ensure her continued leadership in those fields and therein the Fatherland's future success in the world.

He expressed his trust in your father and told him that he's unequivocally confident that the Count has neither need nor desire in either a financial of political sense, nor is he likely to empire-build or seek favour for the sake of reward.

The Fuhrer has given your father the responsibility and authority to act unilaterally in following the path to success for the Fatherland as he, The Fuhrer, envisions it and to bring to fruition all innovation that will be absolute necessary to complete this plan.

He is to accomplish this by organizing and shepherding all the scientific and engineering research and development in these fields; to guarantee, despite all the complications that war will bring, that Germany leads the world in the fields in his lifetime.

He has been instructed to use the best Aryan German minds to facilitate the creation of the scientific and military advances Germany must achieve in order to provide the foundation for a Fatherland that is destined to rule the world.

The Count is to have unlimited financing and a free hand to accomplish his task.

He will report to no one but Hitler and he is to advise the Fuhrer of nothing but successes in all fields. Failures are of no interest; neither is grandstanding.

He expects to hear from your father only when someone in authority is thwarting his progress in some way or when he has dramatically positive results in a specific field.

At the time of their meeting, the Fuhrer made it blatantly clear that he will be far too busy with other tasks on a day to day basis to be involved directly in the long-term mechanics of what needs to be done in the fields of science and technology to achieve his aims."

The Baron paused again. This time, he did it solely for emphasis.

"I would say that your father is, without question acting

under the direct orders of The Fuhrer and with his full and unqualified support "

The Baron released the railing and straightened to his full height then he clicked his heels sharply and began to walk toward the doorway at the end of the observation platform.

"And on that note, I'm going to call it a night and I would suggest you two do the same. You have a very enlightening weekend ahead of you and you will need all the sleep you can get."

CHAPTER THIRTY-FOUR

- Kriegsmarine -

In the case of the German Navy after the Nazis had come to power, two men were primarily destined to determine what the makeup of the German Navy would be at the outbreak of the Second World War on September first, nineteen thirty-nine.

The first was Erich Johann Albert Raeder, an old-liner and a staunch believer in 'Entscheidunggschlacht'.

Born in eighteen seventy-six in Wandsbek, Prussia, he joined the then Imperial Navy in eighteen ninety-five as a 'Seekadett' (Sea Cadet).

Being capable and both politically and socially attuned, he made his rise through the ranks rapidly.

He was promoted 'Fahnrich zur See' (Midshipman Cadet) in eighteen ninety-seven, 'Leutnant zur See' two years later, 'Oberleutnant zur See' (First Lieutenant) by nineteen hundred, 'Kapitanleutnant' (Lieutenant) in nineteen-five and 'Korvettenkapitan' (Lieutenant Commander) in nineteen eleven.

By nineteen twelve he had become Chief of Staff to Admiral Franz von Hipper.

Socially astute and a political creature, Raeder managed to wangle the captaincy of the *Hohenzollern* a few years prior to the start of the Great War.

The *Hohenzollern* was the personal yacht of the last German monarch, Kaiser Wilhelm II.

Raeder formed a friendship with von Hipper and received commendations from the Kaiser, with the intention that both relationships could help to fast track his future naval career.

He served with von Hipper and held several combat commands during the Great War and in nineteen-seventeen was promoted to the rank of 'Fregattenkapitan' (Commander).

He remained in the navy after Germany was defeated and rose to 'Kapitan zur See' (Captain), in nineteen-nineteen.

After the war, in nineteen twenty, Raeder, who despised the current government of the Weimar Republic, which he considered to be weak, ineffectual and anti-military publicly backed the attempted 'Kapp Putsch' lead by Wolfgang Kapp.

The government was able to put down the attempted coup and as a result of his support for it, Raeder found himself distinctly out of favour and the previous rapid rate of promotion in his naval career, suddenly appeared in tatters.

He was summarily transferred out of active service and sidelined into Naval Archives, where he spent two years.

An intelligent and able officer, Raeder determined to make the best of his situation and promptly involved himself in several projects.

He authored studies regarding Naval Tactics and worked on the writing of the History of the German Navy in the Great War.

As a result of his efforts while at the archives Raeder was awarded an honorary degree of Doctor of Philosophy by the University of Kiel.

These accomplishments and his high placed contacts were sufficient to lift the veil that had been left hanging over him due to his involvement in the failed putsch two years previously and he was promoted to the rank of 'Konteradmiral' (Rear Admiral) in nineteen twenty-two.

Shifted back into the mainstream of the service, Raeder once again excelled in his commands and in nineteen twenty-five reached the rank of 'Vizeadmiral' (Vice Admiral).

In nineteen twenty-eight he was promoted to full Admiral and assumed the position of 'Oberbefehlshaber der Reichsmarine' (Commander-in -Chief of the Reichsmarine), ironically taking full command of the Weimar Republic's Navy, at the pleasure of a government which he, now admittedly, only in private, still considered impotent and weak.

* * * * *

- U-boats –

The second pivotal individual responsible for the state of Germany's navy at the out-break of the Second World War was Karl Doenitz.

He was born in Berlin on September sixteenth eighteen ninety-one and was destined to become the architect of the Nazi's upcoming U-boat war.

In nineteen-ten at the age of nineteen he enlisted as a 'Seekadett' in 'Kaiserliche Marine' (Imperial German Navy). A year later he was promoted to 'Fahnrich zur See'.

By September of nineteen-thirteen he'd received his commission as 'Leutnant zur See' (Acting Sub-Lieutenant) and at the beginning of the Great War he was posted to the light cruiser *Breslau*.

In nineteen-fourteen the *Breslau* was one of two ships sold by the Imperial navy to the Ottoman navy.

At that time the Breslau was renamed Midilli and her home port became Constantinople where her task was to engage Russian naval forces operating in the Black Sea.

In March of nineteen-sixteen Karl was promoted to 'Oberleutnant zur See'.

His request for transfer to U-boats was accepted in October of that year and he served on U-39 until his transfer to UC-25 as commander in February of nineteen-eighteen. In September of nineteen-eighteen he was transferred again and assumed command of UB-68.

On October fourth of that year his boat was sunk in the Mediterranean Sea and he became a prisoner of war.

While the war ended in nineteen-eighteen, Doenitz was not released until July of nineteen-nineteen and finally made his way back to Germany in nineteen-twenty.

When he arrived, he picked up his naval career in what had been renamed the 'Reichswehr' (Weimar Republic Armed Forces), a much-restricted force, governed in both equipment and personal by the strict guidelines stipulated by the Treaty of Versailles.

In nineteen twenty-one Doenitz was promoted to 'Kapitanleutnant' in what had now become the 'Vorlaufige Reichsmarine' (German Navy). He was assigned to torpedo boats.

He was next promoted in nineteen twenty-eight to the rank of 'Korvettenkapitan'.

In nineteen thirty-three, six months after Hitler and his Nazi Party came to power in Germany Karl Doenitz received his next promotion reaching the rank of 'Fregattenkapitan'.

In nineteen thirty-four, now a seasoned, competent and respected German seaman, he took command of the naval officer training ship, the cruiser Emden.

He excelled in his new command and by September of nineteen thirty-five, the year in which the name of the German navy changed from Reichsmarine to Kriegsmarine, he was promoted yet again to the rank of 'Kapitan zur See'.

He immediately requested and was granted a transfer to his much beloved U-boats, taking up the post of Commanding Officer of the 1st U-boat Flotilla Weddigen consisting of U-7, U-8 and U-9.

At this time in history the major navies throughout the world were of the opinion that submarines should sail with and be an integral part of integrated surface fleets.

Based on his earlier experience in undersea boats during the Great War Doenitz bucked that general view and began to express the opinion that Germany's U-boats, to be effective, should operate as an independent force.

This was not a view held by the majority of senior German naval officers including Doenitz's immediate superior Admiral Erich Raeder.

While he would not hesitate to voice his opinion if asked, Doenitz recognized that his idea was a minority view and that, even at his current rank, he was not in a position to determine the future of U-boat application autocratically.

He did however strive at every opportunity to present to and make every attempt to convert his peers and superior to his concepts, but tended to tread lightly when the subject was raised.

As Commander of his own Flotilla of U-boats, Doenitz could begin to train and hone his concept of independent U-boat activity.

A disciplined military man, he did this unobtrusively while carrying out his orders to the letter.

By nineteen thirty-seven Doenitz had perfected his ideas for his new type of U-boat application and was eager to see them put into action.

The Treaty of Versailles had been trashed by Hitler and the German military machine, up to that point strangled by the treaty, was being built up in a frenzy of activity.

It was not an easy struggle. All branches of the military were vying for more men, materials and new construction funds.

The mood around him was changing. With war with Britain on the horizon, more attention was being paid to his idea that an unrestricted use of U-boats working independently of surface ships with a mandate to target only merchant ships could easily sever the British lifeline from the United States and Canada, with little or no risk to the boats themselves.

He began to circulate papers pointing out that the destruction of England's oil tanker fleet alone would quickly starve the superior British surface fleet of fuel, leaving it dead in the water; that there was no need to invade the English if they could simply deprive the island of her direly needed seaborne imports of food and materials, in which case the British would have no alternative but to seek a treaty with Germany.

He suggested that if he were provided with a fleet of three hundred of the new type VII U-boats, he could knock Britain out of any future war in a matter of a few months, pressing his point home by going so far as to suggest that the new German navy should consist of U-boats only and that no further funds or materials should go into the construction of surface ships.

There was opposition to his suggestions, but he sensed his ideas for new and different type of U-boat application were beginning to resonate in the marbled corridors of the German hierarchy.

New U-boats were by now being openly constructed, if not yet in the numbers Doenitz would have liked. He had to battle not only the Luftwaffe under the leadership of the powerful Goering, plus the leaders of the surface navy and those of the army and burgeoning SS for funding priorities for his beloved U-boats, but invariably, his own superior, Erich Raeder.

For him it was a frustrating, uphill battle and by the beginning of the war on September first, nineteen thirty-nine the German U-boat fleet consisted of only fifty-seven U-boats and only twenty-two of those were of the new ocean going, Type VII variety.

CHAPTER THIRTY-FIVE

- Daughters –

With just the three of them sitting, a single footman was all that was required to serve dinner.

The Countess sat at the head of the table with her daughters seated to her left and right at mid-table.

Ursula and her younger sister knew from experience that their mother would not allow the conversation to descend to a personal level while a member of the household staff was present. This saving grace would ensure that they could eat the several courses in relative peace, safe from the interjection by the Countess of the expected topic of their current unmarried states, at least that is, until the table had been cleared.

The meal would provide a breathing space, however short, something for which they were both extremely thankful.

* * * * *

- Geneva-

When Hitler became Germany's Chancellor in January of nineteen thirty-three and was briefed on Germany's current situation in the negotiations at the World Disarmament Conference in Geneva he found himself in a very favourable situation.

At that point in time his team stratagem in view of British support was to repeatedly put forward naive offers of restricted armament, knowing that the French would reject these out of hand.

The aim of this subterfuge was give the appearance of

sincere concern as to fairness, the Germans pushing for either the removal of restrictions placed upon them in the Treaty of Versailles, or the application of similar restrictions upon the armed forces of the other European members present.

The French, aware of the huge resurgence of nationalism in Germany under the Nazis, took the bait, hook line and sinker. They repeatedly dismissed Germany's equality in armaments arguments, doing so with haughty dismissals of what, on the surface, appeared to many of the delegates as a reasonably request for fair play.

Time and time again the British stepped up to the plate in an attempt to form a compromise. The Germans were ever prepared to entertain these British attempts to bridge the impasses while the French rejected each in turn.

The Germans, clandestinely suggesting that it was obvious that France had no intention of giving serious consideration to achieving the goals of the conference with a view to fairness for all nations, walked out of the conference a second time in October of nineteen thirty-three.

The British were sympathetic to the German walkout.

Already leaning toward the German point of view with regard to the Treaty of Versailles needing adjustment and now convinced that France, at the conference, had been unreasonably obdurate and therein totally responsible for the German walkout, the British reached a decision that was to later play very handily into German hands.

A discussion held at the highest levels in London determined that any opportunity for future arms limitation talks the British had with the Germans would not be structured in a manner that could be torpedoed unilaterally by the French.

* * * * *

– Sons –

Wilhelm and Eric, nursing a final brandy remained on the observation platform at the rear of the rail car. It was the younger of the two, Wilhelm, who spoke first once the Baron had left them.

"Are you alright with this?"

Eric, who had been gazing off into the middle distance pursed his lips and sucked in a deep breath before answering.

"Yes, I think so. I mean it sounds like a sensible course to take and obviously Father and Heinrich are all right with it. I must admit that I'm curious to find out who else will be involved. I think I can approach it with an open mind and that's all we are being asked to do for now from what I understand - how about you?"

Wilhelm considered for a second, and then cleared his throat.

"It seems to me that Father is just being Father. He's been given a job to do and a free hand to do it. Like always, Dad will dig his heels in and give it his best shot. He's loyal, honest and God knows a good organizer and motivator of men. If the Fuhrer had confidence enough in him to give him the job then I'm of the opinion that it is the duty of any right thinking German to support and assist him in his task. Surely his sons would be expected to jump on the bandwagon."

Eric's serious face softened and he smiled at the description of his father and then nodded.

"Yes, I may be biased but I would have to say that he's well qualified for the job and I'll also admit that I'm bursting with pride at the knowledge that The Fuhrer himself has picked him for such a prestigious position in the New Germany. I'm looking forward to finding out exactly what plan 'B' entails. This could prove to be a very interesting weekend."

* * * * *

- Friedrichshafen - Lake Konstanz –

Friedrichshafen, named for King Frederick I of Wurttemberg, was an ancient city that had been founded on the site of the former city of Buchhorn by the king, specifically as a free port to be used as the shipping and receiving point for his kingdom's trade with the Swiss.

Construction had begun in eighteen-eleven a good seventy years before the first stone was laid for the foundation of its neighbour, Castle von Stauffer.

The new city was planned on a large scale, such that the little village of Hofen was also quickly enveloped in its design. A large Benedictine monastery which had been originally founded in ten-eighty-five was located on the north shore of 'Lake Konstanz' (Lake Constance) in Hofen.

The King who, after having visited the area, fell in love with it, promptly decreed that the Monastery's massive structure be vacated and completely renovated with the intention of using it as his summer Royal Residence.

All goods passing from the King's Royal Wurttemberg state to and from Switzerland moved through the port of Friedrichshafen and across Lake Constance. The port was connected by rail to Ravensburg in eighteen forty-seven and Heilbronn three years later. A ferry running to Romanshorn, Switzerland was initiated in eighteen-sixty-nine, the same year the construction of Castle von Stauffer commenced, at the direction of an ancestor of the current Count von Stauffer.

The Royal state of Wurttemberg, of which Friedrichshafen was a part, had been initially loyal to the French during the time of the Napoleonic wars but found itself incorporated into Germany after the Franco-Prussian War of eighteen-seventy and seventy-one as part of the spoils of war resulting from the Prussian victory.

Friedrichshafen, at the time primarily known for its strong agriculture base, began to industrialize in the late eighteen and early nineteen hundreds. Its change was primarily due to one man.

Born in Konstanz, Grand Duchy of Baden on July eighth,

eighteen thirty-eight, Count Ferdinand Adolf Heinrich August Graf von Zeppelin, who rose to become a German General, was the descendent of a noble family that dated back to the fifteenth century.

He spent his childhood at his wealthy family's estate near Constance and lived there until his death.

As a young man he attended the polytechnic at Stuttgart and being from a military family went from there to the military school at Ludwigsburg. By eighteen fifty-eight he was a lieutenant in the Württemberg army at which time he requested and was granted leave to study science, engineering and chemistry at Tubingen.

Prussia's mobilization for the Austro-Sardinian war in eighteen-fifty-eight resulted in his being called up in eighteen-fifty-nine and he joined the 'Ingenieurkorps' (Prussian Engineering corps).

Ferdinand served as a volunteer in the American Union Army during the American civil war. While there he made a stopover at the balloon camp where the German aeronaut John Steiner was stationed and it was here in Saint Paul, Minnesota that he took his first balloon ride.

At the end of the American Civil War he returned to Wurttemberg to take up a post as general staff officer and in this position took part in the Austro-Prussian War of eighteen-sixty-six where he served with valour and distinguished himself.

Hooked on the wonder of lighter-than-air flight he returned to America in eighteen-sixty-nine to learn all he could from the ballooning expert Professor Thaddeus Lowe.

He then returned to take up active service in the Franco-Prussian war of eighteen-seventy. After that war he became completely preoccupied with the idea of guidable balloons.

He resigned from the army in eighteen ninety-one to devote his full attention to airship design and development.

It took him until the turn of the century to conceive and fabricate an experimental craft and on July the second, nineteen-hundred the Zeppelin LZ 1 made its initial flight over Lake

Constance near Friedrichshafen. That airship remained in the air for only twenty minutes and crashed while attempting to land.

Undaunted, Ferdinand continued to work on his designs, suffering many failures and setbacks, but by nineteen hundred and eight his company was viable and producing functioning airships.

Count Zeppelin died during the Great War in nineteen-seventeen and was thereby spared from being present to witness his Zeppelin manufacturing operation forcibly closed down by the Treaty of Versailles as a result of the Germans losing that war.

Unfortunately he was also absent from the resurrection of his dream under the auspices of his successor Hugo Eckener.

Eckener, a consummate negotiator, was able to work his way around the terms of the Versailles treaty, partially by winning a contract to build an airship for the U.S. Navy as part of a war reparations commitment. He successfully convinced both the U.S. and German governments to support the plan and the result was the construction of LZ 126, later to become the USS Los Angeles. From this success he moved on to the construction of the 'Graff Zeppelin' the most successful ridged airship ever produced.

The craft, Captained by Eckener, completed the first intercontinental flight by airship in nineteen-twenty-eight and circumvented the world in nineteen twenty-nine.

His accomplishments became the toast of Germany and by the early thirties Eckener had become a hero to the German people.

In the nineteen thirty-two German presidential election Eckener intended to run against Hitler, only dropping out when Paul von Hindenburg decided to run for the position again.

Needless to say, the Nazis were not pleased to have such a popular figure challenge their leader.

When the Nazis came to power in July of nineteen thirty-three Eckener made no attempt to disguise his abhorrence of the party. He spoke out strongly and often about the party's policies.

When the Nazis approached him to use his large hangars in

Frankfurt for one of their rallies he flatly refused the request. In a very short period of time any reference to Eckener disappeared from the Nazi controlled media and rapidly slipped into obscurity.

In nineteen thirty-five the Nazis nationalized the company and took it over, using it primarily for propaganda purposes.

The construction of the Zeppelin works had been followed by the opening of other manufacturing facilities in Friedrichshafen.

Founded by Wilhelm Maybach in March of nineteen-nine, 'Luffhhrezeug-Motorenbau GmbH' (Aircraft Engine Building Company), renamed 'Maybach Engine Construction Company' in nineteen-twelve was begun as an enterprise to develop and build diesel and gasoline engines for Zeppelins and railway engines.

During the Great War the company switched production to that of engines for military aircraft and airships. From nineteen twenty-one to nineteen-forty, production shifted back to heavy-duty diesel engines slated for the marine market and the railways. A line of ultra-high-end luxury cars was also initiatedwith success.

When the Nazis came to power the factory retooled to produce the engines needed to power the German medium and heavy panzer tanks. They continued to manufacture these until the end of the war.

Dornier Flugzeugwerke founded in nineteen-fourteen by Claudius Dornier was another company headquartered in Friedrichshafen which found its production restricted by the terms of the Versailles Treaty.

The company was subsequently forced to manufacture their aircraft outside the borders of Germany, doing so in factories located in Italy, Spain, Japan and the Netherlands, producing machines under licence. The aircraft they designed were well received and they were specifically known for their all-metal flying boats produced during the nineteen twenties and thirties. Once the Nazi party became government and demonstrated their general disregard for the Treaty, Dornier closed all their foreign factories and resumed production in the city of Friedrichshafen. Here they produced a variety of very successful military bombers and fighters for the Luftwaffe.

A spin off of the Zeppelin works founded by Ferdinand Zeppelin in Friedrichshafen in nineteen-fifteen was the 'Zahnradfabrik' (Gear Factory), commonly known as ZF. Specializing in engineering, it was set up for the specific task of designing and manufacturing gears for the zeppelins and other aircraft, as these were not available elsewhere.

By nineteen-nineteen ZF sought to avoid the terms of the Versailles Treaty by shifting into the automobile market.

In the twenties and thirties this company quickly became a leader in its field, especially in the area of vehicle transmissions and was in a perfect position to immediately ramp up production to manufacture the merchandise necessary to fulfill the needs of Hitler's war effort once the Nazis took power.

By September of nineteen-forty, Friedrichshafen had become a very important manufacturing sector for the supply of materials needed to keep the wheels, tracks and propellers of the Nazi war machine turning. The Industrial Barons of the area involved in arms production and their shareholders, one of whom was Oberstgruppenfuhrer Count Karl von Stauffer, were all reaping massive returns on their investments and they had become immeasurably important to the Hierarchy of the new German Government.

CHAPTER THIRTY-SIX

- Geneva -

The British made several attempts to arrange for terms that would bring the Germans back to the table in Geneva.

Very pleased at the current situation, the Germans carefully impaired each of these by seemingly earnestly putting forward positions which they were confident would appeal to the British while being totally unacceptable to the French.

This game orchestrated by the ingenious German negotiating team went on for some time until finally on April seventeenth, nineteen thirty-four the French, in frustration, decided to walk out of the conference after stating to the other members that France would see to its own future defence.

* * * * *

- Castle von Stauffer -

The servants, with the exception of the elderly butler, who was of such long service as to be considered a part of the furniture, had been dismissed.

The Countess Erika and her two daughters were sitting around a table, which held a large silver tea service.

The large overstuffed chairs had been placed in a small grouping which was arranged near the lake-facing wall of huge floor-to-ceiling leaded glass French doors, off in one corner of the vast expanse of the large drawing room located on the ground floor at the rear of the castle.

The curtains had been pulled and the majority of the room lay in shadow, the three lamps that had been lit. providing pools of warm glowing light around them but failing to penetrate into the far recesses of the high-ceilinged and lovingly polished wood-paneled room.

The Countess was in great form and had been at it for almost an hour.

First there had been a copy of the guest list for each of her daughters. Those males of a proper age, position and marital status had been carefully underlined and she was determined to provide specifics on each and every one before allowing her girls to leave the room.

As the life histories droned on, both Ursula and Gabriella sank steadily lower into their chairs. When at last the Countess neatly folded her copy of the list in her lap and sat back to await their response it was, as was usually the case, Gabriella who bravely stepped into the breach.

"Mother, I know this is important to you but you are really living in the past. In the New Germany the importance of a family arranged betrothal is no longer necessary…"

The Countess cut her off with a sharp look.

"Perhaps not for the kitchen help, but it certainly is for young ladies of the Aristocracy."

Ursula, who could see that her mother was not at all receptive to such a comment and was fully prepared to support her own point of view made an attempt to intercede.

"What Gabriella is trying to say Mother, is that times have changed for everyone in Germany. However, I'm sure she, as do I, appreciates the trouble that you have gone to and will give every consideration to the young gentlemen you have indicated."

Somewhat mollified the Countess removed her reading glasses, folded them and placed them on top of the list folded in her lap before speaking again.

"Well, I certainly hope so. We are von Stauffers. We have a role to play in the New Germany just as we did in the old. I can understand the boys.

Men need to have some time to sow their wild oats and of

necessity marry later in life to younger partners.

We do not have that luxury. We women must take advantage of our youthful good looks to accomplish a good match."

Gabriella snorted indelicately and then took in a deep breath, before muttering under her breath.

"It's not only men who need some time to sow some wild oats Mother dear."

Her mother lifted her head but luckily did not hear, and Ursula, who did hear, felt her cheeks bloom a faint pink and stood up smoothing her skirt as she moved.

"I'm very tired mother. It was a long drive and I would really like to go to bed now. May we be excused?"

The Countess hesitated for a second and then nodded.

"Yes of course dear. I will be awaiting your father's arrival but there is no need for the two of you to stay up. You will see him at breakfast. We'll have the whole family together for the first time in months."

* * * * *

- Bahnhof Friedrichshafen –

It was approaching three in the morning of Saturday September twenty-second, nineteen forty, when the train pulling the Count's private cars began to reduce speed on the approach to the Bahnhof at Friedrichshafen.

It would be here in the crowded marshalling yards where they would be decoupled from the rest of the train before being re-coupled to a smaller engine which would then shunt them the three miles up the main line to the Count's private spur line.

From there it would travel up the mountainside to the rail barn at Castle von Stauffer.

* * * * *

- Anglo/German Naval Treaty -

With the Geneva conference in a shambles the British were becoming very concerned that the Germans might simply begin building well past the treaty levels and threaten the English control of the seas.

The Admiralty was adamant that a treaty must be reached with the Germans that would limit their future marine force to a *balanced fleet*, bereft of the merchant-hunting pocket battleships and submarines, at no larger than a thirty-five to one hundred tonnage ratio with that of the British.

It determined that if this were accomplished the Germans would be unable to reach that ratio before nineteen forty-two and as such would be quite handily overcome by the British navy should the necessity of war make that inevitable.

Every Weimar Republic government since the Great War had committed small violations of the terms of the Versailles Treaty.

When the Nazis came on the scene in thirty-three they ordered the construction of the first U-boats since the treaty had come into effect.

The first of these were launched in April of nineteen thirty-five.

Hitler made no secret of this breach of the treaty restrictions, and on April twenty-fifth of nineteen thirty-five the British Naval Attaché to Germany was informed that Germany had laid keels for twelve U-boats at Kiel.

This information was brought to the attention of the members of the British commons on April twenty-ninth of that year.

Although shaken by this news, in view of the positions taken by the British at the Geneva Conference, they found themselves in no sound ethical position to publicly challenge this new German disregard of the treaty terms.

Nevertheless they did launch an official complaint with Germany.

The German response was predictable.

They were simply putting into effect the changes that the British delegation to the conference had conceded to the Reich in March of nineteen thirty-four.

The British were left with two choices.

They could threaten armed force to prevent any further breaches of the treaty or they could rely on diplomacy to seek out a workable compromise.

In consideration of the fact that they knew full well that the British people would not support the first of these choices there was really only one path they could reasonably follow.

In reply to the Nazi's response, on May second, nineteen thirty-five the Prime Minister, Ramsay MacDonald, rose in the House of Commons to advise all present of his government's intention to immediately seek out and reach a naval agreement with Germany, with a view to regulating the future growth of the German Navy.

Concluding that section V of the Treaty of Versailles, which was the portion restricting the size and makeup of the German military machine, was now no longer worth the paper it was written on.

The British decided to offer to abolish that section of the treaty if the Germans would commit to returning to the League of Nations, from which Hitler had withdrawn Germany in October of nineteen thirty-three, and the World Disarmament Conference.

At the second London Naval conference held in nineteen thirty-five a summit between the French Premier and the British Prime Minister was arranged.

This meeting resulted in a joint Anglo/ French communiqué being issued that offered talks with the Germans on the subject of arms limitation and potential treaties with regard to individual pacts for Eastern European nations along the Danube River.

Meetings between Hitler and British Foreign Secretary John Simon were scheduled for early march of nineteen thirty-five. These talks had to be postponed when The Fuhrer took umbrage to a British *'White Paper'* proposing a higher defence budget in view of the fact that Germany was in violation of the Treaty of Versailles, by way of contracting a *'cold'* making him unable to attend.

During the period Hitler was recovering from his so called cold he managed on March sixteenth, nineteen thirty-five to find the strength to formally renounce all the clauses of the Versailles Treaty which pertained to disarmament and initiate compulsory military service in Germany.

At a meeting with Simon on March twenty-sixth, nineteen thirty-five Hitler indicated he was prepared to discuss a treaty regulating the scale of future German naval rearmament. The Fuhrer took this seductive suggestion a step further while delivering a speech in Berlin on the twenty-first of May of that year offering to discuss a German Navy at a permanent thirty-five to one hundred ratio of that of the British.

CHAPTER THIRTY-SEVEN

- Ancestral Home –

The small engine pulling the Count's two private railcars slowed and came to a halt once it had drawn the cars past the small spur line whose shimmering moon-lit rails could be seen winding upward from the main line on the valley floor toward the castle, hidden by the thick forest perched above.

The four men had been awakened by the Count's SS-aid just prior to the re-coupling that had taken place in the marshalling yards at Friedrichshafen.

A light meal of bread, sausage, cheese and fruit had been served and consumed while awaiting the main line up the track to be declared clear of traffic in order to provide a window during which the cars could be shunted into the castle spur and then backed on to it to clear of the main line.

The Count and his guests were comfortably seated at the rear of the train on the covered observation platform nursing steaming mugs of fresh coffee.

Once the switching process had been completed and the two cars had been nudged backward onto the spur, the train came to a stop again while the track switch was reset for mainline traffic. This accomplished, the little engine built steam and then began to push the two big cars upward along the single track with determination.

From where the passengers were located at the rear of the train, now moving backwards up the heavily forested side of the mountain, they had a front row seat for the trip up the grade.

The subterranean rail barn was located at the bottom of the east side of the castle which was situated at the top of a minor peak in the range and overlooked the town of Friedrichshafen and Lake Constance in the distance.

* * * * *

– Berlin –

In addition to his offer to keep the German Navy at a thirty-five to one hundred ratio to that of the British in perpetuity during his speech in Berlin on the twenty-first of May, nineteen, thirty-five , Hitler stated "The German Reich government recognizes of itself the overwhelming importance for existence and thereby the justification of dominance at sea to protect the British Empire, just as, on the other hand, we are determined to do everything necessary in protecting of our own continental existence and freedom"

Quite clearly he was very publically extending a sympathetic offer of a reasonable and workable Anglo/German alliance to the British.

The British were ecstatic.

The next day, on the twenty-second of May the British Cabinet voted resoundingly to formally accept Hitler's generous offer.

On May twenty-seventh, Hitler appointed von Ribbentrop to head the German delegation to negotiate the proposed naval treaty on behalf of the Reich.

The German Foreign minister at the time, Baron Konstantin von Neurath, was initially adamantly opposed to the selection of Ribbentrop to lead such a delegation but changed his mind when he began to see that the selection of his unofficial rival for such an important appointment would obviously lead to a dismal failure.

The British would never agree to a ratio of thirty-five to one hundred. Let the upstart von Ribbentrop head the mission; when it failed he would be soundly discredited.

The German delegation arrived in London to start negotiations on June second, nineteen thirty-five.

The inept, inexperienced and diplomatically-challenged Ribbentrop, who at this point in time served in the capacity of Hitler's *Extraordinary Ambassador/Plenipotentiary at Large* and Chief of the Nazi Party organization *'Dienststelle Ribbentrop'* (an alternative foreign ministry set up by Hitler), was completely out of his depth.

In absolute awe of Hitler, Ribbentrop saw this appointment as an opportunity to please his Fuhrer and thereby advance his station. He was absolutely determined not to fail in his mission.

Incredulously, Ribbentrop opened the first meeting on June fourth nineteen thirty-five with the statement indicating that '*The British could either accept the thirty-five to one hundred ratio as fixed and unalterable by the weekend, or the German delegation would go home', and if that unfortunate circumstance were to occur, then the Germans would have no alternative but to build their navy up to any size they saw fit'.*

The British head of delegation, Simon was absolutely flabbergasted, and walked out of the talks.

Ribbentrop was crestfallen but didn't know what to do. He therefore did absolutely nothing which turned out not to be such a bad choice under the circumstances.

The next day several things occurred to shake up the British.

Firstly the British delegation reported to the British Cabinet that after sober second thought they were definitely of the belief that refusing to accept the German ultimatum would give Hitler the green light to build his navy much above the offered ratio to the point where it would become a serious rival for British control of the seas.

They returned to the table and for the next two weeks talks progressed with a desperate to succeed Ribbentrop blindly agreeing to the British positions on various issues relating to how tonnage ratios would be calculated in the various warship categories.

On June eighteenth, nineteen thirty-five the Anglo/German Naval Agreement was signed by Ribbentrop and the new British

Foreign Secretary Sir Samuel Hoare.

Hitler was absolutely thrilled.

He was now utterly convinced that his dream of a future further agreement between Britain and Germany to stand side by side in a foreseeable war against France and Russia was inevitable.

Hitler was to officially name Ribbentrop Germany's Foreign minister on February fourth, nineteen thirty-eight.

* * * * *

- Ancestral Home –

The first view of the castle shimmering in the bright moonlight above the imposing mass of its defensive walls occurred as the observation platform broke free of the dense evergreen stand and then passed through an open portal in the thick wall and into the grounds of the estate.

Despite that fact that all of them had experienced it many times before, that initial glimpse from the rail line had its usual effect upon those seated in the comfortably overstuffed chairs.

Conversation trailed off and heads lifted and slowly rotated as all eyes were drawn to the wonder of the structure's imposing mass spread over its lofty perch at the top of the mountain's peak.

The castle's construction had been commissioned in eighteen-sixty-nine at the direction of the current count's grandfather.

His grandfather had been motivated to build in the area as a result of the then King, Christian Jank Ludwig II of Bavaria, having decided to build the infamous Neuschwanstein Castle on a rugged hill above Hohenschwangau. The King's new castle was to be built on the sight of a much older construction whose ruins his father, King Maximilian II of Bavaria had purchased in order to build the neo-Gothic palace known as Hohenschwangau Castle.

This new structure, finished in eighteen thirty-seven, was then used as the Royal Family's summer residence. Ludwig was King Maximilian's eldest son and he'd spent a good portion of his childhood in this new palace and was obsessively enchanted by its location.

Karl's grandfather Eduard had been a favourite of King Ludwig who later became infamous as the *'Mad King Ludwig'* and wished to have a residence of his own within the relative proximity of Ludwig's new palace.

At the time, the von Stauffer family happened to own an old mansion on a large parcel of land on the top of a small mountain overlooking Lake Constance at Friedrichshafen and Karl's grandfather decided to demolish the structure and build his new castle in the Romanesque Revival style on the site.

Castle von Stauffer, completed in eighteen eighty-five, was the result of this endeavour and had been used exclusively as the family's summer home since that time.

Karl von Stauffer had been born there in eighteen eighty-two, during the final phase of construction.

The estate was surrounded by a massive stone wall that completely enclosed the property, bracketing it down the sides of the mountain to reach and then continue across the shoreline of Lake Constance itself. As a private residence it was in reality not actually a palace but it had been built in the style of castles; it had turrets and towers aplenty. The wall encompassing it served two purposes.

Firstly it achieved the purpose of mimicking the effectively defensive walls historically built to protect castles from attack in the times of knights of old and secondly it provided an impressive degree of privacy for the family while on the estate.

The then Count von Stauffer was a man of considerable wealth and a friend of the court. As a result the structure he commissioned was opulent and constructed on a fairly large scale. When completed it consisted of over one hundred suites and rooms arrayed above the sub-basement and basement storage areas. No expense was spared. The interior was richly appointed and all the modern conveniences were incorporated, including the newest plumbing concepts of the day.

Running water, both hot and cold was available and porcelain toilet fixtures could be found in abundance throughout the castle, in the family's personal suites on the top floor as well as those VIP guest suites on the floor below boasting large, fully equipped, individual, en-suite bathrooms.

CHAPTER THIRTY-EIGHT

- Plan Z -

With the Anglo/German Naval Agreement signed, Hitler ordered the Kriegsmarine to provide him with several plans for the rebuilding of the German Navy.

Of these the Fuhrer chose 'Plan Z'.

On January twenty-seventh nineteen thirty-nine Hitler instructed that the plan be initiated.

When completed it would provide Germany with ten Battleships, four Aircraft Carriers, three Battle Cruisers, three older Panzerschiffe, twelve new Panzerschiffe, five Heavy Cruisers, thirty-six Light Cruisers, sixty-eight Destroyers, ninety Torpedo boats and two hundred and forty-nine U-boats by nineteen forty-five.

Hitler decreed that the larger warships would be built first and that if war were to break out with England prior to nineteen forty-five the large ship-building program would be postponed in favour of smaller craft until these had been completed.

In the short time between the issuance of this order in January and the outbreak of war on September the first, nineteen thirty-nine, just two of the large 'H' class Battleships had been laid down and the components of three new Battle cruisers were in the process of production.

Prior to Plan Z, one Aircraft Carrier, four Battleships, three Heavy Cruisers and six Light Cruisers were already in the early stages of construction.

Upon the declaration of war all work on the 'H' class battlewagons, the Battle Cruisers, some Cruisers and the two Aircraft Carriers already laid down was halted as these large projects would require too much of the essential material available for ship building.

These funds and materials were now to be used for the construction of U-boats.

* * * * *

- Countess von Stauffer -

The Countess Erika, showing no signs of fatigue despite the hour and accompanied by the aged butler, arrived at the highly polished brass elevator doors located on the lower level of the castle von Stauffer's sub-basement. In the summer months she always found the air here refreshingly cool if somewhat stagnant.

As the doors slid open in response to the butler having pressed the summoning button on the control panel set into the stone next to their marble frame, two liveried footmen, manhandling a luggage cart, came into sight at the far end of the corridor and the butler brought them to a halt with a sharp look.

"Once the Countess and I have descended to the rail-carriage barn I will send the car back up for you. Upon arrival below you will wait until the traveling party has gone up. I will ride with them and then return to see to your transportation of the luggage."

* * * * *

- Operation Wilfred -

In March of nineteen forty the English began to prepare a plan for the invasion of Norway, code named 'Operation Wilfred'

The main goal of the planned British invasion was to reach and destroy the Swedish mines in Galliard and cut the Germans off from their supply of iron ore.

It was hoped by the British that this would divert Nazi forces from any imminent invasion of France and possibly open a front in the south of Sweden.

It was also decided that the invasion force would first mine Norwegian waters before they landed troops at four Norwegian ports, those of Narvik, Trondheim, Bergen and Stavanger.

The initial stage of laying mines was scheduled to take place on April fifth, nineteen-forty. It was later postponed to commence on April eighth.

Meanwhile the German's interest in an invasion of Norway was reawakening.

In December of nineteen thirty-nine Raeder took an interest in Vidkun Quisling, who was the leader of the Norwegian National Union Party, the 'National Samling' which had been modeled on the German Nazi Party.

It was a small party with little support or influence in the Norwegian politics of the time. Quisling had served briefly as Norwegian Minister of War in the early nineteen thirties and had been a protégé of Alfred Rosenberg, the head of the Foreign Political office of the Nazi party.

In the summer of nineteen thirty-nine Quisling had, with considerable Nazi support, attempted to sell the idea of German occupation of Norway to his countrymen. His endeavours had achieved little success.

He did however find a receptive ear in Raeder when the two met on December eleventh, nineteen thirty-nine.

At that meeting Quisling informed the Admiral that there was an enormous and impending danger of a British occupation of Norway and further indicated that the Norwegian Government had already signed a secret agreement with the British that would allow such an occupation.

He claimed to be in a position to ensure that the Nazis could, with his help, easily end-run this agreement, taking possession of these necessary bases for themselves. He told Raeder that he had been trying to sell such an idea to Rosenberg for some time but had gotten nowhere.

Raeder took this information to Hitler on the next day. He

told Hitler that Quisling had impressed him but admitted that he had left the impression that he was primarily concerned in advancing his own position in Norway.

Be that as it may, Raeder was adamant that a British occupation of Norway would mean British influence over Sweden and result in an English move to take the war to the Baltic Sea, thereby disrupting the German path to the Atlantic and the North Sea driving a stake into the heart of Germany.

He urged his Fuhrer to meet with Quisling.

Hitler agreed and the meeting was held on December fourteenth, nineteen thirty nine. After this meeting Hitler ordered the High Command to look into how Germany could take possession of Norway.

Hitler met with Quisling again on the eighteenth of December at which time he indicated that he favoured the status quo, that of a neutral Norway, but was convinced that if that neutrality was threatened by the British he would be left with no option but to take action of his own to prevent it.

The Fuhrer provided Quisling with funds and asked him to supply the Germans with an ongoing flow of up to date data on what was transpiring in his country. He ordered the representative in Rosenberg's Oslo office and his naval aid to maintain close contact with Quisling.

Hitler demanded of his own people that Quisling's claims of strong support within Norway be investigated and when this had been done he was told that these claims had been grossly exaggerated.

While Quisling continued to provide ongoing information to the Germans after this time, such information flow from that point on became decidedly one-sided.

The Germans no longer trusted the man to share their plans. Although they did encourage him to believe he was part of their planning it was in fact simply a facade.

On November the thirtieth, nineteen thirty-nine Russia attacked Finland. This action coalesced sympathy for the Fins within the Allied Forces and throughout the Scandinavian countries.

Norway and Sweden had good cause to fear that the Russians might succeed in taking Finland and if that should come to pass simply move on to attack and subjugate each of them in turn.

Quisling quickly informed Raeder, his most appreciative German audience to date, that the Norwegian Government would instantly request military help from the British if the Russians made such a move against them.

The recently signed Russian/Nazi pact had stipulated that Finland was to be considered as outside the German sphere of interest.

If the Germans wished to honour the pact, and at this point in time they were desperate to do so, they were obliged to declare themselves neutral in the conflict between Russia and the Fins.

The taking of this position by the Nazis created a strong wave of anti-German sentiment to sweep through the Scandinavian countries.

Of even more concern to the Germans was the fear that the Allies might declare for the Fins against Russia in this conflict and thereby have their troops welcomed into Norway to prevent the Russians from overrunning Finland.

They had good reason to worry.

The early successes achieved by the vastly outnumbered Fins in defending against the Russian attack served to indicate that the Red Army was an inefficient and ineffective fighting force.

The French, by now convinced that the Germans were preparing for an imminent attack against them, saw this Russian assault on Finland as a golden opportunity.

They proposed to the English that the Allies move to create a Scandinavian theatre of war by taking on both the Germans and the Russians and therein diverting German forces away from their border.

The British, who had no Germans lined up on their borders,

had no wish to initiate a separate war with the Russians and promptly gave the plan a determined diplomatic thumbs-down.

In early nineteen-forty Hitler again turned his attention toward Norway as an increasing allied diatribe directed against the Russian invasion of Finland floating the threat of intent to intercede on the side of Finland heated up. This came to a head on January sixth of that year when the English attempted to get the Norwegian and Swedish governments to agree to allowing British naval forces to enter and patrol Norwegian territorial waters.

Four days later on the tenth of January, Hitler issued a memorandum titled 'Studie Nord', which had just been completed on the first of January, to his High Commands. This document contained the preliminary responsibilities to be assigned to the individual services in the event of an attack on Norway.

The separate High Commands of the German forces had their heads buried in the planning of the attack on the western front. As a result they gave *Studie Nord* only minimal attention; they had bigger fish to fry.

Even Raeder, pushed by his own Naval Staff, had come to the determination that there was no imminent threat of an allied invasion of Norway and it was therefore preferable that Norway continued as a neutral state. Progress on a detailed plan for the invasion of Norway was going nowhere.

Two things were about to change this lack of interest in Norway.

Hitler had intended to launch the German attack against France and the Low Countries before the end of January nineteen thirty-nine.

By mid-January he changed his mind. Two factors led to him making this decision.

The first was a change in the weather conditions making them less favourable for attack and the second was the unfortunate forced landing made in Belgian territory by a Luftwaffe Major who happened to be carrying a copy of the German plans for the invasion of France with him at the time.

Hitler decided that the invasion could not go forward before the end of March.

The pressure now came off the German High Commands who immediately gave a sigh of relief.

Hitler's immediate attention shifted away from France and back to Norway.

Hitler, who had been chaffing at the bit to continue the offensive against the Allies since October of nineteen thirty-nine and was now frustrated at the need to delay the invasion, channelled his aggravation over inactivity into a thorough study of the Norwegian problem.

Hitler's general frustration left him heartily displeased with the lack of the separate commands to reach decisions.

On an individual basis they continued to vacillate, continually flip-flopping on their positions, never finding a solid footing.

Such activity was then compounded by a seeming inability to reach a common cause with each other in any other planning endeavour.

This ineffectual behaviour on the part of all of them had been driven home to Hitler and was very clearly demonstrated in regard to *Studie Nord*.

Hitler determined to take such planning operations down a new path. On January twenty-third nineteen-forty he ordered *Studie Nord* recalled.

On the twenty-seventh he directed his de facto minister of war, 'Generalfeldmarschall' (Field Marshal) Wilhelm Bodewin Johann Gustav Keitel, the head of the 'Oberkommando der Wehrmacht' (Supreme Commander of the Armed Services), to send letters to the Commanders in Chief of the Army, Navy and Air force ordering that all future military planning operations would be removed from control of the separate forces and forthwith conducted as the sole prerogative of the 'Oberkommando der Wehrmacht' (Armed Forces High Command).

Hitler informed Keitel that all future planning responsibility would now fall to him and would be carried out under the direct supervision of the Fuhrer who was the only person capable and equipped to determine the overall direction of the war.

To accomplish this task he was to form a working team which would be designated the Armed Forces High Command and would consist of an operations staff consisting of one officer from each of the services who Keitel considered to be suitable for operations work and who had training in organization and supply.

This was to be done immediately and its first assignment was to be the planning for 'Operation Weseruebung' the code name for the drawing up of a plan for the invasion of Denmark and Norway.

CHAPTER THIRTY-NINE

- Weekend Plans -

The Count, his sons and the Baron had gone their separate ways, each to get settled into their own suites on the top floor of castle, but before parting had agreed to meet at the stables at five for a pre-breakfast ride on the grounds of the estate.

The Countess Erika visited her husband briefly in his rooms to touch base with him in regard to the plans for the weekend.

They had a short discussion and then she excused herself to retire to her own apartment to get some much needed rest before breakfast was served.

The Count opened the adjoining door between their quarters and then bent his lips to meet hers briefly.

They shared a smile before she passed through and then he closed it behind her and turned to change into his riding clothes which his aide had finished laying out on his massive, intricately carved and highly polished mahogany four-poster bed.

* * * * *

- The Krancke Plan -

On January twenty-ninth, nineteen thirty-nine the Chief of the Finnish Army, Field Marshal Carl Gustaf Mannerheim, publically appealed for allied help to stem the Russian attack on his country.

The French, still very much interested in taking on the Russians directly with the hope of drawing the Germans into a front on Scandinavian territory to relieve the Nazi pressure forming on their own borders, pushed for an elaborate plan which included the blockade of the port of Murmansk combined with Balkan operations and the landing of troops in both Sweden and Norway.

The British, in no hurry to escalate hostilities on the one hand but feeling the pressure to aid the Fins on the other, saw the Finnish appeal as a possible opportunity to make landings in Norway that, under these new circumstances might be welcomed by the Norwegians. They suggested a much more modest plan, one which would give them the chance to have their fleets welcomed into Norwegian territorial waters, occupy the Norwegian ports and stem the flow of Swedish ore to the Germans.

The British held sway in the diverse discussions and in the end the main thrust of the allied support was aimed at operations confined to Norway and Sweden while ostensibly only doing so in order to bring forces to bear on the Finnish front.

This resulted in a response to the plea from the Fins by the Allied Supreme War Council. It consisted of a plan to send an expeditionary force scheduled for arrival by the middle of March to land directly at Narvik and move from there by rail to the eastern terminus at Lula, occupying Kiruna and Gallivare as they moved. Once they had established two allied brigades along the line, two more brigades would then be sent on to Finland.

The new German staff for Operation *Weseruebung*, as ordered by Hitler had been formed and on February fifth nineteen forty, it first assembled as directed by the Fuhrer, as a newly created department of the Operations Staff, Armed Forces High Command.

The senior officer of the group was Captain Theodor Krancke, the commanding officer of the cruiser 'Admiral Scheer'. On this date there was no representative on the part of the Luftwaffe present. This was because Field Marshal Herman Goering, smarting at Hitler's decision to move planning away from the separate forces and consolidate it under the direct control of the High Command which reported directly to the Fuhrer, chose to boycott the newly formed Operations Staff.

He felt that, as the Luftwaffe was to play a major role in the operations against Norway, he should be directly involved in the planning of the operation. He had therefore not found time to select a representative from his staff who would be authorized to speak on behalf of the Luftwaffe

This childish response, typical of many of those who made up Hitler's inner circle, who exhibited a tendency to hang on to and expand their personal power and influence at every opportunity, was certainly not unique among the leaders of the three arms of the German armed services.

However, those in charge of the army and navy were sensible enough to know better than to display an openly obdurate reaction in respond to Hitler's firm decision. The Fuhrer was not a man who suffered disobedience lightly.

It soon became apparent to Goering that he had bitten off his nose to spite his face and he promptly made his selection of an officer to represent the Luftwaffe on the new planning staff.

The new High Command planning staff was shocked to find that relatively little of the previous work done with regard to occupying Norway and Denmark by the planners of the separate arms of the German military was of any real value. It became immediately apparent to them that Hitler had been right to consider all the earlier work as next to useless and pitifully incomplete.

As a result of the Russian invasion of Finland and the Allies response to it, the various arms of the German Armed Forces found themselves under the gun to work together.

Hitler's insistence that the individual representatives chosen to represent each of the services not only be suitable for operations work, but also trained in organization and supply saw to it, that although they initially had no major resources to assist them, the right men for the job were now sitting around the new High Command operations-planning table.

The newly formed group first looked at what they had inherited.

This consisted primarily of the less than helpful and uncoordinated memoranda that had been produced individually by the three arms of the German military after December nineteen thirty-nine.

Thanks in no small part to Quisling, there was also some limited information on Norwegian military installations.

All in all, this gave them little more than suggested tentative points for departure of the invasion troops.

For the preparation of general background information on the enemy and the production of maps for the invading forces they found themselves having to rely on things like travel guides, tourist brochures and hydrographical charts.

In addition they were forced by the need for secrecy to restrict the size of their staff and do most of the legwork themselves.

They had no previous German experience that could assist them in the endeavour.

What had worked historically would not help them in the planning of modern warfare.

They quickly determined that if they wished to author a successful invasion, they would have to pioneer an entirely new approach to a modern form of deployment.

On the fourteenth of February the German tanker *Altmark,* who was carrying three hundred British seamen captured earlier as a result of actions against British merchantmen by the cruiser *Admiral Graf Spee,* steamed into Norwegian waters on its return trip to Germany.

The Norwegians, sticking to their stance of neutrality, although strongly suspecting that the tanker was transporting English nationals being held against their will, made no move to interfere with the ship's movements.

Six British destroyers appeared on the horizon and the *Altmark* accepted the escort of two Norwegian torpedo boats as it took refuge in a fjord.

Entering Norwegian waters in open disregard of the orders of the Norwegian Government and strong protests of the two escorting Norwegian ships, the British destroyer *Cossack* steamed into the fjord, sent a boarding party onto the *Altmark* and forcibly removed the prisoners.

The Norwegians were embarrassed and Hitler was furious. On February nineteenth he ordered a speed up of the planning for the invasion of Norway.

Despite all the obstacles in their path, the planning group, under Krancke's leadership, dug their heels in with a passion and within three weeks they had produced an effective plan which contained a complete outline of the technical and tactical requirements required for a successful invasion.

Coordination in the attack was a mandatory requirement with a view to making the best use of the element of surprise. The simultaneous landing of troops in a variety of locations was paramount.

The principle centers of industry and population, Trondheim, Narvik, Oslo, Kristiansand, Arendal, Bergen and Stavanger had to be taken in one synchronized swoop.

Accomplishing this would mean the loss to the Norwegians of eight divisions, one half of their entire strength, all but wipe out their artillery capability and bring the vast majority of their airfields under German control.

This was to be accomplished by the use of six German divisions, these to be deployed half by the air and half by sea.

As Goering had envisioned it would be a primarily airborne operation.

The Luftwaffe's *Seventh Air Division* would supply eight transport groups and five battalions of parachute troops in the first wave and follow up with the transport of the *Twenty-second Infantry Division* (airborne) over the next three days.

General Alfred Josef Ferdinand Jodl, Chief of the Operations Staff of the High Command and Keitel's second in command suggested to Hitler that the matter was now complete and should be placed into the hands of a Corps Commander and his staff for active development. Hitler agreed and Lieutenant General Nikolaus von Falkenhorst, Commanding General of *XXI Corps,* was subsequently chosen for the task.

On February twenty-first at noon Falkenhorst reported to Hitler and was offered the task of advancing the *Krancke* plan and when and if it was initiated, taking overall-command of the invasion. Falkenhorst agreed to review the file presented him and supply his answer to Hitler within twenty-four hours.

The next day von Falkenhorst advised Hitler that he had completed his review and felt the plan had merit and that he could support it. His appointment was made official on that day.

The Wehrmacht General moved quickly, forming a selected working staff in Berlin, drawn from XXI headquarters personnel, on February twenty-sixth.

Von Falkenhorst's staff studied the *Krancke plan* and began to tweak it. The first decision they had to make was what to do about Denmark.

A naval supplement to the *Studie Nord* had strongly supported the necessity of taking of bases in Denmark with the emphasis on the importance of those at the northern tip of Jutland in order to facilitate vital air and naval control, over and on, the Skagerrak Strait.

The triangular strait, bounded on the southeast by thecoast of Norway, the southwest by that of Sweden and the Jutland peninsula of Denmark connects the North and Kattegat Sea area where it opens to the Baltic Sea.

The Krancke plan had expressed the opinion that these necessary bases in Denmark might be secured through diplomatic means, strengthened by a threat of military occupation. Falkenhorst's staff supported the need for the bases to achieve the necessary goals set out by Hitler but was not prepared to even consider endangering the entire operation by counting on any such accommodation being reached through diplomatic means.

Denmark would have to be occupied by force.

On February twenty-eighth General von Falkenhorst sat down with Keitel and outlined a plan of attack that included the taking of the Danish state in conjunction with the other targets. It included the assignment of two additional divisions of troops to accomplish this task.

He was adamant that one other problem had to be addressed and that concerned the timing of the Scandinavian invasion.

In his view the concept of aggressively opening up the attack on France and the Lowland Countries, already tentatively scheduled by the Fuhrer for mid-march could not be accomplished in conjunction with the current troop commitments set aside for the move on Denmark and Norway.

Army High Command acknowledged that certain specific and specialized segments of the German military machine would be needed in both and they could not be in two places at once.

Adjustments in the specific deployment of forces planned to date in relationship to the Scandinavian assault would have to be made. It was recommended that the commitment of parachute troops to *Weseruebung* be reduced to four companies and that one regiment of the Twenty-Second Infantry be held back in reserve.

The reductions in troops and the additional occupation of Denmark were personally approved by Hitler on the twenty-ninth of February.

On March twenty-first Hitler issued the 'Directive for Case Weseruebung'. It was a bold move calling for testicular fortitude on the part of everyone involved and requiring the advantage of surprise to succeed.

The entire operation was to be portrayed to the peoples of the occupied countries and the world as a peaceful occupation, a reasonable step toward ensuring the continuation of Scandinavian neutrality.

In his directive Hitler appointed Von Falkenhorst as Commanding General, Group XXI, to be in sole charge of the operation, which he now designated as *Weseruebung Sued* (South for Denmark and *Weseruebung Nord* (North) for Norway.

He made it extremely clear in this document that during the operation the Commanding General would take instruction from and report to only one man.

Adolf Hitler.

CHAPTER FORTY

– Working Weekend –

Breakfast at the Castle von Stauffer had been a family affair, with the only outside guest being Baron von Kliest, who was in all but name considered one of their own.

It had been a relaxed event, leisurely taken, but as the dishes were being cleared from the table that easygoing ambiance was interrupted by the sound of the family's pack of German Shepherds heralding the arrival of the first cars being admitted through the main gate which was located between the estate's gate-keeper's lodgings and the dog kennels.

The Count and Countess excused themselves from the table and made their way out of the sunshine-filled morning room and worked their way to the front of the castle where the butler was in the process of lining up a pair of maids and four footmen in preparation for the receiving of guests.

The Count had dispatched his own staff car and driver to the Friedrichshafen Bahnhof to meet the morning train from Berlin where a group of four were expected; by the sounds of the dogs, he expected that others, arriving by car, were also on their way up from the gate house.

A few moments later he stood, dressed in full uniform, beside Erika.

They were backed by the staff in the shade of a porte-cochere in front of the large double wood panelled doors of the main entrance of the castle.

His earlier surmise was given substance as the first of a parade of vehicles appeared from within the tunnel-like recesses of the long, tree-lined and carefully graded driveway.

His own staff car was in the lead. Riding inside behind

his driver were two uniformed staff officers of high rank, one SS and the other Wehrmacht, accompanied by their wives and two handsome young officers of lower rank, both of whom could be clearly recognized by their features as offspring of the vehicle's other passengers.

Two more open black chauffeured Mercedes-Benz 770 series II staff cars followed, both showing signs of the long overnight trip from Berlin and carrying senior uniformed members of the armed forces, the first members of the Kriegsmarine and the other Luftwaffe personnel. A fourth closed limousine brought up the rear.

As the vehicles swept to a stop the drivers quickly exited and opened doors for the waiting passengers.

The array of uniforms alighting from the vehicles had become the norm in wartime Germany and was unremarkable but when the last car in the line, an impressive nineteen thirty-nine Maybach SW 38 closed limousine gave up its cargo consisting of four gentlemen in impeccable business dress, the other guests took note.

These were powerful men of business whose faces were well known in Germany and their attendance at the Count's weekend retreat was a surprise to all in attendance with the exception of himself and the Countess.

* * * * *

- Weseruebung

-

To observe that Hitler's *Weseruebung* directive, when circulated, was not well received by the commanders of the Luftwaffe and Army would be a gross understatement.

It was the Navy's leadership that had first brought forth the concept of occupying Norway and subsequently Denmark to Hitler's attention.

It was the Navy who had supplied the most senior officer to

the newly constructed joint planning group, and it was the Navy who had supplied the largest input into that planning.

The attack against the Allies scheduled to roll westward through the Lowland Countries and occupy the north of France was a major undertaking and Hitler had tentatively indicated that such a strike would take place in mid-march.

Neither the leaders of the air force nor those of the army wanted any part in a splitting of troops and equipment in order to fight in what they determined to be a secondary and far less strategically important theatre of war.

The Wehrmacht and Luftwaffe position on a Scandinavian invasion plan had been both ongoing and unchanged from the time of Raeder's first suggestion of it.

Hitler's formation of a separate joint-planning group under the direct control of the Armed Forces High Command had been hard enough for them to swallow and now with one stroke of the pen Hitler had dismissed their concerns about a second front in Scandinavia, and he had done so without even consulting them.

An astounded General Franz Halder, Chief of the General Staff of the Army, noted in his diary on March second, nineteen-forty that, to date, he had not "exchanged a single word" with Hitler on the subject of Norway. This was a man who had, since nineteen thirty-three, always been a part of any strategic military planning, including that of the western campaign against France and the Lowland Countries.

Despite being routinely in disagreement with Hitler with regard to military planning and deployment matters since the Nazis had come to power and thereby definitely not one of the Fuhrer's many yes-men, Halder had a tremendous amount of training and experience behind him and was determined that he had a responsibility to make his views known, be they for or against what the Nazi leader had in mind.

Halder was both amazed and affronted that at Hitler's direction the Armed Forces High Command had ordered a variance in the strategic stationing of various sections of his

Wehrmacht troops, without so much as discussing the matter with him.

For their part the Luftwaffe protested strongly that the use of the Seventh Air Division demanded for the Scandinavian front as well as other Luftwaffe units would jeopardize their effectiveness in the battle looming on the western front against France and the Low Countries (Operation Fall Gelb).

On March second the allied forces of Great Britain and France formally submitted requests to both Sweden and Norway asking for the right of transit for troops which they would be sending to the aid of the Fins.

In response Hitler lashed out at his detractors in both the Luftwaffe and Wehrmacht demanding that they stop their bickering and that the forces he had determined as necessary in his earlier directive be assembled as ordered. This was to be completed by the tenth of March in time for the invasion of Denmark and Norway to launch on the thirteenth with the landings to take place on March seventeenth. This was later postponed to April.

The three Commanders in Chief, Army, Navy and Air force were ordered to attend a meeting with him on the Fifth of March.

At that meeting the Commander in Chief of the Luftwaffe, Field Marshal Herman Goering, obviously frustrated and short-tempered, blustered on for some time about his having been kept in the dark about the entire planning operation for *Weseruebung* and bold-facedly claimed that all planning in that regard had therefore suffered from a lack of his input and as a result was worthless and would have to be redone.

Hitler made no comment regarding Goering's tirade. He simply repeated the facts.

The Allies were committed to providing support to Finland against the Russians They could only do that by landing in Scandinavia and had in fact clearly indicated by applying for right of transit for their troops, an intention to do exactly that and soon.

This intention allowed the Germans to justify their occupation by claiming that the reason they did it was solely to prevent the Allies from abusing Scandinavian neutrality.

Hitler made it clear that he had thoroughly reviewed the plans prepared for Germany's invasion of Denmark and Norway and had determined that they were properly drawn.

He indicated that he intended to direct the invasion personally and then invited anyone at the table to question his ability to bring it to a successful conclusion.

Predictably no one demurred and Hitler received instant commitment on the fulfilment of the forces designated for the invasion from all three Chiefs.

On March seventh Hitler decided to add some additional formations to the invasion and issued a directive accordingly fortified by the order that the disposition of forces was now final and no longer subject to change. The two operations, *Gelb* for France and the Lowland Countries and *Weseruebung* for the Scandinavians were now irrevocably separated from each other.

Hitler was done discussing the matter.

There was not even a resulting peep of discontent from the Chiefs.

The British plan for landing in Norway had first been scheduled to begin with the mining of Norwegian territorial waters on April fifth, nineteen-forty. This was subsequently postponed to April ninth due to a disagreement with the French.

The German's invasion forces commenced their attack on the night of April eighth/ninth.

Interesting times were ahead.

CHAPTER FORTY-ONE

- Play Time -

Ursula and Gabriella, accompanied by two female friends invited for the day to come up from the city of Friedrichshafen which nestled on the lake below the castle, their brothers, Wilhelm and Eric and the two young officers who had arrived with their parents from Berlin by train had broken away from the older guests.

The Countess had pointedly spoken to Ursula and her sister regarding the pair shortly after their arrival, explaining that each held the promise of rapid promotion and stood in line to inherit both a title and extensive business holdings from their fathers.

Put simply, they were put on notice that these were men to be considered as good catches.

As the sun reached its apex in the clear sky above the estate they formed in a group around the outdoor pool nestled in the centre of the inner gardens located on the first of the terraced steps of green that led downward from the front of the castle to the shimmering lake below.

Two liveried staff maintained a small bar beside the changing houses at the east side of the patio that surrounding the big heated pool and were kept busy supplying drinks as needed, light snacks from the kitchens, fresh towels and clean ashtrays.

Gabriella wore a bathing costume that left little to the imagination. It displayed a great deal of her golden, and in anticipation of improving her tan, well-oiled skin.

She was currently perched on a stool at the bar, drink in hand, holding court before the young officers.

Both of them were in bathing costume, clearly displaying impressive physiques and healthy, tanned good looks.

It bespoke of an interesting weekend ahead for Gabriella.

Each was giving rapt attention to her every gesture.

Wilhelm and Eric were in their element frolicking in the pool with their sister's well-formed and nubile female guests from the city below.

Ursula, conservatively swim-suited, lay on a chaise reading a novel and sipping iced tea.

The Count and his male guests were sharing the aroma of good cigars and whisky in the billiards room and the Countess was giving tea to their wives and daughters in the solarium which overlooked the pool below.

* * * * *

- Denmark –

The Nazi land invasion of Denmark which took place on April ninth, nineteen-forty was the shortest in recorded military history.

Despite the fact that they knew of Germany's intentions, the Danish Government had forbidden the taking of any defensive action in order to forestall provoking the Germans.

The German planning had taken warfare into the modern day, Coordination of army, navy and air force troops, the first effective use of paratroops and Blitzkrieg tactics overwhelmed the Danish forces in a battle that lasted less than six hours.

A leaflet drop by a wave of Luftwaffe planes over Copenhagen containing a threat to bomb the civilian population if immediate capitulation was not forthcoming coupled with a promise that the Danes would be given political independence in domestic matters after the occupation, was enough incentive to cause the government to capitulate.

* * * * *

– Arrivals –

The remainder of the guests had arrived over the day, the last arriving shortly after four. Pre-dinner cocktails were slated for eight with dinner itself to follow at nine.

By late afternoon the group of young adults around the pool had swollen to twelve. Glistening, oiled golden skin was apparent wherever one looked and two more footmen had been added to the staff working at the pool.

Ursula had given up her book an hour ago, accepting responsibility to fulfill the role of co-hostess as the numbers increased.

Despite herself she was now quite enjoying the pool and the attentions of a young, buff and blond Adonis-like Luftwaffe pilot who had to her delight, turned out to look even better in formfitting swimming trunks than he had in uniform.

As a result, it wasn't until sometime later that she realized that her younger sister was no longer at the pool.

Ursula had, some years ago, slipped into the role of mentor for Gabriella who had at the time exhibited a tendency to what had been politely referred to at the time by her mother, as having a somewhat flamboyant personality.

Her mother could call it whatever she liked. The truth was that Gabriella was obsessed with sex and had been ever since her breasts had begun to bud.

Ursula drew in a deep breath and her features clouded with frustration despite her attempt to maintain the atmosphere. The young Luftwaffe officer didn't seem to pick up on the change and she managed a smile as she excused her-self and started to cross over to the bar to speak with the liveried server.

There is only one person in this family who is more eager than her mother to see Gabriella safely married off. And that person is me.

* * * * *

- Gazebo -

The large Gazebo at castle von Stauffer stood at the centre of a Japanese garden, two terraced levels below that of the pool.

It was off to one side of the property in an area screened from its surroundings by tall weeping willows whose branches had been left untrimmed and allowed to trail against the neatly cut grass in the gentle breezes that swept up off the lake below.

Screened against insects it was unheated and normally opened by the removal of its large wooden shutters in early spring and left open to the elements until the cooler temperatures of fall begin to arrive in the autumn.

From experience Ursula knew it as a location favoured by Gabriella for clandestine trysts with members of the opposite sex while she was in residence at the castle.

The narrow gravel paths leading through the willows and weaving in and about the gardens and ponds were always kept beautifully raked clear of footprints by the gardeners and it was this fact that served to confirm Ursula's first guess as to where Gabriella was likely to be found.

There were definite signs that more than one person had used the path very recently.

As she approached the screened doorway leading into the Gazebo she was fully expecting to find her sister 'in flagrante dilecto' with one of the two young officers who had arrived with their parents on the early train from Berlin.

The murmuring splashing sounds provided by the artificial stream running over a series of rocks before entering the pond to the right of the doorway had masked any sound coming from within but as she opened the doorway she could clearly hear the sounds coming from the grouping of couches in the centre of the room.

She let out a deep sigh before she entered the dimly lit room and slammed the door sharply behind her.

The sounds stopped and she was not surprised to see two

heads, followed by a view of Gabriella's firm hard tipped breasts on one side and the golden fleece-covered chest of one of the tanned young officers on the other, both glistening with a layer of perspiration , pop up over the back of the couch.

She was, however, taken aback when yet another head, that of the second young officer Gabriella had been entertaining earlier, face flushed and covered by a sheepish grin, popped up beside the first two.

Gabriella, Gabriella, sister of mine. Is there no end to what you will do for a sexual thrill? Please if there is a God let them both be wearing protection.

A wide smile of recognition formed on Gabriella's innocent features. Ursula placed her hands on her hips.

"Your absence at the pool has been noticed…"

Gabriel, breathing heavily, took a second to respond.

"Ursula dear…since you're here… won't you join us? There's more than enough to go around."

Both young men were by this time on their feet and madly scrambling to locate their discarded swimming trunks and pull them on.

Ursula shook her head in momentary disbelief, pausing just long enough to study the bodies of the two naked men, both of whom were very obviously in a state of advanced arousal, before she spun on her heel and left the Gazebo.

She had done so solely for the purpose of confirming that there was a God of course…lord knows she had harped enough regarding protection against pregnancy over the past number of years.

Obviously her little sister had taken note and was ensuring she had her own supply close at hand at all times.

Circumstances aside, it had been a very pleasing and stimulating view and it was times like this she had to admit to wondering which one of them was the smart one, she or Gabrielle.

CHAPTER FORTY-TWO

- The Countess Entertains -

Before dinner cocktails for the guests were provided in what was referred to as the great room, a magnificent sixty by sixty foot square with deeply polished, mahogany paneled walls, which were a beautiful backdrop to the many large ancestral portraits on display.

The floor was black-marbled, the ceiling thirty-feet-high oak-beamed and one entire wall was made up of huge French doors which led out onto a flagstone patio of identical size.

There were two massive open-hearth stone fireplaces, one centered in the wall at either end of the room, but the huge logs stacked within these remained unlit in consideration of the unusually warm temperature for the time of year.

In further acceptance of the wonderful weather, the French doors had been swung open and the perfumed scents from the gardens beyond drifted in on the soft breeze to circulate around the room.

Small clusters of armchairs and couches arranged around coffee tables were spread around the edges and down the centre of the big room and the Count and Countess, drinks in hand, moved from one to the next to speak briefly with each party before moving on.

The seating had not been pre-set by the Countess as would be the case for dinner.

Left to their own devices the guests had formed arrangements which tended to be reflective of generation, rank and profession.

Uniforms were much in play and dominated the scene. Each military grouping tended to be of a singular rep-resentation:

officers of the Luftwaffe, Kriegsmarine, Wehrmacht and SS, accompanied by their wives, sitting with their comrades in service and two small groups which consisted of barons of industry had been formed in the center of the big room.

Four footmen in livery, holding trays moved continuously, circulating among the crowd providing refills as required.

* * * * *

Dinner was announced precisely at nine and the guests, now numbering fifty-two were partnered for the entry into the large dining room across the hall from the great room.

As chance would have it Ursula found herself partnered with one of the young officers who had been entertaining Gabrielle earlier in the Gazebo. She was relieved to find that the handsome young man had the decency to flush slightly and lower his eyes as he offered his arm.

Gabriella, who was slated to follow her older sister into dinner, had inherited the second officer involved in the Gazebo Ménage a Trois as her escort and within seconds of taking his arm she was batting her eyes at him and deep in conversation.

The final course was served at ten forty-five in the evening and when it was finished the gentlemen retired to the library for cigars and port while the ladies crossed to the screen-enclosed covered patio on the west side of the castle for tea and a fireworks display.

The display would be unique in Germany in that such displays and celebrations once common in many parts of the State had been forbidden since the beginning of the war.

The normal wine festival fireworks display provided each year at this time by the von Stauffers had therefore required a dispensation and the Count had received it from the highest authority.

Finding Hitler in an upbeat mood at a meeting earlier in the year on the eve of the successful French campaign he had made the request with the explanation that since Lake Constance was one of the designated low cost recreation areas chosen for the workers of the Reich, such a display would be enjoyed by those taking advantage of a State-approved break from their labours.

Hitler had agreed with the idea.

En route to the patio the Countess drew her daughters aside to speak briefly with them. She addressed Gabriella first.

"Well dear, you seem to be getting along very well with the young SS Captain. He is from a very good family and has a bright future ahead of him."

Ursula arched her eyebrows and Gabriella grinned.

"Yes mother, I'm certainly enjoying his company."

He Mother nodded and managed a hopeful smile before turning to address her oldest daughter.

"But you Ursula! Why you hardly spoke to your young man at dinner."

Ursula shrugged.

"Well it's been a long day, Mother. I guess I'm just tired."

Her mother stiffened her back.

"Be that as it may dear, you are not getting any younger. You have an obligation to take advantage of any opportunity that presents itself."

Gabriella pursed her lips to hold back a smile.

"Mother's right Ursula; you need to take advantage of any opportunity that arises...now may we be excused Mother. The fireworks will be starting shortly."

The Countess nodded and Gabriella spun on her heel and headed out into the hallway. Before Ursula could move, her mother placed a restraining hand on her elbow.

"I think we may have a possible candidate here; she seems to be very attracted to the young man and he's obviously interested in Gabriella."

Tired of putting up a false front Ursula snorted, shook her head, and turned to follow her sister, her words drifting back over her shoulder to her mother.

"Oh yes Mother, he's more than interested all right, and he is not alone. But not in the way you imagine, I'm afraid. I do not think he will be offering my little sister a ring any time soon."

* * * * *

- Unwilling Ally -

Over the evening of September twenty-third to twenty-fourth nineteen forty the British bombed Berlin in a reprisal attack for the German bombings of London.

Hitler was appalled and the corpulent and ever-preening Luftwaffe head, recently promoted 'Reichsmarschall des Grossdeutschen Reiches' (Reich Marshal of the Greater German Reich), and to this point undisputed deputy to Hitler, Herman Goering, who had publicly declared that his Luftwaffe would guarantee that Germany's capital was never bombed, felt the second wave of cold air creep into his heretofore strong personal relationship with the dictator.

The first hint of frost had been as a result of the Luftwaffe's inability to secure dominance in the skies over the English Channel in preparation for the invasion of Britain.

Goering, who had felt himself secure as top man in the power-grasping, rag-tag entourage who made up Hitler's inner circle suddenly began to have second thoughts and those who stood quietly but deviously in line for that top spot, notably Himmler and Bormann, now took every opportunity when in Hitler's presence to put Goering down and elevate their own prominence within the circle.

* * * * *

- First Step to Final Victory -

The library was one of the largest rooms in the castle.

It consisted of floor to ceiling windows on its outside wall and with the exception of the double studded oak door and massive opened-hearth stone fireplace, was filled with bookshelves on the other three.

The current Count, as did his father and grandfather before him, read voraciously.

All were avid collectors in their time of rare and first-edition volumes.

Eight of the men who had sat for supper, most members of the younger generation, had now excused themselves from the library after enjoying a glass of port and a cigar.

They had done so at the request of the Count who had quietly explained to each on an individual basis that weekend or not there was a war on and urgent matters on the highest level needed to be discussed.

Immediately after the last of these men left, six members of the staff under the butler's supervision entered and at the Count's instructions began to rearrange the furniture.

The three intricately-carved matching mahogany reading tables that normally ran end to end down the center of the room were now moved into a 'u' shape and placed in the middle of the room.

The comfortable arm chairs that had been arranged in the four corners in small clusters around reading lights were carried over and placed along the outside edges of the tables. Four matching crystal carafes containing crushed ice and water were placed on padded bases in a line along the centers of the tables and identically patterned stemmed glasses placed in front of each chair.

The butler placed the gold embossed name cards at each table placing and then let his gaze meet the Count's before turning to gather the other staff and marshal them out of the room.

The Count's SS-aid followed the staff out of the room and pulled the big double doors firmly closed behind him, and then he shifted a chair from the hall wall and placed the back of it against the doors before sitting down.

Inside, the Count bolted the big doors before turning around and walking back to the tables where he took a seat at the center of the table that formed the bottom of the 'U'.

An ornate gold inlaid gavel and base rested on the table to his right and he picked it up and brought it down sharply.

The various conversations ceased and the Count cleared his throat before speaking.

"Gentlemen the hour is late and we have much to discuss. Shall we begin?"

Without consultation the Count had determined that rank would take precedence in the seating, and that included his sons who were seated at the far end of the table on his left.

The only exception was the fact the four industrial barons in attendance bracketed him at the head table, two to each side.

The Count waited until all were seated and then let his eyes rove around the three tables.

"There will be no official record kept of this gathering. No notes are to be taken. Is that understood?"

There were a few exchanged looks and a pen and small notebook which had been withdrawn from the inside pocket of a Wehrmacht general's tunic promptly returned to whence they had come.

The Count nodded in satisfaction and continued.

"This is a gathering of like -minded men. Most of you know each other and by the time this meeting is over everyone here will be familiar with our membership. I have been asked to arrange this meeting in order to allow the men in this room to reach a consensus as to how we are to proceedwith our common goals."

He paused and then nodded.

"Yes, I said common goals. I understand that the majority of you have, for the most part, kept your thoughts to yourselves, a very wise decision if I may say so, in consideration of today's Germany. But each of you has previously expressed your thoughts on the matters concerning us to at least one other person in this room, or you would not be here tonight.

I want to make something very clear to all of you before we move forward. What we set out to accomplish today will be of the utmost importance to the future of the Fatherland and it is sanctioned at the very highest level of the Party. That said, the organization formed by those in this room together tonight, will be a secret group. Its activities will not be discussed with anyone who is not sitting with us tonight and it will not be a matter of public knowledge, and when I say that I am telling you that no one who does not have a need to know of its existence will know. In some cases those persons who will not be informed of our existence may well be your superiors."

The Count reached for the carafe before him, poured a glass and raised it to his lips. There was much shifting about in chairs and expressions of unease were, if varied as to degree, nearly universal.

Several sets of eyes moved around the table meeting those of others and murmured comments were heard.

The Count set his stemware down and opened his mouth to speak again. Immediately all attention was riveted on him.

"To ensure that what I have just said does not give you the wrong impression I am going to tell you the reasons for such measures."

The room was dead quiet now.

"Firstly, we are at war and while what we are going to set into motion this evening is only the reasonable and realistic initial phase of the planning required to assure that we win that war, common knowledge of it could lead to a short-term sense of defeatism among the German people, something to be avoided at all cost.

Were it to happen, it would serve to undermine Germany's amazing military successes achieved thus far and it is something we must not allow to happen. What we want to accomplish as a group is the creation of a well-thought-out fall-back plan that is organized and ready to go into action if and I repeat if, we should be unable, for whatever reason, to achieve the Fuhrer's vision for the future of Germany through military means.

I'm certain that each man in this room realizes that knowledge of such a fall-back plan, if made available to the general public would not serve our current course well. At my meeting with Adolf Hitler when the Fuhrer asked me to come out of retirement he said to me, and I quote, 'I am only one man. My task is monumental and I must of necessity rely on others to independently and without my direct oversight, carry out my wishes. I trust that you will do that for the Fatherland.'

I am also only one man and I cannot fulfill the responsibilities I have been given without your help, and like The Fuhrer, I trust that you will do that for the Fatherland."

He let the last words hang in the tomb-like silence of the room for a few seconds before continuing.

"If there is any man in this room who feels he is unable to join in this project, let him leave the room now. There will be no recriminations, no loss of stature or position for doing so. But you must make that decision now; it will not be an option at any later time."

Some heads turned inquisitively, but no one made to abandon his seat.

The Count refreshed himself from his stemware.

"Very good, gentlemen. Now let's get the foundation of this new organization, which I have chosen to code name 'Operation Fatherland', firmly entrenched.

I am going to select from those present, individuals who will chair the committees who will be responsible for the various arms of our new endeavour.

Each chair will have absolute control of his particular area. He will in turn choose a maximum of three others from this room to assist him in his specific area of responsibility. If in some cases the chair is outranked by another member of his committee, rank will hold no sway.

Let me repeat that. Rank will hold no sway.

Each chair will be held solely responsible for any decision or action taken by his group.

The chair of each group will report to one person only and that person will be me. Each committee will act independently of the others.

They will act as what I will call a 'cell', as a single part of the entire operation.

No one but me will know who sits on which committee. From this day forward no one on any committee will contact anyone else in this room who is not a member of their individual committee. All other contact will be through me. Let me qualify the word contact.

The only exchange of any kind between non-committee members of this organization will between you and me and by contact I mean the discussion of any matter regarding anything to do with our activities, no matter how small the issue or how urgent.

I and I alone will know the entirety of the organization's makeup and the overall operations it sees fit to undertake. If circumstances occur where I am not available for any significant period, one of my sons will act as an emergency intermediary. Are there any questions about this restriction on communication among members of our group?"

The room remained silent.

"Right then, I am now going to give you a general overview of what our aims and achievements must be, the specifics as to what responsibilities each committee will have, how we are to be financed and the full scope of our end goal. Once that has been completed this meeting will be over and there will never be a second such occurrence.

From that point on there will be no occasion outside of a committee conference where more than two men in this room will make contact about anything to do with our activities and in that eventuality, one of those men will be me. "

CHAPTER FORTY-THREE

- A Necessary Alliance -

It was on the morning of Monday September twenty-fourth that an already displeased Hitler was to find out that his previous high expectations for Spain's assistance in the taking of Gibraltar might be suffering a setback.

Hitler considered Gibraltar's demise as a British holding an absolutely necessary precursor to bringing the British to the treaty table.

During the Spanish civil war Hitler had provided Franco with military units and he had extended credit to the rebels for supplies of materiel to the tune of over two hundred and twelve million dollars. In return for a portion of the raw materials these holdings could produce, the Nazi leader had even gone so far as to promise that Germany would recognize Spanish claims to French holdings in Morocco.

Nazi Germany had played no small part in assisting Franco in the winning of the Spanish civil war and to Hitler's mind he had more than earned Franco's support in the taking of Gibraltar.

This expected tit for tat response had been strengthened for Hitler by the earlier replacement, in October of nineteen thirty-nine of then Spanish Foreign Minister Juan Beigbeder Atienza, a staunch supporter of the British, by Franco's brother-in-law, Suner, who was an outspoken German adherent.

It had been further solidified in June of nineteen-forty, shortly after the defeat of France, when the Spanish Ambassador to Berlin had presented a memorandum in which Franco clearly declared that he was ready, with a few condit-ions, to enter the war and stand beside Germany and Italy against Britain and her allies.

At the time the memorandum arrived in Berlin, Hitler along with all his top military advisors was heady with the ease in which France had been overcome by the German 'Blitzkrieg' (Lightening War).

They had therefore taken no action on Franco's offer in that it was considered to be unnecessary in the shared view that England would be invaded successfully by Germany in short order.

Since that time things had changed.

The British invasion operation had been delayed indefinitely and the new goal was to bring England to her knees and force her to the treaty table.

In order to accomplish that end he needed Spain's assistance in taking Gibraltar.

However, at a meeting between Foreign Ministers Suner and Ribbentrop held on this date, the Spanish representative had diplomatically but firmly refused to agree to any resulting claims as spoils of war after the taking of Gibraltar, on the part of the Germans in regard to a number of militarily-strategic but relatively small islands lying just off the African coast.

The Germans wanted these holdings for use as military bases and were absolutely astounded that Spain would take such a position immediately after Ribbentrop's effusive offer of substantial African territory to the Spanish as their spoils resulting from such a successful joint conquest against Gibraltar.

When the matter of the refusal on the part of the Spanish to agree to Germany's ownership and control over the islands reached The Fuhrer's ears, Hitler was incensed.

Outwardly he'd harangued Ribbentrop for not taking a firmer stand on the matter of the islands.

Inwardly The Fuhrer reached the final decision to become personally involved in any further discussions with Spain.

These he informed his Foreign Minister, would in future be conducted on the highest level, one on one, between himself and Franco.

* * * * *

– Ursula –

Ursula remained after the fireworks for a nightcap with the others under the attentive gaze of the handsome Luftwaffe pilot who had singled her out earlier by the pool.

She found him, somewhat surprisingly, as attractive from the point of view of intelligence and well-mannered behaviour on the inside as he had been from a physical point of view while frolicking in the form-fitting trunks on the pool deck earlier in the day.

More importantly he was expressing obvious interest in her.

Somewhat cynical when it came to men, Ursula was endeavouring to determine if her mother might have had something to do with the delightful windfall sitting across the table from her, his legs below that table taking every opportunity to brush lightly against hers, bringing with each brief contact, a delicious tingling sensation of warmth.

She was not so engrossed in the young man that she failed to notice Gabriella drifting off in the direction of the Gazebo with the same two young officers she had been entertaining earlier in the day, one on each arm.

She was however, intrigued enough with the deeply tanned Adonis, whose deep blue eyes never left her, to decide not to interrupt a second attempt by her sister at satiating whatever urges possessed her with regard to the two young officers she had in tow as the three of them skipped, yes
skipped, down the pathway toward the Gazebo in the darkness.

You're on your own sister dear. It's been a long time since a man as interesting as this one has given me a second look. As rare as that is, it compels me to not pass up the chance to get to know him better.

* * * * *

Hitler looked up from the sheets of statistical reports he had been reading and smiled across his desk toward his young Kriegsmarine, U-boat liaison officer.

"Excellent! Excellent, finally some good news! That bloody Raeder does nothing but whine - at least Doenitz and his U-boats are making the British bleed. If he can keep this up he'll soon bring them to their knees."

The young, crisply-dressed U-boat officer nodded his agreement as Hitler looked up at him.

"If all my officers had taken up the torch of war with the determination demonstrated by your commander, we would have had a treaty with the English by now.

His eyes flickered over toward a subdued Goering who was standing near the window and who made no comment and then returned to his Kriegsmarine aide.

"Please extend my compliments to the Commodore. Tell him I am very pleased with the results of his efforts to date and that if these U-boat successes keep up, he may rest assured Germany will express its appreciation in a manner
befitting his energies in the defence of the Fatherland."

The aide snapped his heels together smartly and lifted his arm in a sharp salute.

"Ja wohl, mein Fuhrer!"

* * * * *

- Leaders -

The Count had a single, ringed lined pad and pen on the table in front of him. The first few pages had notations and he referred to them now.

"To begin I must explain why I am now acting contrary to my own security rules to speak to you gentlemen as a group.

I do this because it will save time since I will have to explain myself to you only once which I would have to do individually were I to follow the guidelines I have laid down as to meetings of members of our group. It will also allow for an initial exchange between all of us that I believe will be beneficial to all in attendance. I therefore encourage you to ask any questions of the others that may present themselves to you as we progress and I emphasize that this will be the last such meeting between us.

Having selected you gentlemen as our committee heads, I now intend to assign your specific departments but first let me explain why the good Baron and my two sons have joined us at this table.

My own responsibility in our joint venture will be that of planning, strategy and overall supervision.

My sons will find it necessary on occasion to act as my intermediaries; hence they will need to be in on the ground floor of our operation.

I will utilize the Baron, Doctor von Kliest as my council and to provide me with guidance on a day to day basis. As you are undoubtedly aware, the Baron is one of our leading scientists in the field of medicine. Perhaps you are not aware however, that he is the world acclaimed leader in the areas of eugenics and reproduction. As such he will play a central role in structuring the advances in this area that will serve to provide Germany with the racially pure, genetically-sound manpower of vastly superior intelligence and physical strength that will be necessary to meet the needs of a future Fatherland.

He works toward that goal now, but he shares the concerns of the men who have come together here this weekend, and while he labours toward accomplishing it, he realizes that its success will, of necessity, be a long term project.

He informs me that it will take at least twenty or thirty years to begin to produce the adult offspring and decades to reach the numbers that will make such a program fully effective.

He knows that his research is nearly completed and has a vision of what miracles it can produce.

His frustration lies in the knowledge that the results of that research cannot achieve success in the relatively short term that a war of attrition, both in the sense of manpower and materials, something that appears likely due to the threat of a two front struggle, will mean. Years cannot provide him with the timeframe he will require to capitalize on his research to the point where it can make a difference to Germany's future. It will take decades."

He leaned back in his chair and briefly removed his reading glasses, rubbing the bridge of his nose and them putting them back into place

"The Baron needs infrastructural support, gentlemen, and he needs time. Not months, not years but more than likely a generation.

Given that amount of time and financial and material support he tells me he now has the expertise to create for the Fatherland a master race, a race so superior in every way that the rest of the world will bow to it in awe. If he can do that, and I believe he can, Germany will be a world leader in every sense and it will have cost not one droplet of German blood."

He looked from man to man.

"Operation Fatherland's sole job will be to provide him with the sustenance he requires to accomplish that goal and you gentlemen will be the corner posts of that operation."

There was a firm rap at the door and the count nodded to Wilhelm and then the door. Wilhelm stood and crossed to open it. The butler stood holding a large silver tray bearing a sweating champagne bucket containing a single large dusty bottle.

"I'm following the Count's instructions, young master."

Wilhelm recognized the magnum for what it was and took it gingerly from the tray in both hands.

He allowed the butler, tray now under one arm, to look after closing the door and as he turned back to face the others his father smiled.

"Ah yes, I had forgotten - a very special vintage, gentlemen.

Let us pause in our labours and take time to celebrate our wonderful new challenge and to give this bottle the attention it deserves by using its contents to toast the Fatherland and then we can proceed."

CHAPTER FORTY-FOUR

- Norway -

On April fifth, nineteen-forty France and the United Kingdom officially notified Norway of their right to deny German access to Norwegian resources.

A day later the Norwegian Government sent a report to the British Admiralty indicating that ten German destroyers had sailed for Narvik.

On the seventh of April Royal Air Force reconnaissance planes reported that there was an increase in movement by parts of the German Fleet. The British Home fleet, joined by the Second Cruiser Squadron, shifted position in order to patrol further northward.

On the morning of April eighth, nineteen-forty the British destroyer *Glowworm* was steaming in heavy fog on her way to rejoin the battle cruiser *Renown* when she came across two German destroyers, the *Bernd von Arnim* and the *Hans Ludemann*.

The two destroyers were part of the German *Weseruebung* operation naval force transporting troops destined for Trondheim and led by the heavy cruiser *Admiral Hipper*.

The German destroyers tried to break off the engagement and signalled the force leader for assistance.

The *Hipper* quickly responded to the request and arrived on the scene within minutes but initially had difficulty in distinguishing between the *Glowworm* and the von *Arnim* in the heavy fog.

Upon reaching certainty of the *Glowworm's* identity, the *Admiral Hipper* opened up on the destroyer with salvos from her full accompaniment of eight inch main guns.

The fourth salvo struck pay dirt and the *Glowworm*, finding herself definitely outgunned began to make smoke in an attempt to break off from the heavy cruiser.

The modern German warship carried radar-directed armament and the smoke that now shrouded the destroyer was of no deterrent. The *Hipper*, steaming at high speed, had by this point reduced the distance between the antagonists and her four-point-one inch guns could now be brought into action.

Considerable damage on the Glowworm resulted, during which time the destroyer had managed to fire five torpedoes at the heavy cruiser. *Hipper's* Captain had held to a bow-on attack against the destroyer in order to offer the smallest target for a torpedo attack and all five fired torpedoes missed.

The heavily damaged *Glowworm* dropped back into her own smokescreen in an attempt to bring her remaining torpedo tubes into action for a second launch. The much larger *Admiral Hipper* bore straight into the smoke and when in sight of the destroyer turned to ram her. The distance between the two ships was too short to allow the *Hipper* the time to come round to a position where she could use her bow to cleave the destroyer and the resulting collision between the two ships came about as the bow of the *Glowworm* struck the cruiser just abaft the port anchor throwing a German sailor overboard.

During the collision the bow of the *Glowworm* broke off before the remainder of the destroyer raked the side of the cruiser ripping several holes in her hull and taking out the forward torpedo mounting.

The Admiral Hipper took on considerable water as a result but the leaks were soon isolated and no mortal damage resulted. The destroyer now engulfed by fire drifted off and a short time later her boilers exploded and she slipped below the waves. The German heavy cruiser stopped her engines to take on survivors.

The German sailor lost overboard during the collision was not found but several of the British ship's complement were taken aboard.

Later on the morning of April eighth the *MS Rio de Janeiro,* which had been requisitioned to transport troops and equipment to Bergen was spotted off the picturesque seaside village of Lillesand, Norway by a Polish submarine.

On board were three hundred and thirty solders, six two- cm. Flak thirty, four ten point-five Flak thirty-eight anti-aircraft guns, seventy-three horses, seventy-one vehicles and two hundred and ninety tons of provisions made up of feed, fuel and ammunition,

The ship was scheduled to arrive at Bergen shortly after the occupying troop landings there had been completed.

The Polish sub *ORP Orzel*, operating under British command, signalled for the ship to stop and it acquiesced. The Polish submarine Captain then signalled ordering that the ship's papers be brought over to the sub and that the ship be surrendered or it would be sunk. There was no response and the ship was subsequently hit by a single torpedo and began to take on water.

At noon a Royal Norwegian Naval aircraft arrived on the scene and began to circle. The Polish submarine fired a second torpedo and this struck the ammunition on board which caused an explosion. The ship sank. Approximately one hundred and eighty men survived and were rescued by local Norwegian vessels.

Denmark was successfully occupied on April ninth. The Norwegians were ill prepared for an invasion based on the Nazi *Blitzkrieg* model.

The German ten thousand man initial force which participated in the attack was not particularly large by military standards.

However, the achievement of complete surprise in the method of attack coupled with the smooth delivery of all the committed forces by sea and air in a single coordinated and synchronized blow proved to be extremely effective.

Seaborne troops occupied the primary ports along the Norwegian coast from Oslo to Narvik. Paratroops, the first ever deployed, quickly took the airfields located at Stavanger and the Norwegian Capital of Oslo. A Luftwaffe commitment of eight hundred aircraft easily mastered the country's airspace.

A solid foothold was quickly achieved in the key military and population centers: Kristiansand, Stavanger, Narvik, Bergen and Trondheim.

There had been strong resistance against the seaborne troops which had been transported to Oslo by the German cruiser Blucher, which had been subsequently sunk by shore batteries in the area of *Oslofjord* shortly after having disgorged the troops.

This resistance was overcome upon the arrival of the bulk of the paratroops, who had secured the airport, as they moved from the airfield and into the city,

A German force, specifically assigned to capturing the Royal family and the Norwegian Government at *Midtskogen*, failed in its task due to the efforts of a ragtag group of committed defenders.

On April tenth five British destroyers entered Ofotfjord (Narvik Fjord) to find that ten German destroyers awaited them. An immediate battle broke out between the opposing sides and each lost two ships before the British retired.

The German cruiser *Konigsberg* lying off Bergen was attacked by aircraft and sunk. The Norwegian Government fled the capital of *Oslo*. Vidkun Quisling stepped into the void, declaring himself the head of a replacement Norwegian government.

On April twelfth *Konigsberg* surrendered to German forces without a fight.

On the thirteenth of April the British battleship *Warspite* with an accompanying screen of nine British destroyers sailed into *Narvik* to deal with the remaining complement of eight German destroyers and handily destroyed them.

April fourteenth brought a landing of British troops at *Namsos* and *Harstad* and a joint British/French force was prepared for landings at *Trondheim* and *Narvik*. German paratroops dropped on *Dombas* and successfully blocked the rail and road networks in southern Norway. They managed to hold their position for five days before surrendering to Norwegian troops. Quisling was forced out of power on the fifteenth and the British

Guards Brigade landed at *Harstad* on the fifteenth of April.

On the sixteenth the British landed at *Namsos,* and the next day at *Andalsnes.* On the eighteenth further British troops landed at *Andalsnes* and the French at *Namsos.*

German forces kicked the British out of *Steinkjer* on the nineteenth and on the twentieth German air raids destroyed the *Namsos* harbour to prevent further landings while German forces moved north out of *Oslo* to *Lillehammer* and took the town the next day before moving northward to challenge the British forces.

On the twenty-second the British landed more troops at *Andalsnes,* in the hopes of supporting the troops north of *Lillehammer,* who were now under superior German attack.

By the twenty-fourth of April the German forces in *Narvik* were besieged and further landings were planned to force their surrender.

Despite the reinforcements provided for the British fighting north of *Lillehammer* the Germans forced them to retreat on the twenty-fifth and Norwegian forces began to attack the Germans bottled up at *Narvik.*

The tide had definitely turned in favour of the Germans and they began to push hard. The Allies decided to withdraw their forces from *Namsos* and *Andalsnes* on the twenty-seventh and abandon their effort against the German forces at *Trondheim.*

French troops arrived at *Harstad* on the twenty-eighth.

The Norwegian Royal family, with their government, evacuated to *Tromso.*

The German forces coming up from the south linked up with the *Trondheim* troops

On April thirtieth the Allies began to evacuate their troops from *Andalsnes* and completed the withdrawal on May first. The next day the German forces entered to take that city while the allies evacuated *Namsos* and landed a joint French/British force at *Mosjoen* to block the steady German advance toward *Narvik.*

German dive-bomber's attacked the evacuation force, sinking

the French destroyer *Bison* and the British destroyer *Afridi* on May third.

CHAPTER FORTY-FIVE

- Family -

Ursula paused in the hallway just before the door to her apartment. She was flushed and a little light-headed. She leaned back against the coolness of the wall as she lifted her right hand to her mouth and touched the back of it with her lips precisely where it had been kissed only moments ago.

A gentleman to boot!

She wouldn't have invited him into her bed, but she had been prepared to accept a kiss to cap the evening. She had in fact been hoping for such an outcome. Instead he'd met her eyes and held them as he took her hand and raised it to touch his full lips, before bowing gracefully and bidding her a good night.

It had been brief, but it had left her breathless and although she felt like she was probably reacting like a lovesick schoolgirl experiencing her first crush, it left a promise of something more and she was very much looking forward to their next meeting.

The sound of approaching footsteps drew her out of her reverie and she pushed off the wall and quickly reached for the handle to the door leading into her apartment. She opened it and was about to enter when she heard her mother's voice.

"Ursula dear, I'm glad I caught you. I've just been to Gabriella's rooms to say goodnight. I rapped but got no answer. Have you seen her? And what exactly did you mean earlier by your comment about Gabriella not being offered a ring?"

What the hell…why not just tell her and get it over with?

Yes Mother, you'll find her down at the Gazebo performing God-only-knows-what number of sexually, acrobatic contortions with not one but two young men, which is why I think it highly unlikely that either one of them would be the slightest bit interested in offering her a ring!

Ya right...her mother would turn apoplectic instantly.

Ursula bit her tongue and closed her eyes tightly for a second, clearing her mind, divesting herself of the temptation.

Well at least I know how to take her mind off Gabriella and stave off any further enquiries - at least until the threesome has worn itself out and called it quits for the night.

She took a deep breath and straightened her back before turning to face her mother.

"No Mother, I don't but I'm glad you're here. That young Luftwaffe pilot I met at the pool this afternoon..."

Her mother's troubled features cleared instantly as though wiped from her face by an invisible hand and she began to smile.

"Yes dear, isn't he a treasure. Now he's one of the ones I was telling you and Gabriella about, you remember. I know his mother and well quite frankly he's quite a catch. Why I..."

Ursula cut her off.

"Yes that's the one I mean, Mother I would really like to learn all I can about him. Would you mind stepping in and enlightening me, or are you too tired?'

Her mother was already inside the room and pushing the door closed behind her,

"Well I am tired dear, but under the circumstances..."

* * * * *

- Western Front –

On May tenth, nineteen-forty Hitler launched Operation Fall Gelb (Case Yellow) the German attack against the Lowland Countries and France in the west.

The unprovoked military occupation of Belgium, Holland and Luxembourg followed that of Denmark and Norway in rapid succession.

The Allies continued to support the Norwegian forces for the remainder of the month of May but they quickly began to realize that they were fighting a losing battle and now that they were facing the ferocity of Hitler's unleashing of the *Blitzkrieg* of *Gelb* they had neither the forces nor the stomach to consider any further involvement in Scandinavia.

On June first, nineteen-forty, France and the United Kingdom informed Norway of their plans to evacuate their troops from the country.

This was accomplished by June eighth at no small military cost to the allies.

Abandoned, the government of Norway instructed its forces to demobilize on June ninth and the surrender of Norway to the Nazis was completed on June tenth, nineteen forty.

* * * * *

- Chain of Command –

The Champagne bottle was empty.

The Count picked up his notes and began to speak again.

"I have broken your committees down into the following categories and have selected with care, considering both your areas of expertise and current military assignments where applicable.

The first of these will be finance. For this important post I have selected the only civilian member of our group."

He raised his eyes and nodded across the table to the Baron Friedriech von Bauer.

"While we will be primarily financed through funds I control in my current position as head of scientific and military research and development within the Reich, there is an additional source of funds that may well present itself due to our subjugation of populations in the areas we have recently conquered militarily.

Further to those resources, the Baron and his peers in industry have been good enough to advise me that they will make unlimited funds available to us in the event such a need should arise. It will be in his hands to see that our efforts are adequately financed both now and into the future. He will choose the remaining members of his committee"

The SS General sitting to the Baron's left, the only man in the study who was not of aristocratic birth, turned to face him.

"How much money are we talking about?"

The Baron took the time to light his cigar before responding in a flat, matter of fact voice.

"In my vocabulary the word 'unlimited' has only one meaning, Herr General."

The General arched his eyebrows and Count von Stauffer smiled.

"Are there any further questions on our financial situation, gentlemen?"

There were no takers and the Count continued.

"SS-General Dieter Bichler will be responsible for the committee holding the dual responsibility for security and recruitment. He will also work in conjunction with Friedriech with regard to ensuring our ability to gain access to certain valuables that will come our way as a result of Germany's military conquests to date.

For those of you who may be unaware, Dieter is currently in a position where he holds authority within the Reich in regard to the seizure of such articles from our newly subjugated lands and their removal to the Reich for safekeeping."

One of the Wehrmacht General's brows furrowed but when the man made no comment, the Count moved on.

"The transport committee will be headed by our Luftwaffe comrade, Major General Gunter von Schmidt. He informs me that his current appointment gives him access to transport to allow for the movement of anything located within the new Reich territories."

The Count raised his eyes from his notes, inviting questions but there were none.

"General Gerhardt von Konig will chair supply and Colonel Helmut von Brunner, procurement.

All of you will report to me on an as needed basis and you will receive instruction, requests and advisements from me as your assistance is required to meet one of our operation's needs.

Each of you will be individually accountable for the actions of your committee members and all operations originated by your committee."

He glanced up and let his gaze move around the table, inviting questions and, finding none, turned back to his notes.

"You may at any time address any specific concerns you have directly to the committee chair who leads that area of expertise. For example, if General von Konig needs transport arranged he would simply contact Major General von Schmidt to make such arrangements. You may feel free however to advise me with regard to any situation about which you are unsure.

Any concerns of a security nature are to be immediately referred to General Bichler for remedial action on his part, and General Bichler will be the final authority in any case of a security breach.

I urge you to keep your communications secure. There is to be nothing between you in writing under any circumstances and nothing said that isn't on a face to face basis under secure circumstances.

It goes without saying that you will not share any information on our operation with anyone who has not been previously vetted, and that is to include immediate family. We are playing a high stakes game here. None of us should forget that, not even for a moment.

Are there any questions gentlemen?"

He glanced around the table and smiled. When no one responded the set of his shoulders softened for the first time since the group had entered the room.

"Good and now having finished our business for today we can allow ourselves the luxury of considering tomorrow as a day of rest. The only exception will be brief individual meetings for each of you to take place between myself and my aides to allow for a free exchange of ideas relating to your specific fields of expertise. I have set a simple agenda for each of these meeting and they will be scheduled tomorrow based on your individual times of departure. One of my sons will advise you of the specific times at breakfast.

Now, I suggest that we all find our beds as it is not long to dawn. Monday morning will see the launch of 'Operation Fatherland' and all our workloads will suddenly be increased immeasurably. "

He stood, clicked his heels and saluted.

"Gentlemen, today we have set the cornerstone for a fallback plan to ensure a positive long-term future for Germany in the catastrophic event that we should lose our current struggle - Heil Hitler!"

CHAPTER FORTY-SIX

- A Long Day -

At least temporarily satiated, Gabriella was the last member of her family to climb into her bed on Sunday morning.

It was minutes before five, and the fading night sky was showing the first signs of the coming dawn in the east.

* * * * *

- Berlin -

German Foreign Minister Joachim von Ribbentrop was meeting with his Spanish counterpart Ramon Serrano Suner who was in Berlin for the purpose of further discussions on Spain's entry into the war and Hitler's proposed attack on the British naval base at Gibraltar.

Attempts to arrange the Spanish cooperation Hitler had counted on for the invasion of the island had been going on for some time and getting the Spanish nailed down was proving to be difficult.

Franco was a very cautious man and was unwilling to commit himself to taking sides in the war unless he could see definite and specific advantages for Spain.

To date, to Hitler's frustration, the Spanish dictator had effectively sat on the fence, claiming to be 'neutral' in the conflict.

The previous day's round of meetings between the two men at the Reich Chancellery had left the Spanish Minister unsettled and uncomfortable.

He sensed that von Ribbentrop's superior and condescending attitude, which had been clearly demonstrated during those meetings, bespoke of Hitler's growing impatience with Franco's hesitation to commit and he approached the evening meeting with no small sense of trepidation.

It therefore came as somewhat of pleasant surprise to find that they were to be joined by The Fuhrer himself and that upon his arrival Adolf Hitler seemed to bend over backwards to extend an aura of warmth and politeness to him.

Buoyed by this unanticipated reception Suner was quick to confide to The Fuhrer that he greeted the Nazi leader not only in his capacity as Spain's Foreign Minister but also as the personal agent of General Franco.

Hitler, well briefed before the meeting, was thoroughly aware of Suner's background particulars. He knew that the Minister was married to the sister of Franco's wife and did indeed have Franco's ear. Some time ago however, Hitler had also reached the conclusion that dealing with any intermediary at this point would not bring about the commitment from Spain that he required.

He listened politely as the Minister's prepared speech, which when paraphrased simply repeated the line that Spain had been taking all though the talks so far, had rolled forward off the politician's silver tongue.

Spain would join Germany in the war when it had recovered from its own civil war. It would however, have to become self-sufficient in foodstuffs and war material before it could seriously consider the matter.

Hitler ignored the statement completely and began to patiently explain to Suner that Europe had to be organized into a single political unit and that Africa would then become a protectorate of that body.

Spain would have to become part of that unified body and she would have to play her part in the taking of Gibraltar.

Suner demurred, saying that the taking of the island naval base couldn't be accomplished without artillery and Spain would need the big guns before taking part.

Hitler waved a hand in dismissal of the comment and swept

into a lecture clarifying to the Spaniard that nothing could be further from the truth.

He ended by stating unequivocally that his Stuka dive-bombers would do the job, and Spain would have no need of Artillery.

Suner left the meeting feeling both impressed by Hitler and uplifted in spirit.

He did in fact have his brother-in-law's ear and he was well aware that Franco had been impressed by the Nazi's short and effective defeat of the French in June and that his master had taken notice of the fact that Italy, under Mussolini, had, in hopes of being on the winning side of the conflict and thereby benefitting from any resulting peace treaty, promptly declared war against France and her allies as a result of that military success.

The result of Germany's whirlwind success against France and the Lowland Countries was impressive and Franco's political stripe certainly biased any decision he might be expected to make toward the fascist side of the coin, but the Spanish dictator was still unsure of what the future might bring.

The failure of Germany to manage to take the next obvious step to remove Britain and a potential second front from the equation weighed heavily upon him.

At the end of their conference in the chancellery Hitler had suggested to Suner that a meeting should be held between the two leaders in the near future to discuss the matter on the highest level.

Hitler wrote directly to Franco the next morning reiterating and driving home his vision of the future of an alliance between Germany and Spain.

He painted a picture of a swift victory at Gibraltar and a resulting German-guaranteed rosy future for the Spanish and emphasizing the sharing of prominence with Spain on the world stage and of the vast spoils, both in territory and riches such a conquest would bring about.

* * * * *

– Meetings –

Staff, under the watchful eyes of the butler and housekeeper, provided two breakfasts for the weekend guests on Sunday morning.

The first, held at seven and laid out in the morning room was, as had been anticipated, lightly attended but the second at nine, kept the servers hopping.

All family members of the household attended the second seating with the exception of Gabriella, who slept through both.

Having broken his fast, the Count retired to his study where he, the Baron von Kliest and his sons met in turn with the five newly appointed committee heads.

The Count had arranged for these separate conferences with the primary intent of allowing his boys the chance to ask questions of these powerful men and gain a basic understanding of what 'Operation Fatherland' was designed to achieve.

He was not surprised to find Eric's interjections, in view of the rank and position of the individual men in attendance, to be few and well thought out, nor to find his younger son Wilhelm's, who had always been less in awe of those holding high position, to be of a frequent and pragmatic nature.

At these meetings the Count offered each of the committee leaders a place on his private railcars which would be leaving shortly after noon for the return trip to Berlin.

All readily took him up on the offer despite the fact that two of them had arrived in their official staff cars and had originally intended to return to Berlin by road.

* * * * *

– Return to Berlin –

By the time the party of men descended by elevator to the lower sub-basement, a small switching engine had already attached itself to the two cars and hauled them out of their shelter below the castle. They stood in readiness to return them to the marshalling yards and a Berlin bound train scheduled to leave within the hour.

Their number was such that the bedroom car would be filled by guests and Eric and Wilhelm would be sharing the servant's quarters in the Count's main car for the duration of the trip.

His military aide was to be billeted separately in a compartment on the passenger train which had been designated to haul them north once they'd reached the marshalling yard at Bahnhof Friedrichshafen.

The short trip down the private spur and onto the main line went without a hitch and after twenty minutes the Count's two railcars were being coupled to the rear of a passenger express train destined for Berlin with a caboose added behind them.

The yards were even more congested than they had been on their arrival early Saturday morning freight cars lined up as far as the eye could see.

Many of the awaiting flatcars held vehicles similar to those they had seen heading northward as the train pulling the Count's cars had been sidetracked, in order to allow the passage for northbound freights, when they had earlier made their way south from Berlin. These flatcars carried chained down battle-worn and soiled Panzers III's (tanks) and halftracks.

Almost as many of the remaining tracks were crammed with yet more flatcars, these loaded with row upon row of identical heavy wooden boxes.

As the Count's party settled into the comfortably-upholstered armchairs provided in the observation lounge area at the rear of the train the Count nodded out the window toward the closest of these box-loaded flatcars and said to no one in particular.

"Gears manufactured here in Friedrichshafen at ZF gear factory. They're headed for the 'Krupp - Gruson Werk' in

Magdeburg."

Wehrmacht General Helmut von Brunner nodded in agreement.

"Yes, part of the upgrade for the new Panzer Mark 'IV - E.'"

Wilhelm stared out at the seemingly endless line of flatcars and shook his head.

"That's an awful pile of gears…"

Von Brunner nodded.

"Yes and we're going to need them all and more I'm sure. The new Panzer IV - E is the fifth production model of the 'IV' medium tank. Among other things the upgrades over the 'D' version bring better armour. It will have fifty millimetres of bow armour plate and thirty millimetre steel plates added to sides and front of the superstructure. The tank crews will certainly appreciate the extra protection, as I'm sure they will the new seven point five centimetre 'KWK .40' main armament.

Perhaps now when they run up against a British Matilda tank, as they did in France, they will be able to pierce the enemy's armour and put them out of action rather than having to watch in frustration as their shells bounce off."

A whistle sounded then moments later the car lurched and they began to move out of the station as they switched track and pulled into the wake of a long twin-engine military train of loaded flatcars trailing a manned and sandbagged flack gun platform.

CHAPTER FORTY-SEVEN

- The Spanish Civil War –

Despite his decision to only postpone Operation Sea Lion, the plan for the invasion of the British Isles, rather than cancelling it outright, Hitler still had to deal with the possible threat of having to face a two-front war.

Having concluded that the invasion was impractical if not impossible at this point in time due to the lack of both the required naval and air supremacy in and above the English Channel, he now determined that his only avenue toward accomplishing this would be through the determined application of a combination of military pressure and diplomacy.

Despite several previous rebuffed attempts at bringing the English to the treaty table, The Fuhrer still fervently harboured a sincere hope that he could succeed in his attempts to convince the British to join him in the fight against bolshevism, even if only as a silent partner.

Unable to invade England with his military due to a lack of air and sea superiority, Hitler began to form plans to force them to the table by other means. In addition to diplomacy he had several military options he could use to bring England to her knees and force her to settle for his terms.

On the diplomatic side of the coin he saw what he was offering the English as an honourable peace. It included agreement to a non-occupation by German troops and relative independence for the British Isles, but a change in foreign policy that would definitely meet Germany's needs, terms he considered exceedingly generous to them under the circumstances.

He felt he could pressure the English from a military point of view in a number of ways. Germany would continue to bomb

London. The massive naval base at Gibraltar would have to be taken. This would prevent the British Navy from operating in the Mediterranean which would assure Germany a successful assault against North Africa and the Mideast and stretch the shipping lines between England and her Far East holdings to the point of making them un-defendable in a naval sense.

He would use his U-boat fleet and the Luftwaffe to cut the English supply line from America and Canada via the Atlantic Ocean and effectively put the British Isles under siege, isolating and starving them into submission.

In the interim he would use the Luftwaffe to terrorize the city of London, thereby breaking the spirit of the average British citizen with the aim of encouraging them to force their government to sue for peace.

Hitler needed the assistance of newly Fascist Spain under General Franco in order to carry out his plan to remove Gibraltar from British control. He felt confident that such support would be forthcoming should he ask for it.

There was good reason for him to expect this. Over several years Hitler had carefully groomed his relationship with Franco. He had done this for several reasons.

On a political level he was strongly interested in seeing the establishment of another right of center, dictatorial, authoritarian regime on the border of France.

The Fuhrer was planning to go to war and he needed all the allies he could get.

By supporting Franco in the Spanish civil war Germany would be provided with a platform to safely test the effectiveness of its military forces, in particular the fledgling Luftwaffe and that could be done on foreign soil and with relative diplomatic impunity.

The Spanish Civil War commenced on July of nineteen thirty-six. The insurgents, led primarily by military officers, attempted a coup which failed but left them in control of approximately thirty-five percent of the country.

General Franco, a Spanish military officer who was sympathetic to the rebel cause, was at this time in charge of the Spanish Moroccan Colonial Forces which were based in Spain's colony in northern Morocco. He commanded the only effectual military armed forces available to Spain and these, if made available to the rebels, could turn the tide in their favour.

Unfortunately for the Rebels and Franco the Spanish Navy had remained loyal to the Spanish Republican government and as a result Franco had no means available to him to rapidly facilitate the movement of the troops from Morocco to mainland Spain.

Franco had turned to Adolf Hitler for help.

He sent an urgent request to the Germans requesting air transport for his troops to assist him in getting them across the Strait of Gibraltar.

In acquiescing to this request Hitler reached his first overtly military decision since taking power.

The Spanish Civil War lasted for three years during which Soviet Russia supported the Republic with aid, advisors and weaponry. Support for the rebels, both military and financial, flowed from Germany and their fascist ally Italy throughout their triumphant campaign.

Units of the German Luftwaffe took an active part in the fighting and quickly proved their worth.

This was personified in the nineteen thirty-seven terror bombing of the Spanish city of Guernica which they left a flattened, smouldering wasteland.

In April of nineteen thirty-nine the rebels under the Franco controlled Falange party's leadership proved to be successful in the civil conflict and subsequently took over the government of Spain.

The depth and effectiveness of the Nazi's participation in aiding the rebels resulted in German military units being provided superior positioning during Franco's victory parade through Madrid in the summer of thirty-nine.

To Hitler's way of thinking, Franco owed him big time and

he believed he had every reason to expect solid support from the Fascist leader in his future plans to negate the British Naval presence in Gibraltar.

Air attacks on London would be maintained, if with reduced eagerness on the part of the officers in charge of the operation and lessened enthusiasm on the part of many German pilots. The bombing of London had continued daily since September nineteenth, nineteen-forty.

On the twenty-first of September the British Government officially ordered citizens to make use of the London underground system as air raid shelters.

In the crucial aircraft numbers game the Luftwaffe was not doing well, losing about twice as many planes as the British defenders.

Outwardly Hitler appeared to have completely lost interest in Operation Sea Lion, the planned invasion of England by one hundred and sixty thousand German soldiers. There was not even the slightest hint from him that he might be reconsidering his recent decision to postpone the invasion indefinitely.

* * * * *

- Kaiser Wilhelm Institute -

In view of the recent unseasonable high temperatures in Berlin, the windows running the length of the two outside walls of the Count's corner office at the Kaiser Wilhelm Institute were open to take advantage of the prevailing soft breeze.

There were four men in the room seated in comfortable thickly-upholstered, leather-covered chairs.

The chairs were arranged around a circular boardroom table that sat in the corner of the large room, situated to one side of the doorway which led in from his secretary's office.

Despite the open windows which allowed a cross flow of gently moving air, the four officers had removed their tunics and were working in shirtsleeves.

The Count, a notepad and pen in front of him, was speaking. Dr., the Baron von Kliest and the Count's two sons were listening attentively. At the Count's instructions the inlaid leather table in front of each of them was empty of writing implements.

A sweating glass of ice water stood on a thick coaster before each man with a freshly filled insulated pitcher ready to provide refills resting on a tray in the centre of the table.

"...and I think we have reached a consensus as to which parts each of us will play in the day to day administration of Operation Fatherland."

He raised his head and glanced around the table before continuing.

"Let me reiterate then and if you have any comments or changes to suggest, feel free to express them. Eric, who is assigned full time to my staff, will act as my aide in terms of the day to day operation of our endeavours.

Wilhelm, who has been assigned by the Reichsfuhrer SS as his representative on my staff will as one of his duties, carry out that responsibility but he will do so in a reciprocal manner.

He will ensure that Himmler is kept abreast of our accomplishments here at the institute in all fields with the exception of matters relating to Operation Fatherland, which the Fuhrer has determined, are for his ears only.

He will also act as our eyes and ears in relation to the activities of the Reichsfuhrer with regard to anything the SS may be undertaking that might in any way negatively affect Operation Fatherland.

Heinrich will provide the rest of us with progress reports on his developments of the eugenics program, which we recognize as the primary tool needed to successfully reach our long-term goals, that being the creation of a world dominating Aryan populated future German nation. Are we all in agreement?"

Nods from the other three were returned by the Count.

"Wilhelm, you indicated earlier that the SS-Reichsfuhrer had suggested that your other duties would mean that you would be involved in both the SS Eugenics and 'Lebensborn' (Fountain of Life) programs. Are you yet aware of what part you are to play in these and how much of your time they will take?

Wilhelm exhaled and placed his cigarillo into the ashtray in front of him before responding.

"Herr Himmler has instructed me to get up to speed on both. It would appear that with regard to eugenics, I will be spending a fair amount of time in the company of the good doctor here..."

He turned to smile at the Baron.

"...he, being the German expert in the field. My duties will be to keep the Reichsfuhrer up to date on all progress in the field."

The Count smiled.

"I guess that is to be expected. After all, the entire financing for this particular research is currently funded by the SS. I see no conflict here, providing that no part of our specific plans for Operation Fatherland's intended extraneous use of that scientific research is revealed to those other than the Fuhrer. I myself will provide that information. It will be for his ears only."

Wilhelm nodded in understanding.

"Yes of course, Father. Now in relation to the Lebensborn program, my duties will apparently be in the form of assisting in the administration of the entire program."

He flushed slightly.

"I am also to be used as the subject of posters promoting the programme, so you will all have to get used to seeing my brooding, heroic Aryan features peering out at you from every lamp standard in the near future I'm afraid."

Eric turned to face his brother and grinned.

"Taking an active part in the programme then, are you Wilhelm - a major part of the fountain of youth."

Spontaneous laughter filled the large room and the sound of shifting chairs and the flick of lighters soon followed as the Count stood and stretched.

* * * * *

- Security Breach -

The Count and his two sons, who had all taken up residence in the family mansion in Berlin upon their new assignments, bade the Baron good evening in the parking area outside the institute and then entered the Count's awaiting staff car.

The driver was given instructions to take them to the Bahnhof where they were to meet and pick up the Countess who had remained behind at Lake Constance to close up the castle for the season.

She would be arriving by train shortly.

The car was about to move when a horn sounded from the rear and a second vehicle pulled around to draw up beside the Count's.

The closed sedan sporting SS number plates stopped and the driver leapt out to open the far rear door.

SS-General Dieter Bichler exited the back seat and approached the rear of the Count's glistening black, open Mercedes 770 series II 150. He smiled at the occupants and then clicked his heels and bowed slightly.

"Count von Stauffer, I'm glad I was able to catch you before you left. Might I have a word in private please?"

The Count met his driver's inquisitive gaze and nodded in the affirmative.

The uniformed chauffer swivelled his head back to the front and shut the powerful motor off. He started to get out with the intention of opening the door for the Count but the General imperiously waved him back into his seat and opened the Count's door himself.

Leaving the door open, the two men walked a short distance away to a spot where they could not be overhead. Dieter got straight to the point.

"We've had a slight incident Karl…"

The Count opened his mouth to speak but the General raised a hand and continued.

"Nothing to worry about. I've taken care of the matter but I thought you should be made aware."

The Count nodded and Dieter continued.

"It seems that two of the junior officers who were in attendance at the initial conference at the lake and drove back to Berlin by staff car felt it necessary to discuss our business in a general sense over a few steins at a roadside inn on the trip back. They were overheard by one of my people who happened to be sitting at a nearby table. No damage was done and the situation has been dealt with."

The Count frowned and shook his head.

"Not even twenty-four hours after being told, my God! Thank you Dieter, I knew I had the right man for the job when I chose you. Thank you for setting them straight."

The SS-General smiled, his deep blue eyes glittering coldly.

"Actually Karl I didn't bother wasting my breath. You will no doubt hear about the dreadful accident - too much drink - over a cliff I'm afraid - no survivors. I will see to it that all those present at the lake for our meeting learn of their fate. I believe such news will go a long way toward preventing any future gaffs of this nature."

His heels met sharply and he raised his hand in salute.

"Heil Hitler, and please, convey my regards to the Countess and your lovely daughter Ursula when you meet their train."

The Count's driver was holding the door when Karl stepped back to the Mercedes and climbed in. His father's face was drained of colour and Eric took note.

"Are you all right Father, bad news was it?"

The Count managed a forced smile as he sat down and shook his head.

"It was nothing of major consequence - just an unfortunate accident apparently."

My God, I'm already lying to my family. How many secrets will I have to keep locked away in the dark dungeons of my mind before this is over?

And how did the General know about his wife's arrival by train? More disquieting, Bichler had indicated he knew something I did not. Why would Ursula be accompanying her mother? To the best of his knowledge she had intended to return to Berlin by car with Gabriella. Did the SS know more about his intimate family affairs than he did?

He nodded to his driver and the open staff car pulled away from the curb and headed for the train station.

CHAPTER FORTY-EIGHT

– Problem Child –

The driver of the Count's massive, black Mercedes 770 series II W 150 cabriolet staff car, which bore SS plates and fender runes, did not need to concern himself with the vehicular congestion in front of the Anhalter Bahnhof in Berlin, the largest train station in Europe.

He wheeled the big black vehicle into one of the restricted VIP parking spots that fronted directly on the main entranceway, pulling up behind a closed Luftwaffe-plated sedan.

The thick ant-like pedestrian traffic, much of it in uniform, making use of the main entrance, entered and left beneath an impressive façade festooned with long, red, hanging banners emblazoned with black swastikas, circled in white.

Busy but disciplined, this flow of humanity gave little real indication of the frantic activity involving the arriving and departing passenger trains and the ever-growing number of military trains that were shunting and forming up in the huge marshalling yards behind the massive building.

As the driver opened the rear door the Count spoke to his sons.

"You two go on in and meet your mother, and apparently Ursula.

I'll send the driver in to help with the luggage after he lowers the jump seats.

The two of you will have to use them on the way homeif your sister is, as I have been advised, traveling with your mother.

Ursula and the Countess joined Karl on the spacious rear seat of the staff car and their luggage was spread between the passenger seat beside the driver and between them and the two boys who rode in the two jump seats between the passenger compartment of the big Mercedes and the driver.

The Count greeted them and as he waited for the driver to close the doors and return to the front seat he mused on Ursula's presence.

Obviously the SS did know more about his family's activities than he did. General Bichler had been correct in his suggestion that Ursula would be accompanying her mother.

It was a small thing to be sure, but it gave him pause and served to cause him to reconsider his earlier assessment of what steps would have to be taken to guarantee his family's safety in relation to the activities of 'Operation Fatherland'.

In those few seconds he made the decision to take time to re-evaluate any future action he initiated with a view to weighing what steps they would require to ensure that those he loved were insulated from any repercussions which might result.

That done he turned to address the two women.

"I thought you would be returning with your sister, Ursula?"

The Countess responded.

"It's Gabriella's driving dear. Poor Ursula had enough on the way down to the Lake and didn't have the stomach for the return trip."

Ursula, who had indeed used that very excuse for accompanying her mother, knew full well that what had been a sufficient excuse for her mother would not be adequate for her father.

She watched him carefully after her mother had spoken and reading his expression decided that she had better come clean. "Well that and the fact that she managed to find what she obviously considered a better companion for the trip back and asked if I would mind returning with Mother."

The Countess Erika arched her brows and spoke in a flat tone once she had turned to face her daughter.

"Well really Ursula, and who might that be?"

Ursula frowned and shrugged her shoulders.

"It was one of the young officers who came down for the weekend."

The frown slipped from the Countess's face to be replaced with a quizzical expression.'

"Without a chaperone - not very sensible I must say!"

Ursula let out a sigh and shrugged her shoulders.

"Well she is twenty-one years old Mother, and this is nineteen thirty-nine, after all.

Besides her car is only a two-seater. Where do you suggest we could have put the chaperone - in the trunk?"

The Countess straightened her shoulders and settled back into the comfortably-padded leather seat. Her face coloured slightly and she pursed her lips briefly before responding.

"Don't be flippant, Ursula. You know exactly what I mean. Why wasn't I consulted about this?"

Ursula sensed she'd gone too far and attempted to placate her mother.

"It was all rather last minute Mother…I only knew about it when she was about to leave.

There really wasn't any discussion or any time to have a discussion for that matter, kind of spur of the moment I'm afraid, and you were busy with the staff at the time."

Somewhat pacified but definitely not happy, the Countess snapped back.

"Well, I blame you dear. You know full well that Gabriella has difficulty making proper decisions about this kind of thing. It was very inconsiderate of you …"

Karl saw the flush start at the base of his daughter's neck and begin to work its way upward.

He did not support his wife's view that Ursula should, at this point in their lives, be held solely responsible for her younger sister's actions.

It was time for him to step in before a full blown argument erupted.

He cut his wife off in mid speech.

"Who is this young officer? What do we know of him?"

Ursula recognized that her father was attempting to diffuse the situation and bit her tongue. She gave the Count an appreciative look and used her quick mind to shift the topic slightly into an area where her mother would feel more confident.

"Well, Mother could give you a better explanation of that. He was one of the men she specifically invited. You remember Mother, the good-looking SS-Officer..."

The Countess seemed to relax instantly as her mind shifted direction as she began to force it back to the contents of the guest list.

"Well of course. He's of good family, and well thought of apparently, if considered somewhat unruly in terms of his social life, but be that as it may, the very idea of her returning to Berlin alone with this young man, un-chaperoned, I mean, what will his parents think of our Gabriella when they find out? This is hardly the way to initiate a good match."

Wilhelm stepped into the breach to support his twin sister.

"From what I saw of Gabriella over the weekend I don't think an un-chaperoned trip back from the Lake with this young fellow is going to make a great deal of difference when it comes to securing a good match for Gabriella with his family."

Ursula met his gaze and gave him a slight nod and a brief smile of thanks.

The Count could see his wife's mouth open to respond and he broke in, nodding in the general direction of the driver as he spoke.

"Well I suggest we leave this matter for now. We can discuss it privately at dinner."

The Countess's eyes flickered to the driver in reaction to the Counts nod and she pursed her lips.

"Yes, you're right dear."

Her eyes shifted to Wilhelm's.

"But I won't have this subject casually buried, Wilhelm. If there is something your father and I need to know about Gabriella, you have a responsibility to the family to see that we are so advised. This whole Gabriella situation has gone on far too long as it is and we will not bury our heads again. We will deal with it tonight."

CHAPTER FORTY-NINE

- Battle of Britain -

The end result of the 'Luftschlacht um England' (Air Battle for England) was a surprising disappointment for the Nazis.

At the beginning of the conflict the Germans had a rough ratio in aircraft strength of three to one in favour of the Reich, British numbers in the neighbourhood of sixteen hundred and the Nazis at approximately four thousand.

After taking France, there was no particular advantage to be had by either air force in relation to distance to targets, in that the Germans could now fly from airfields in France.

There were many and varied reasons, running the gamut from strategic target selection to types of aircraft involved, why the Germans lost this air battle but one particular factor stood out: the invention of radar.

Robert Watson-Watt is credited with the invention of the British radar system.

Ironically, Watson-Watt accomplished his task by building upon the initial research on the subject done by the German Heinrich Hertz in eighteen eighty-eight who discovered that radio waves could be *bounced off* objects.

Further experimentation and development on this concept took place in the early nineteen hundreds when another German, Christian Hulsmeyer took up the task and as a result patented a system for use of such waves on shipping in nineteen hundred and four.

Watson-Watt began his task in nineteen thirty-five when he was asked to investigate the possibility that the Germans had invented, what was then termed as a *Death Ray* weapon based on radio waves. He was to research to see if such a thing was possible and if so to duplicate it for the British military.

Watson-Watt, starting from the original German research with radio waves soon determined that the *Death Ray* was a myth; however he did discover that radio transmitter could create a *bounce back* echo from an airplane up to two hundred miles away.

Needless to say the value of such a defensive system in a time of war was immediately apparent to the powers that be and the project was put on the front burner.

By the start of the war the British had a *chain* of radar stations spread along the south-east coast of England. These 'CH' (Chain Home) stations were built in fixed positions on high cliffs facing out to sea. They transmitted a broad beam of radio pulses which blanketed a vast area out over the English Channel.

Once German aircraft had crossed over these shore stations they were lost from the radar and then became the responsibility of the *British Observer corps* personnel who were responsible for continuing to pinpoint the direction speed and numbers of craft from that point on.

Low flying aircraft could escape detection by the steel tower mounted *CH*, which rose up to a height of three hundred and sixty feet, by dropping low enough to come in below the pulses. This shortcoming was successfully addressed in nineteen thirty-nine by the creation of '*CHL*' (Chain Home Low) radar.

CHL was low mounted on a two hundred foot tower and had a rotating aerial which transmitted a narrow beam rather than a broad pulse.

It was unable to measure the height of incoming planes but is could detect aircraft flying at five hundred feet at ranges of up to one hundred and ten miles.

Research on radar continued throughout the war on both sides, bringing overall improvements but at the time of the Battle of Britain the British had the edge.

Early on in that conflict the Germans tried to destroy the radar towers but they did not give the radar system the consideration it deserved at the time. When his first attempts at destroying them through bombing the towers appeared relatively ineffective, Goering decided to change tactics and search out what he determined as better targets.

In its infancy, the system was not without its glitches but it did serve to accomplish one important task.

It went a long way toward eliminating the element of surprise from any German air attack launched from France.

It provided an edge that the outnumbered British defenders desperately needed.

* * * * *

- Safe Harbour –

The last course had been served and the family was now alone in the dining room.

"Is what Wilhelm says true Ursula? Has it gotten this bad?"

Mother is right. It has gone on far too long. If it hasn't happened already, soon Gabriella's activities are going to become common knowledge in the social circles of Berlin and once that happens there will be no hope for a good marriage for her. Not only am I completely out of my depth in trying to babysit her - I'm bloody well fed up with trying.

She looked across the table at her brothers and then turned to face her father who had posed the question.

"I would say it's worse, Father. Mother is right. Something must be done if we want to get her married and hopefully settled down and it needs to be done soon."

The Countess Erika had gone pale over the past few minutes. Inwardly she had known it was serious but she had really no idea it had gotten this far out of control. Tears of frustration began to form in her eyes and the Count spoke forcefully in an attempt to stem the flow.

"Alright, obviously something must be done. Erika you apply yourself to making up a list of men who would be suitable and who would, for whatever reason, have been unlikely to be involved socially within Gabriella's circle of friends in the Berlin area over the past year or so. What she needs is a firm but loving husband who will be strong enough to keep her in check and satisfy her needs while accepting her buoyant and spontaneous nature."

Eric, with some difficulty, withheld a smile.

So that's what they call it now, is it Father?

The Count continued.

"Wilhelm, we need to get her involved in some type of employment that will hold her interest. She is nearing the completion of her nurses' training and I don't believe it would be good for her to find herself assigned to some field hospital after she graduates. I'm wondering if you couldn't find her a spot within the Lebensborn Program. She is good with children and they must need nurses. If you could find her a position that she finds challenging and satisfying perhaps she'll be less inclined to look for outside stimulation. Couple that with a caring husband and we might achieve a balance that will help her to accept a more responsible lifestyle."

Wilhelm nodded.

"Yes, I'm sure she would do well and we do need nurses. The organization is in a stage of rapid expansion as a result of the Scandinavian territory we have recently occupied. As we speak, new staff is being sought for openings in Norway.

I would make one suggestion with regard to a husband. I don't think he should be from the military.

I know that will radically cut down on the choices Mother will have, based on the fact that the majority of eligible men of her age are already in the military, but I think if this is to have any chance of success, Gabriella is going to require stability. She will not find that with a military man who is bound to be transferred about.

Or if Mother can't find a suitable civilian, perhaps a military man who is likely to be permanently stationed in a non-combat role here in Berlin, maybe someone under Father's command;

someone with a scientific, engineering or medical background who will almost certainly serve out the war far away from the front lines and spend his nights sharing a bed with Gabriella."

Karl took a few seconds to absorb his son's suggestion.

The boy is on the right track.

He found himself a little surprised at the maturity and soundness of the ideas expressed and yet he knew he shouldn't be. Of his two sons, Wilhelm had always been the deep thinker and while he might often be at odds with his oldest boy when it came to positions on political matters he had always been very aware of Wilhelm's abilities to problem solve with a maturity far beyond his years.

"I think you've hit on the right approach Wilhelm, although I think it important that we also consider removing her from the Berlin area with a view to getting her out from under the weight of peer pressure exercised by her current circle of social acquaintances."

And hopefully away from any prattle which is no doubt being circulated locally by so-called friends who are prone to unhealthy gossip about her current reputation in regard to her activities with men.

"Your mother and I will work together on the selection of a good mate and I will rely on you to secure her a position that will not only appeal to her, but absorb her in her work. If we select carefully I believe we have a good chance at harnessing her outgoing personality and high energy level in such a manner as to reverse the situation in which she currently finds herself."

<u>Other books by Patrick Laughy</u>

The Little Black Book

Alumni

<u>Coming soon</u>

Continuation of the 4th Reich series
and
Atlantis-a fantasy series

www.ingramcontent.com/pod-product-compliance
Lightning Source LLC
Chambersburg PA
CBHW062127170626
46813CB00002B/597